# *An Ancient Haunting*

## Lily Ash – Book One

### Kate Innes

## Mindforest Press

First published in 2024 in Great Britain by Mindforest Press
www.kateinneswriter.com
ISBN 978-0-9934837-9-0
Copyright © Kate Innes 2024
A catalogue record for this book is available
from the British Library.



Cover and internal artwork by Anna Streetly @magpiemateria
Cover graphic design and maps by MA Creative
www.macreative.co.uk

Quote from *The Iliad* used under Creative Commons Attribution-ShareAlike 3.0 United States License for 'Homer. The Iliad with an English Translation by A. T. Murray, Ph.D. in two volumes. Cambridge, MA, Harvard University Press; London, William Heinemann, Ltd. 1924.'

**Plan of Palace** – from *A Handbook to The Palace of Minos at Knossos with its Dependencies* by J. D. S. Pendlebury, 1933 – reprinted by Cambridge University Press in 2014. Plan adapted for legibility by Mike Ashton of MACreative.

*Good-bye-ee!* song composed and written by R. P. Weston and Bert Lee, 1917

The ancient joke in Chapter 14 was inspired by John T. Quinn's translation of *The Philogelos* (Laughter-Lover) 4th-5th century CE

# An Ancient Haunting

## Lily Ash – Book One

Kate Innes trained as an archaeologist and worked in museums, but now she enjoys time-travel by writing historical fiction for children and adults. Having lived across three continents, Kate has settled in the ancient landscape by Wenlock Edge in Shropshire with her family. She enjoys exploring ruins, walking her dogs in the woods, teaching creative writing and meeting readers of all ages.

Find out more about Kate's writing at
www.kateinneswriter.com


**Children's Fiction:**

*Greencoats* – Shortlisted for the Rubery Book Award 2022

*An Ancient Haunting – Lily Ash Book One*


**Medieval Adult Fiction – *The Arrowsmith Trilogy*:**

*The Errant Hours*

*All the Winding World*

*Wild Labyrinth*


**Poetry:**

*Flocks of Words*

*For my son*
*Jim*

*Therein furthermore*
*the famed god of the two strong arms*
*cunningly wrought a dancing-floor*
*like unto that which*
*in wide Cnosus*
*Daedalus fashioned of old*
*for fair-tressed Ariadne.*


*The Iliad*, Book 18, line 590, by Homer

# Glossary

*Antío* – (Greek) Goodbye
atelier – (French) workshop or studio, especially one used by an artist or designer
*bien sûr* – (French) of course
*chevalier* – (French) knight
*Efcharistó* – (Greek) Thank you
*Eínai fílos mou o Michalis* – (Greek) Michalis is my friend
*Ephor* – (Greek) the head of an archaeological ephorate, responsible for managing archaeological sites and museums and matters related to antiquities in their region
*fílos* – (Greek) a male friend
*Geiá* – (Greek) Bye (or Hello)
*Kalispéra* – (Greek) Good afternoon/evening
*Kaló apógevma* – (Greek) Good afternoon
*Koíta* – (Greek) Look
*Kyrie/Kyria* – (Greek) formal title, used like Mr and Mrs
*N'est-ce pas?* – (French) Isn't it?
*Poseidon* – Classical Greek god of the sea and earthquakes
*Pos se léne?* – (Greek) What's your name?
*Se efcharistó pára poly* – (Greek) Thank you very much
*tsikoudia* – (Greek) a grape-based brandy distilled in Cretan villages, also known as raki
*yaourti* – (Greek) yoghurt

# Plan of the Palace

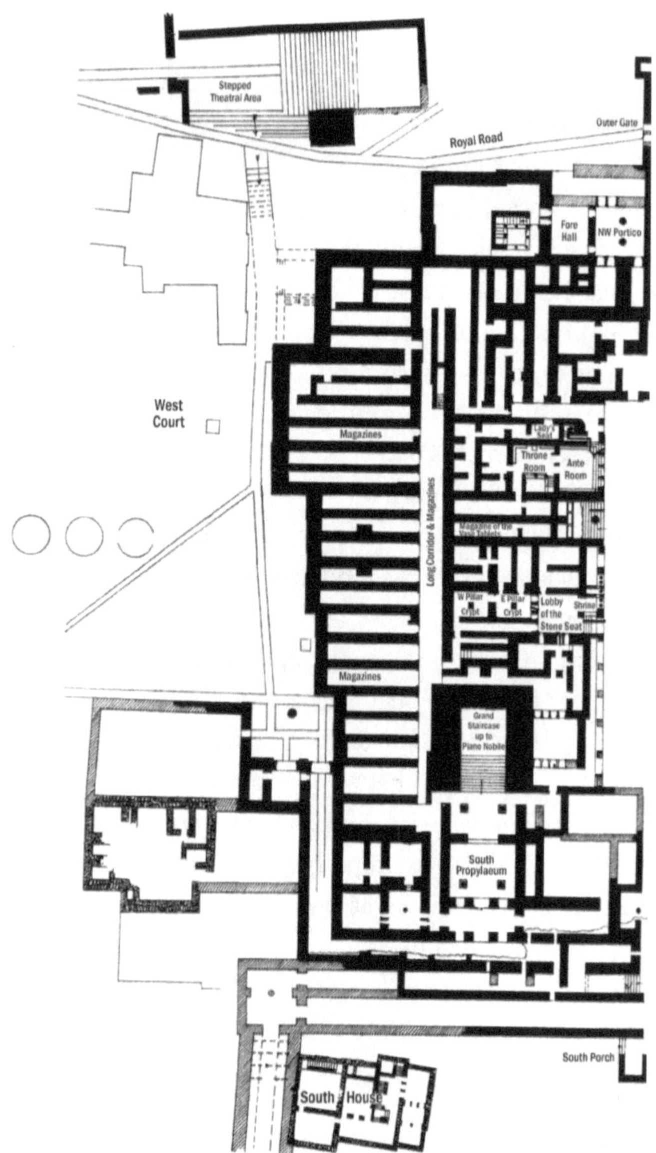

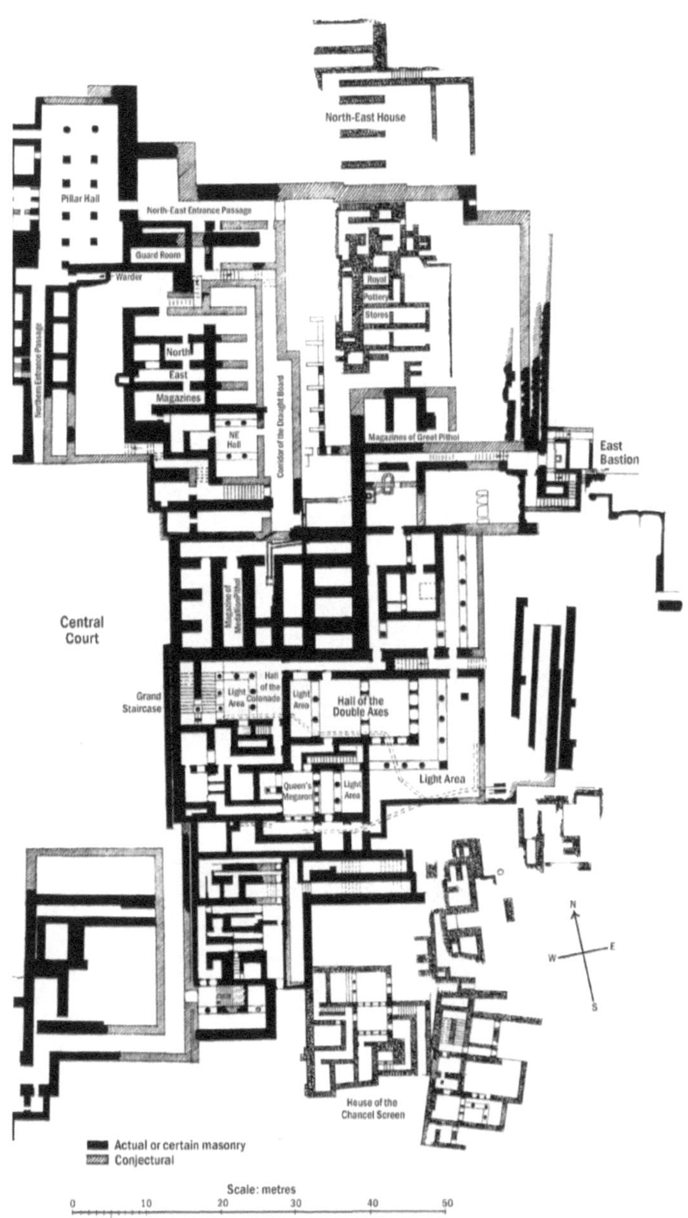

North-East House
Pillar Hall
North-East Entrance Passage
Guard Room
Warder
Northern Entrance Passag
North East Magazines
NE Hall
Royal Pottery Stores
Corridor of the Draught Board
Magazines of Great Pithoi
East Bastion
Central Court
Magazine of Medallion Pithoi
Grand Staircase
Light Area
Hall of the Colonade
Light Area
Hall of the Double Axes
Light Area
Queen's Megaron
Light Area
House of the Chancel Screen
N
E
S
W
Actual or certain masonry
Conjectural
Scale: metres
0    10    20    30    40    50

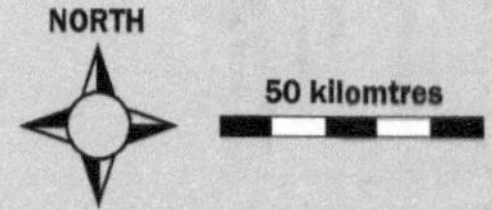

GREECE
AEGEAN
SEA
Athens
Piraeus
NORTH
50 kilomtres
CRETE
Día
Heraklion
Karteros
Mount Ida
Knossos

# 17<sup>th</sup> December, 1929
# Daggerhill School

Although Daggerhill claims to be a boarding school for well-off girls of a lively nature, we aren't provided with many comforts. Perhaps if the common room had more than a few broken chairs and an almost empty bookcase, the spirit who haunts me would have used a cushion to hit Mabel.

As it was, Frank chose an old dictionary, which he threw straight at her gloating face.

I imagine Mabel will spend quite some time in the dentist's chair while they attempt to reconstruct her cruel smile. I try to feel cheerful about this as I wait for the headmistress to arrive, hands behind my back, standing the regulation three paces away from her desk. But Frank is still present and still angry.

I'm angry, too. No matter how hard I try to obey the rules, I'm always being set up for trouble – by the living or the dead.

It's cold in Madame Mercator's study. The fireplace produces more smoke than heat. I don't think I've been warm since I arrived here in September, but at least the windows in this room aren't broken. In fact, they look very expensive: two stained glass panels depicting the Christian virtues. On a plinth in between stands a tall Chinese vase which holds all that remains of Madame Mercator's husband, who died of some tropical disease far from home, back in the days when, one supposes, she had some charm.

Mabel bullied me from day one. I was late for the start of term because my train broke down. When I finally arrived, it was past bedtime. I was shown upstairs to the high-ceilinged dormitory. All the girls in Form Two were pretending to be asleep, but, as I walked to the very end of the room, I could see the gleam of their eyes watching me.

Of course there was a nasty surprise under the thin blanket, followed by stifled giggles as I took the soaking sheets off the mattress and slept under my coat. So Matron had me down as a bed-wetter from the start – and it became my nickname.

Mabel is the ringleader. No one survives at Daggerhill unless they pay her, in one way or another. Coins, sweets, prep, dirty work, attacks on her enemies. She certainly deserved a taste of her own medicine, but I can't tell Madame Mercator that. She thinks Mabel is an angel, and I'm a devil.

'And I wonder whose fault that is, Frank?' I say in my head.

*You were about to be tortured by her again, so don't start blaming me for defending you!* He shouts back, as usual.

'She bullies me because you invade my mind even when I'm not alone, and I look like a lunatic. Go away, Frank! You'll just make things worse!'

*You're so ungrateful. Next time I'll just leave you to be kicked around, shall I?*

I can hear the headmistress's footsteps approaching the door.

'Frank – get out! Please!'

*No, this is the fun part! Headteachers are always so stupid when they're angry.*

The door swings open.

'Lily Ash! I should have known it would be you.' Madame Mercator slams the door behind her and clenches her fists inside their lace cuffs. 'Stand up straight! Don't think you can hide from me by cowering there near the floorboards!'

My small size has always infuriated her for some reason. She keeps her eyes on me as she stomps over to her desk. Frank is seething. I can hear him swearing at Madame inside my head.

'Yes, Ma'am,' I manage. It's very hard to concentrate on both the living and the dead, and it always makes Frank furious if I can't pay him the attention he demands.

Madame Mercator is squinting at me with her narrow eyes, as if I'm a disgusting insect that's stung her and she's just about to hit me with a rolled-up newspaper. But it's not going to be a newspaper. Her silver-handled cane hangs from the special holder attached to the side of her mahogany desk. Her hand reaches out for it, moving like an automaton.

'I'm sorry –' I begin.

Madame is gripping the cane as if it's the hand of her dearest friend.

'Silence! I've heard all your excuses, each one more ridiculous than the last. It's clear that the report we received from your last school was entirely accurate. You're a cruel and wicked girl. I'd hoped we could reform you, but you are beyond help.'

It's always the same. No point even trying to explain, as no one will believe what is actually happening to me. All I can do is attempt to minimise the damage. I close my eyes and take a deep breath. I must force Frank out. He's capable of turning a bad situation into a catastrophe.

*You can't tell me what to do. You're just a girl! I'm not going anywhere!*

His voice is fainter but still taking up too much space in my head. The cane smacks down on the desk.

'Don't you dare ignore me!'

Madame Mercator looks angrier than I've ever seen her before. Thin face the colour of an overripe plum. Nostrils flaring like a stampeding bull.

'Yes, Ma'am,' I whisper. There's no way out of this. The pair of them are pulling at my mind, and soon, very soon, there'll be consequences.

'Mabel's father will be absolutely furious, and the school will be inspected, thanks to you!' Madame shouts.

*All of daddy's money can't make miserable Mabel's teeth grow back!*

I try to look sorry, but I no longer know what my body is doing. It's all I can do to keep from collapsing. Madame Mercator leans her free hand on the desk, her voice high-pitched, cracking.

'I hope you realise you've changed Mabel's life for ever. She may never marry after the damage you did to her teeth!'

*A lucky escape for any man –*

'Shut up, Frank!'

There's a long, shivering pause. The two conversations have crossed. I've spoken out loud, not in my head.

The headmistress's mouth is hanging open. She might be silent, but Frank isn't.

*Don't you dare tell me to shut up! I'm the only one you've got, Lily Ash! Without me, you'd be dead at best!*

I put my hands on my head, trying hard not to scream. Frank is building up to a real tantrum, and if I don't force him out –

The cane swings through the air, and I instinctively dodge.

'How dare you speak to me like that! Stand still, hold out those filthy hands of yours. You'll be leaving this school but not before you have been punished for your appalling behaviour!'

I run for it. Even the cold winter of Northumberland will be better than this. I'll find a tree to sleep under. I'll ride under a train. But she's faster than she looks and grabs me by the arm before I reach the door. I'm stronger than I look, but even so, I can't break free from her grip. The cane is raised to hit my head not my hands.

That's when he does it. Imagine a small tornado about the size of a ten-year-old boy. In a rush of energy, he goes straight for the Chinese vase.

I raise my free arm to try to stop him – as if I could.

I've never seen Frank, so I have no idea what he looks like. But I know he's smiling as he lifts the vase from the plinth and throws it straight into the fire, where it smashes into a thousand sooty pieces.

# Chapter 1
## 10<sup>th</sup> January, 1930
## The Manor
## Glascott under Wychwood

Much as Madame Mercator wanted to be rid of me, there was no reply to her letters demanding my removal. She locked me up in a stripped-bare room in the infirmary over Christmas.

By the time the one remaining member of my family arrived back from wherever he'd been, and I'd travelled on three different trains back to the Manor, the signs of the caning she'd given me had faded.

But not my memories of it.

Up to that moment in the headmistress's office, I'd been afraid of talking about what happens to me, about who I really am. But not any more. I'm going to tell you everything. It matters that you, most of all, understand. If you ever read this, you'll know what actually happened, not the rubbish they accuse me of.

You, my mother, will know the truth.

That's all I can hope for as I stand before yet another enormous desk, waiting for the latest verdict on my life.

'I'd be grateful if you'd *listen* to me, Lily Ash!'

There's good reason to pay attention to Uncle Leonard at this particular moment. But, try as I might, I can't. He sits hunched over the leather blotter. I can see his breath in the cold air and his moving lips, but Frank is back, tugging at my mind, making ordinary conversation impossible.

Bang!

'Lily!' Uncle Leonard is standing now, his fist clenched on the leather desk pad. He smashes it down again.

'Yes, Uncle?'

'I'm beginning to see why my father threatened to send you to the asylum.'

I'm sure you remember how horrible Grandfather was, Mother. But he'd never have actually sent me to an asylum, because that would've killed Grandmother. They're both dead now, of course. I wonder if you even know that? She died from being worried and crying all the time, he from the shock of losing all his money in the stock market crash.

So now I'm in the hands of Uncle Leonard. And you must know what your brother is like. Not remotely interested in children. Although he might be if I were dead, as he's an archaeologist.

'That vase was the final straw. Daggerhill School won't take you back, and I have important work on an excavation abroad.' Uncle Leonard sinks back into the curves of his ornate chair, and props his head on his hands. 'I just don't know what to do with you.'

There's a long silence. The fire hisses and pops. The grandfather clock ticks in the hall. Even Frank is quiet now. Maybe listening, too.

'I'm very sorry, Uncle. It wasn't me. It was – a cat. It jumped onto the plinth and knocked the vase off.'

He shakes his head slowly.

'Lily, no one believes your stories any more. So don't even try to convince me that a *cat* caused an expensive Chinese vase to fly across the headmistress's study.' Uncle Leonard examines an ink spot on the blotting paper. It resembles an hourglass. 'You'll have to go somewhere – somewhere secure.'

I don't like the sound of that.

The housekeeper and gardener have been 'let go'. Half the furniture in the Manor is already covered in white, ghostly sheets. But I could stay. I wouldn't bother anyone, and no one would bother me.

'I'll be fine here, Uncle! The chickens are still laying. I know how to boil an egg and light a fire.'

His eyes remain fixed on the ink spot.

'And when the coal is gone? When there's no one to wash your clothes? You'll live here like a savage, just like your –'

He stops himself in time, shuts his eyes and runs his hands through his thin hair.

'You cannot stay here alone, and there's no money to send you to yet another boarding school after all the damages we've had to pay. I don't *want* to send you to an orphanage, but that seems the only solution. You'll be looked after until you reach your majority. Perhaps they'll find you work.'

'Uncle, please –'

'Don't argue!' His eyes flash pale blue, then return to the desk. 'There's nowhere else. The Manor will be boarded up until I return, when, with luck, I'll have some funds. I might be able to send you to another school in a year or two.'

'But I'll be beaten, starved –'

'Don't be ridiculous,' he interrupts. 'You've been reading exaggerated stories from last century. Modern orphanages are regularly inspected. They're clean and sanitary. There's no luxury, but having silver cutlery hasn't exactly turned you into a proper young lady. Quite the reverse.' He risks a quick glance at my frayed, stained dress. 'In the orphanage you'll learn to behave. That's all I can do.' He gets up suddenly, the chair rocking back on the thin carpet. 'Go and pack your things. We leave in the morning.'

I look around the room, trying to think of a way to change his mind. The ancient artefacts in the glass display cabinet vibrate at the edge of my senses. The books are silent on the shelves, but their pages are crammed with ideas.

'Why are you standing there in a trance? Go to your room! I have business to conclude before I leave.' My uncle's voice trembles, but there's no mercy in the set of his shoulders.

I go to the door feeling even angrier than when Madame Mercator locked me in the punishment cupboard. But I turn the brass handle and shut the door behind me carefully. I can't afford to slam it and make Uncle Leonard more furious.

Children don't leave orphanages. An uncle who has no family, no wife, no interest in anything other than ancient civilisations doesn't return to look after his niece. He will take me there, and I'll never come out.

The hall is full of the sound of time going by – precious seconds flung back and forth by the pendulum of the clock. Tick by tock, the orphanage is getting nearer.

I run for the stairs.

Frank doesn't like it when I'm angry. He doesn't visit when I'm happy either. He comes when I'm sad or frightened, which is more often than not. At first, he made me more frightened. I was only six when he started talking to me. I'm nearly twelve now, but I still know practically nothing about him, except he's hot-tempered, ten years old and likes to throw things, especially at bullies. However, sometimes he has good ideas.

I run up two flights of stairs to my room and shut the door. Sitting down on the bed, I take two deep breaths, fold my hands in my lap, half-close my eyes. Once I've cleared the anger from my mind, it doesn't take long for Frank to come back.

*What was that cold fish saying to you? I couldn't hear through all the shouting in your head!*

'I told you to leave me alone, Frank. You've already got me into trouble in every school, and now I'm going to be sent to an orphanage, thanks to you!'

*You know that's not why. It's because your uncle is scared. He's convinced there's something wrong with you, and you'll stamp on his spectacles, or smash his precious bits of already broken pot, or spill ink on his white sleeves.*

'Don't be horrible.'

*You've probably thought of doing all those things. And who can blame you? Anyway, he's afraid, and you need to make him even more afraid.*

'How will that help? If he's sending me away because he's scared, making him more so will only make it worse!'

*Threaten him! Tell him that you'll cast a spell and all his hair and teeth will fall out. That should do the trick.*

I almost smile at the thought of Uncle Leonard trying to talk in his clipped, precise voice without any teeth.

'There must be another way. I don't like being frightening.'

*Fine. You think of something better if you're so clever. Something weak and girly.*

There's a moment of heavy silence as I try to think of something that will be neither.

'I could run away, I suppose.'

*Where to? You'd be picked up by the police and then taken to the orphanage, stupid! I should know.*

'I just want to stay here! I don't mind being alone. I need to think of something!'

*You're never alone. Don't you know that by now?* His tone is exasperated.

Despite his words, I can feel Frank fading away, and I'm not sorry. It always leaves me feeling exhausted if he stays more than a few minutes.

*I'll follow you to the orphanage or wherever you go, Lily. I can always find you.*

I'm not sure if that's meant to be a comfort or a threat.


I put my plan into action after midnight. Frank's idea about scaring my uncle out of taking me to the orphanage is the only one available at short notice. I'll speak to him in a language that he understands, using his own obsession to make my point. It will, in a way, be justifiable.

Uncle Leonard is not a deep sleeper, and I must pass his door on my way down to the library. The house is freezing. It's hard to be stealthy whilst shivering, but at least I don't have to worry about waking Mrs Jones, the housekeeper, in her room by the back stairs. She's already gone, leaving a pot of lumpy porridge as a parting gift.

A slice of moonlight falls diagonally across the parquet floor of the hall. It's enough to see by, for now. I stand for a moment, screwing up my courage. The key to the library is kept on the back of the cellar door, alongside the key to your old bedroom. I used to steal that key too and try to conjure you there. It never worked. And that's one of the reasons I know you're definitely not dead, Mother.

The trick to the cellar is to fill my mind with a song. If I'm singing, the voices don't come through to my conscious understanding. If I stop singing and hear what the spirits are actually saying, my uncle will find me in the morning, lying on the cellar floor, too exhausted to move, my chance gone. I know this from bitter experience. It took me a week to recover last time, and it's left me with a horror of the place.

The song that works best on these occasions is *Good-bye-ee*. Do you remember? You used to sing it to me before bed. You sang it just before you left.

*Good-bye-ee, Good-bye-ee,*
*Wipe the tear, baby dear, from your eye-ee.*
*Though it's hard to part, I know*
*I'll be tickled-to-death to go.*

I start to sing it very quietly under my breath and slowly open the door. I keep singing as I feel for the key. I'm still singing when I knock the key off the hook, and it clatters down the stairs. I carry on singing as I step down into the blackness, patting blindly around on each step for the key.

*I'm trapped! Under the coal. Please help me! I can't move.* A girl – very young.

*Touch my stash, and I'll kill you!* Male – vicious.

*How dare you disturb me? I'll make you pay for this!* Old man – up to something.

The conflicting cries of the dead are almost drowning me out. I sing faster. A little louder. On the fifth step, I finally feel the key, cold on my fingertips. I force myself back up the stairs, crawl into the hallway and slowly push the door closed, the key clutched in my palm.

Frank, that good-for-nothing, so-called friend, is nowhere. The least he could do is keep the other voices away, but he won't stand up to them. He's all talk.

I'm gasping for breath. It seems impossible that Uncle Leonard can sleep through all the noise. But he hears nothing in the house except the creak of the floorboards, the rattle of the windows and the fall of sticks down the chimneys from the jackdaw nests. Nothing of the restless dead. I'm like a magnet to them, and he's just an ordinary piece of metal.

I get to my feet and stand for a moment, listening to the hall clock and waiting for my heart to slow to its rhythm. Then I make my way over to the library door.

The lock is well-oiled. I slip inside the dark room, feel my way to the fireplace and find the box of matches. The candles on the mantlepiece give enough light to see the cabinet of treasures on the opposite wall. The key to it is in the desk. The desk key is under the carpet.

You may be wondering how I know all these things. I sound like a thief. But I don't steal things – unless it's absolutely necessary. I'm just very observant. I have to be.

I sift through the contents of the lower right drawer of the desk, find the little key on its silky ribbon and head for the cabinet, avoiding the squeaky floorboard just to its left. Uncle Leonard's bedroom is, as you know, right above the library.

I reach in and pick up a small stone slab that was, according to the label, originally part of a wall frieze in the tomb of the daughter of an Egyptian scribe. A girl called *Menka*. It is carved limestone with a hint of red and blue pigment tracing the girl's beautiful profile and the sky above her. The hieroglyphs below her name are what I need.

The stone is cold in my hand.

Visions of the ancient past begin to fill my mind.

# Chapter 2
## 11<sup>th</sup> January, 1930

After leaving the threat on Uncle Leonard's desk, I can't sleep a wink. I'm still freezing after my experience in the cellar, so I get dressed and sit in my clothes under the covers until I hear the clock strike six. I'll make breakfast and prove that I can look after myself.

The fire in the range is nearly dead, but I manage to revive it with some sticks and a shovelful of coal from the scuttle. It takes ages for the kettle to boil, and all the time I rehearse how I'll behave and what I'll say when Uncle Leonard finds the message. I'm sitting in Mrs Jones's rush-seated chair by the range, where it's warm. So warm I fall asleep with the eggs in a saucepan on top. And that's where Uncle Leonard eventually finds me.

At the sound of his voice, I jolt awake.

'The eggs are boiled dry!'

'Sorry, Uncle.' I leap up from the chair and burn my hand on the saucepan trying to get it off the hotplate. I guess he hasn't been in the library yet, by his ordinary grumpy demeanour.

'For heaven's sake,' he mutters. 'How long have you been sitting there?'

'Would you like some tea? The pot is warm,' I say in the brightest tone I can manage.

He gives me a strange look and reaches for a cup from the dresser.

'Put those eggs in the bin. I'll have my tea in the library. We leave shortly. Are you packed?'

I nod mutely, but he's already gone, carrying his cup and saucer. I go to the kitchen door holding the saucepan with a tea towel. It's just getting light. The sunrise is muted, but at least it isn't raining. I breathe in the winter air and walk across the yard towards the garden gate. No point wasting eggs. Maybe the foxes or badgers will eat them.

Behind me the house is silent. He'll have seen the message by now. My fate depends on his reaction. I find myself praying, if that's what it is, to the Egyptian god *Thoth*, who helps scribes and writers, to give strength to my message. Although, in truth, the hieroglyphs I've copied with a fountain pen are an empty threat. I have no more power to curse than a hen.

Mist is rising from the river at the bottom of the garden. The place where I first heard Frank's voice looks eerie and beautiful. Why do I only have a troublesome spirit following me and no real, living person who cares for me? I've been asking that for years with no answer.

There's a choked shout behind me. Uncle Leonard is standing in the kitchen doorway, his face pale. He beckons me with one long finger. I walk through the garden gate and into the kitchen, leaving the pan in the sink. He's gone ahead into the hall and is waiting by the library door. I stand a safe distance away, looking down at my wet shoes. My feet hurt. My shoes are too small, but this is definitely not the right time to ask my uncle for new ones. He bends his narrow head towards me.

'Take that disgraceful display off my desk, then go and get your case.'

I look up, but he's turned away and is staring at his pocket watch.

I walk into the shadowy library.

All is not as I left it.

The fragment from the tomb wall is on the desk where I placed it, and the scrap of heavy paper with the hieroglyphic curse written in black ink is also there, looking clumsy and childish. Copying the figures was tricky in the candlelight.

But around it is a thin, pale, indistinct circle. I approach the desk cautiously, peer at it, touch it with my fingertip. It's fine golden sand. Desert sand. I rub it between my finger and thumb, and a shiver travels through my body. The sand lies on the leather desktop as if slipped from a palm between fingers, encircling my naive attempt at a curse.

I'm sure it frightens me more than Uncle Leonard, because he doesn't know that I didn't do it.

You might be wondering how I learnt to write hieroglyphs and why I chose that language to frighten Uncle Leonard. You've been away a long time.

You probably don't know that your brother has excavated in the Valley of the Kings in Egypt. And you won't be aware that, when I've been here in the summer holidays and told to stay out of my grandparents' way, I studied the books from this library under my bedcovers. I've worked my way through most of the interesting ones, and, as a result, I've taught myself a few useful skills, including decoding the most basic hieroglyphic signs. The story of the translation of the Ancient Egyptian language is interesting. But you know that already. Your name is in the front of that book, on the dedication page.

*Rosetta Ash.*

I'd never written a curse before. I didn't take it seriously enough. But my back was against the orphanage wall, and now I've opened a door I didn't intend to. I should've known better and not listened to Frank. He's always getting me in trouble.

I touch the Egyptian wall fragment with the tip of my finger. It's very cold. Maybe just as cold as the room, but it feels colder. I back away. What is the most respectful thing to do now that the Egyptian spirits are involved? Should I leave the display here in the library to gather dust?

I touch it again – pressing my hand on the carving. A vision comes down across my eyes – clear as water: a girl lying on an inlaid ebony bed in a room lit by smoking clay lamps. It's *Menka* looking straight into my eyes, her finger pointing at my chest. She's a young girl, but also an old spirit with a penetrating stare. She's dead, but not at rest.

Her tomb has been desecrated, her portrait and name removed. The spells written so that *Menka* can navigate the world of the dead have been taken from her tomb and separated from her body. I must replace this fragment of it, which states her name and curses anyone disturbing her. I must return it to Egypt. To her mummy.

If I don't find a way, she will remain in my mind, trapped in limbo, pointing at me accusingly, as if I was the one who hacked her name off the wall with a chisel. I quickly promise to bring it back to her, and, to assure her of my sincerity, trace the Egyptian hieroglyph for 'vow' in the air with my finger. *Menka* lowers her hand slowly, holding me with her eyes until the door to her shuts.

I grip the edge of the desk – blinking, disoriented. The library squirms unnaturally.

'Aren't you finished yet? We have a train to catch!' That snaps me back to Oxfordshire. Uncle Leonard is shouting from the hall. He doesn't even want to enter the room.

'Coming, Uncle.'

I quickly open the cabinet and lower the wall fragment into place, whispering the vow again. I have no desire to be haunted by yet another spirit. Back at the desk, I scrunch the hieroglyphic paper up in my fist. I'll deal with it later. The sand will have to stay there. It came from another realm. Perhaps it will go back, but I won't show disrespect by sweeping it up and throwing it away as if it were common dirt.

I shut the library door behind me and stand with my back against it. Uncle Leonard glares at a point just above my head.

'I see you are willing to do anything to make my life difficult, even feeding me to crocodiles.' His voice is shaking. I can't tell if it's from anger or fear. 'Perhaps you assumed I was returning to Egypt!' He smiles strangely. 'Well, I don't believe your curse. A schoolgirl who thinks she can command ancient gods!' Little drops of spittle accompany his sarcasm. 'But you have no scruples, no discipline, and I cannot risk you harming other children.' He turns away and yanks his coat off the stand. 'You'll have to come with me.'

I must look as horrified as he does.

'Let me stay here, Uncle! I promise I'll take care of the Manor.'

'A girl on her own in an old house with no servants and no income? You're quite mad.' He strides to the door. 'Meet me at the end of the drive. The train leaves in twenty minutes.'

'But where are we going?'

'Don't you know?' he asks sarcastically. 'I thought someone like you could see the future.'

'No, I only see the past.'

His head snaps round.

'Don't be impertinent!'

He grabs his hat and valise – and slams the door behind him.

Better or worse than an orphanage? It's hard to say what being with my uncle is going to be like. But I've no intention of leaving the Manor empty-handed. Who knows when I'll be back? There's time to take something of you. Just a small thing, if I'm quick.

I climb the stairs two at a time.

# Chapter 3
## The Ashmolean Museum
## Oxford

Uncle Leonard doesn't say a single word to me on the train journey. He stares out of the window as if his life depends on it, and I don't dare ask again where we're going. But it's soon obvious. Oxford is only a short journey away. I run to keep up with him through the streets, dodging students in black gowns. My uncle is tall and quick. He won races for the University before the war, as you probably know. But it's hard to imagine him being anything like the many loud, cheerful students cycling along these roads.

Uncle Leonard eventually slows down in front of a grand building covered with pillars and statues. At the top of the wide steps leading to the huge door, he takes me to one side.

'It's crucial that I'm *not* disturbed during this important meeting with Sir Arthur. If you so much as touch a speck of dust on any of the statues, I will take you directly to the constable. Is that clear?'

I nod.

I've heard plenty about Sir Arthur Everett, his great wealth and amazing archaeological discoveries. Perhaps you have too? In any case, I understand that he is much more important to Uncle Leonard than I am.

'Sit where I tell you, and wait quietly.'

Echoes of past lives reverberate through museums if you have the ears to hear them, and they are overwhelming places if you do. I cross its threshold with my arms folded, intending to touch absolutely *nothing*.

Uncle Leonard points to a marble bench just inside the door. Opposite is a desk where a grey-haired, heavily-bearded man is sitting in front of a ledger and a telephone. I perch on the cold stone. The old man looks up as Uncle Leonard approaches him, listens, nods and picks up the black telephone. Soon Uncle Leonard is walking away towards a marble staircase. He glances back at me just before turning the corner, as if he thinks I'll already be smashing things or turning cartwheels down the galleries.

The old man is looking at me through thick spectacles. It's hard to tell what expression he wears under his beard. I duck my head and start swinging my legs to warm them up. My pinched feet are two blocks of ice, and my stomach is rumbling. In the galleries beyond the desk there are voices I can't afford to listen to.

'Come here, please.' The old man is leaning over his desk, beckoning me.

I shake my head.

'My uncle told me to stay here.'

'Poppycock. I'm in charge of visitors to the museum, and you are a visitor. So, I am asking you to come here, girl. It's not far.' He tilts his head.

I get up reluctantly and approach his desk.

'What have I got in my hand?'

He's holding out a clenched fist.

'I don't know, sir.'

'Well, guess! Don't stand there like a haddock!'

The old man is beginning to remind me of a teacher I had when I was eight years old.

'Maybe a button?'

'No. You have two more guesses. Think, child!'

I glance towards the stairs.

'My uncle wanted me to stay on the bench.'

'As if it matters if you are on the bench or ten feet away at my desk!' he rumbles. 'If you're inside the oldest museum in England, you may as well gain something.'

I try to think of a clever answer, but there's too much on my mind.

'A grain of sand.'

'What an *extraordinary* guess.' He cocks his head and twists the clenched fist to and fro. 'No. It's not a grain of sand. You have one more guess.'

'Or what?'

His smile makes his wiry beard expand.

'Or you don't get to keep what's in my fist.'

Fists don't necessarily contain things I'd like to keep. Things like bruises and black eyes. But I don't think this man is threatening me. He has smile wrinkles around his eyes.

'Please may I have a clue?'

'Would the Sphinx give you a clue?' he chortles. 'Very well. As I'm not the Sphinx at the crossroads, I will. In my hand I have five minutes of happiness.'

It doesn't take long to work it out, despite my limited experience of that emotion. I smile back at him.

'It's a sweet.'

He opens his fist slowly to show a toffee wrapped in green waxed paper.

'Open your palm.' He places it on my hand.

'Thank you, sir.'

'It seems that you're not accustomed to being given treats, young lady.'

I stare at the toffee and shake my head very slightly. I'm small for my age, so he probably thinks I'm much younger than I actually am, and the tears that have filled my eyes will not surprise him.

'Well, in that case, put this one in your pocket.' He produces another toffee, this time in pink paper. 'And quick, pop that one in your mouth.' There's something probing about the look he gives me before waving me away from the desk. 'That'll keep you out of trouble.'

And somehow, it does. I sit on the bench for nearly an hour, barely sucking on the toffee, and I'm not troubled by Frank, or the voices from the sarcophagus, or the urns full of bones. The rich sweetness of the toffee fills every part of my head.

The old man doesn't speak to me again. He's busy with a party of tourists and then a group of students who make various demands. When, eventually, Uncle Leonard reappears, striding towards the door, he raises his head from the ledger and winks at me. I try, unsuccessfully, to wink back and follow my uncle into the freezing, drizzly afternoon.

We are back on the train heading further south when I think it might be safe to ask a question.

'Where's your new job, Uncle?'

He looks up from his book, catches my eye and swiftly shifts his gaze to the window.

'You won't have heard of it. It's an island in the Aegean Sea. Crete. Now part of Greece. A long way from here. We're catching a ship from the London Dock tomorrow.' And he puts his nose back in the book.

But my heart begins to race, because I know that when *you* left, it was by ship. You weren't going to Greece. You were going to India, and when you arrived, you promised you'd send for me. But you never did. Grandfather told me you'd died, and for years I believed him.

Not any more.

Greece is in the Mediterranean, and the Mediterranean Sea is joined to the Red Sea by the Suez Canal. Ships must travel through it to get to India, or go thousands of miles out of their way around the whole of Africa (I did pay attention in school when I thought it might be useful). Maybe I can escape from my uncle, stow away on a ship going all the way to India, and find you. Uncle Leonard doesn't want me. He'll be glad if I vanish.

The rest of the journey is a blur of buildings swishing by and plans going through my head. But there's one thing I really must do before making my escape – get a bigger pair of shoes. I can barely walk, never mind run at the moment, and, for better or worse, I know I'll be doing plenty of running very soon.

My uncle has never been to a shop where they sell ready-made shoes before, that's quite clear. All his shoes have been handmade to fit him. He stands fidgeting while the store assistant measures my feet. She stares accusingly at him and says that my toes are nearly turning under themselves in these tiny shoes.

He pays for the cheapest pair they have in my size, and then he has to feed me. Even a confirmed bachelor eventually realises that children need food. But he leaves me to eat my meat pasty and cabbage alone in the guesthouse dining room. He's going to his club for one last night before leaving the country. I should wash and go straight to bed. We must be up early, he says.

I'm not sorry he's gone. I need some time alone to talk to Frank. I particularly want to tell him about the overseas journey and ask if he'll still visit me. Part of me wants to be free, but without Frank I'll have no one to talk to. No one who understands who I am.

The bathwater is tepid, so I quickly wash and rub myself hard to get warm. Then I lay out my clothes on the chair and climb into the narrow bed. The sheets are freezing, the bedspread thin. I hop out of bed and put on my socks and jumper. Sitting under the covers, I take a deep breath and half-shut my eyes.

*Took your time, didn't you? Gallivanting around London!*

'Hardly. I just got a pair of shoes and ate a pasty.'

*Just a pasty! It's been years since I had a pasty. And you tease me with your dinner.*

'It was horrid. Full of gristle.'

*Good! Having fun with your uncle? He's such a jester! What japes!*

'He's barely speaking to me.'

*That's not surprising.*

'It was your idea!'

*I didn't mean for you to use a real Egyptian curse, idiot! Only make him think you might.*

'I didn't try! It just happened.'

*You don't know your own incredible strength, do you?*

Sarcasm drips from every word.

'What will happen now?'

*He's got to look after you, or he'll be attacked by a gigantic crocodile.*

'Not really?'

*What did you expect?*

'But – what if I run away from him, far away, but I'm perfectly safe and healthy with my mother?'

*If you come to harm, wherever you are, he'll be eaten by a Nile crocodile.*

'We're going to Greece, Frank. Not Egypt.'

*Well it's a good thing you didn't include snakes in your curse. There are plenty of those in Greece. Just think of Medusa!*

I shake my head. Real life is frightening enough without mythical, snake-haired she-monsters who can turn you to stone.

'I thought Uncle Leonard would let me stay in the Manor, but we're leaving on a ship tomorrow and sailing across the Mediterranean. Will you come with me?'

*Where else would I be? At the maharajah's pleasure dome?*

'Do you really mean it? You'll stay with me no matter how far?'

*Wherever you go, I go. And that's a curse on me!*

He treats me to a rude noise from his collection.

'Please don't cause trouble and throw things, Frank. I don't want Uncle Leonard to be angry all the time. I need to stay inconspicuous. You understand, don't you?'

There's a faint buzzing in my ears.

'Frank?'

He's gone.

I lie back against the pillow, taking shallow breaths. After a moment, I force myself out of bed and onto the cold floorboards. I want to check my suitcase. Under the lid, inside the cloth lining, is the photograph I took out of the frame in my grandparents' bedroom. I hold it in my fingertips.

Rosetta Ash: long blond hair tied back under a white cap, in the Red Cross uniform you wore during the Great War, taken before I was born. Whatever happens, I'm going to find you, Mother, and this photo is going to help me do it.

## Chapter 4
### 12<sup>th</sup> January, 1930
### Tilbury Dock, London

Tilbury dock at nine a.m. just before a large steamer sails is a busy, noisy, confusing muddle. As soon as we get off the train it's pandemonium. Entire families with their servants, followed by porters wheeling trollies of luggage, clog the walkways. Sellers of fruit and jellied eels compete for our attention. Somewhere on board a band is playing. The notes sound sad in the morning fog.

Uncle Leonard's heavy trunk was sent ahead from Oxford. We go to the baggage hall before we embark to make absolutely certain it's been loaded. We're too late. No one can answer his query as the ship is only minutes from departure.

Uncle Leonard is like a bag of cats about it. Whatever is inside is *absolutely critical to his work*. Eventually he gives up trying to find out, and, just as the deafening horn sounds for the last time, we run for the ship.

Perhaps you felt like this when you left eight years ago, heading to India? Breathless on deck after the climb up the gangway, looking over the railing, alone, nervous yet excited as the brass band plays the National Anthem and the view begins to change.

But were you alone? If only I could remember things clearly. All that remains is the warmth of your arms holding me against your shoulder, the *Good-bye-ee* song and the tears. *I'll send for you soon*, you said. Or have I imagined that?

The deck is too cold for most people, and, once the huge ship is tugged away from the landing stage and everyone has waved until they're exhausted, most of the passengers go below to have a cup of tea and thaw out.

Uncle Leonard is looking around unhappily.

'I should be on the *Viceroy of India*, first class, not on this old packet.'

The 'old packet', a steamer named the SS *Moldavia*, is impressive enough to me. But I've never travelled by ship before, and my first experience will be in third class, the only place available at short notice on this sailing.

'How long will it take, Uncle?'

'A week, if we're lucky with the weather. An eternity if we're not.' He shrugs his coat tighter. 'Come along.'

I follow reluctantly. Although I'm very cold, I'd rather stay on deck. The sight of the port growing smaller, the sound of the gulls and the smell of the engines are novelties. My new shoes squeak on the deck as he holds the heavy door open for me, and we're sucked into a smoky, crowded room.

'Tourist Class,' Leonard mutters, coughs, and pushes towards the bar.

The first three days through the English Channel and across the Bay of Biscay are terrible. While I'm busy being violently sick in our cramped cabin, Uncle Leonard, who has a stomach of iron, establishes that his trunk has been stowed in the hold and becomes slightly less bad-tempered. By the time we reach the southern point of Portugal, the weather improves, the swell eases, and I'm able to go on deck with the other pale, weak passengers.

My only coat is too short to keep out the wind, but it's better than nothing. I thrust my cold hands into the pockets, and my fingers wrap around two objects: the toffee the old gentleman at the museum gave me in the right pocket and a crumpled piece of thick paper in the left.

A shiver runs down my spine.

It's the curse. I've been carrying it around with me like the albatross around the neck of the Ancient Mariner. We did that poem at school. It's not the ideal story to contemplate when you're at sea, as all the characters have a truly terrible ocean voyage.

I hold the paper in my fist and consider throwing it overboard. But the ship is moving fast through calm waters. The curse will fly out behind me, onto the deck below. I shove it back to the bottom of my pocket. I'll have to steal someone's matches and burn it later.

Sudden dizziness and a wave of pressure in my head make me grip the railing and close my eyes. Immediately I see a huge crocodile opening its jaws inside a circle of fire. Its eyes are oily green with a slit of deep black, mouth full of long, jagged teeth, armoured tail scraping and crashing. It speaks in a hissing, liquid voice I barely understand.

But this much I do: the power of the curse conjured inside that circle of sand is now inescapable, all around me and inside my tingling skin. It doesn't matter where Uncle Leonard and I are, or the distance between us. The great river Nile enters the Mediterranean, and, ultimately, its water flows in all oceans and seas. There's nowhere beyond the reach of this spell.

Burning the paper will only make matters infinitely worse, because that insult will cause the great Devourer of the Dead – the crocodile daemon *Ammut* – to eat my heart after I have died, trapping me in *Duat*, the Egyptian Underworld, with no chance of rest or paradise. My prayer to *Thoth* to give power to my words was foolish indeed. He's the god of judgement and hieroglyphs – and *Ammut* serves him.

The spirit I've wakened with those curse hieroglyphs from *The Book of the Dead* is incredibly powerful. I've no idea how to undo it. But clearly, I mustn't give my uncle any reason to mistreat me. Even though he's grumpy, indifferent and rude to me, I'd rather not watch him being mauled and swallowed by a crocodile.

It takes all my strength to open my eyes. I'm crouching on the deck clinging to the post of the railing, all my limbs trembling. That deathly, stinking mouth hovers on the edge of my vision. I stand up slowly, blink and look around. No one has noticed my strange behaviour because everyone else on deck is leaning over the opposite railing, pointing and making excited noises.

I haven't been able to keep anything down for two days, but I suspect the toffee might stop the shaking. I unwrap it and pop it in my mouth.

'Come over here! You're missing the show!' A tall woman in a red beret is waving at me from the other side of the deck. 'Here, stand in front of me for a good view!'

I smile and shake my head, my mouth full of sticky, delicious sweetness.

'Come on! I promise it'll make you forget your seasickness.' The woman beckons me again.

I stagger across the slippery deck towards her, and she pulls me to the railing. Dark oblong shapes break the surface of the grey, rolling sea. A sudden blow of air and water, like a fountain in a park only much higher, with rainbows in the spray. A dorsal fin, thin and sharp, and the hint of the long, long body before it sinks below the water.

I count three whales before the boat leaves them behind.

The red beret woman sighs happily.

'Wasn't that simply lovely?'

I nod, my mouth full of toffee that I don't want to swallow too soon.

'I've always wanted to see whales, and here they are playing alongside the boat! Fin whales, I believe. The second largest animal in the world. And I heard someone say there were dolphins at the bow just before breakfast.' She wipes sea spray from her cheek and looks thoughtful. 'I hope there aren't any whaling ships nearby. I couldn't bear to see them hunted. Could you?'

The idea of it makes me feel a bit sick again. I shake my head vigorously.

'What's your name?'

I push the toffee to the side of my mouth.

'Lily,' I manage.

She smiles and holds out her hand.

'Hilda Pendleton. How old are you, Lily?'

'I'll be twelve soon.' It comes out muffled but apparently understandable. I put my thoroughly-shaken hand back in my pocket.

'Will you? You look younger than that, but I daresay you will grow like a bean when you get going. When I was a teacher, all my pupils did that. One day they'd be up to my waist and the next day up to my eyes!' She smiles widely.

I smile back and begin to inch away. Luckily a man grabs her arm, pointing and talking about something on the horizon. I'm sorry to appear rude, but Frank is pulling at my mind, and I don't want him to start throwing things around the ship as if it's a skittle alley because I can't talk to him.

Luckily there are lots of places a small girl can hide here, even surrounded by hundreds of people. The most convenient is under the canvas of the nearest lifeboat.

'What do you want, Frank?'

*Some toffee!*

'Very funny.'

*Stupid of you to end up on a ship. I had to search and search to find you.*

'Why? I thought you could find me anywhere.'

*Of course I can. It's just harder away from the land. I don't like it out here. Too much water.*

'Well, you did find me, more's the pity. Guess what! They have a mail room on this ship. The letters and parcels are going with the ship all the way to India.'

*So what?*

'So, I'm going to write a letter to my mother and slip it into the postbag.'

*To what address?*

'I don't know. Do you?'

*I'm not a postmistress!*

'Well, do something useful for a change and help me find out.'

*I'm not at your beck and call, Lily Ash.*

'But I'm at yours? That's not fair. I still don't know who you are or why you're talking to me.'

*Fine, I don't want to talk to you any more anyway.*

'I didn't mean that. Don't be so touchy.'

*Go and write your pointless letter. You have no idea how the world works. You think you can write 'Rosetta Ash' on an envelope and the post-wallah in India will comb the country to find your long-lost mother? What a stupid plan.*

'Stop being horrid. That's not all I'm going to do. I'm going to leave Uncle Leonard and travel to India myself.'

*Oooh! Such a big girl, planning a quest!*

'I don't want to talk to you when you're like this.'

*Well, you'd better toughen up. You're not in a girls' school any more, and if you insist on going to India with no money and no map, you're going to need me.*

Typically, he chooses that moment to leave.


I see Hilda Pendleton again in the evening as I'm walking along the narrow deck past the dining room window. The window is open a crack to let the tobacco smoke out. She's sitting at a table with Uncle Leonard and the man who'd been with her on deck.

I've already had my tea, and I'm not allowed to sit with the adults, but my hearing has always been excellent. I crouch in the dark underneath the window and manage to listen to most of the conversation.

It turns out that her husband is also an archaeologist and they're going to work on the same site as Uncle Leonard, although they're going to Egypt first and will meet us in Crete later in the spring.

'What a wonderful coincidence, isn't it, John?' Hilda Pendleton exclaims. 'We've heard so much about you, Mr Ash, and it's marvellous you are coming out to join the crew at Knossos.'

A strange name – Knossos. It gives me an odd feeling, almost like fear.

'Your fame precedes you, Mrs Pendleton. I understand there is no hill or mountain you cannot conquer.' I've never heard my uncle being charming before. It sounds odd in his mouth, like an unfamiliar language. 'And you must tell me of your exciting discoveries at Tel el Amarna, Mr Pendleton.'

'Call me John.' A clink of glasses. 'It's an amazing site. We've yet to find the true treasures, but we will. Very soon. You must come and see it for yourself.'

Uncle Leonard grunts as if agreeing, but I suspect he won't be going to Egypt voluntarily for some time.

'Amarna is unique in Egyptian history, like Knossos is for the ancient Greek world. Unique and very important.' John Pendleton speaks like a sword thrust, direct and quick. 'Your work has mainly been in classical antiquity, is that right, Mr Ash?'

'Before you launch into all that, John, let's do the social pleasantries!' Hilda Pendleton interrupts. 'I know how keen you archaeologists are to get down to the stratigraphy straight away and forget about normal life.' She laughs. 'Are you married, Mr Ash?'

'Leonard, please, Mrs Pendleton. No, I'm yet to join that happy band.'

'But you have a child with you? A young girl? I saw you come on board together. So pretty. Amazing grey eyes – almost silver! And soon to have a birthday, I understand.'

Uncle Leonard clears his throat. I suspect all the words he'd like to say about me are stuck in there.

'That's my niece, Lily. Unfortunately there's no one else to care for her, so she's my ward for now.'

'How sad!' Hilda Pendleton says, and seems to mean it. 'What a difficult situation for you both. But you have the opportunity to teach her so much through travel. It's the making of a modern young woman. It certainly was the making of me.'

There's a pause. Uncle Leonard is probably gulping his drink.

'Indeed, Mrs Pendleton. Although my main concern is to keep her safe, for my sister's sake.' Another spasm of throat-clearing. 'Mr Pendleton, do tell me of your last meeting with Sir Arthur. I want to make sure I understand his instructions about the priorities for this season at Knossos. I understand it's suffered considerably from neglect and earthquakes.'

After that, there's nothing of interest to me. Just a long, tedious conversation about the Great War, the damage it did to Crete, and the latest refinement of a 'pottery sequence'. Being an archaeologist sounds rather dull.

But Hilda Pendleton doesn't think so. She contributes to the discussion enthusiastically. And, what's more, I can understand most of what she says. I wonder whether she'll ever travel as far as India. I can imagine her being an interesting and useful companion on that long journey.

# Chapter 5
## 16th January, 1930
## SS *Moldavia*
## Mediterranean Sea

It occurs to me that you may know nothing of my life since you left me. So, while I'm waiting for the ship to reach the next port, I'll try to bring you up to date.

After you left, they found a nanny for me. She looked after me as best she could, considering she was older than Grandmother and quite deaf. But she stroked my head when I was sick or upset, sang to me and made up stories about my daddy. This was confusing because Grandfather had told me I didn't have a father.

When Nanny was dismissed and I was sent to school, it was made very clear to me by the other girls that I *must* have a father. Probably a very unsuitable one, and besides that, I was certainly illegitimate and so they couldn't possibly be my friends.

I wonder what you'd have told me about my father. I'd appreciate the truth, Mother. I think I deserve it.

You must be twenty-nine by now. Your birthday is in April. You'll be thirty when I am twelve. Anyone can do the calculation. You were still very young when you left me, and I'm always being told that young people are foolish and irresponsible. I don't think you were, but that is what they want me to believe: that you left me because you didn't want to take care of me.

Since Nanny left, I've really only had Frank to look after me. He must have died when he was ten, because that's how old he is whenever I ask him. I'm older than Frank now, although he was much older than me when I first heard him.

It was a spring day in 1924, and I was standing by the river at the bottom of the garden. I was sad that Nanny had been dismissed and that Grandfather was sending me away to boarding school that very afternoon. I was frightened too.

Living in Glascott Manor, I'd always been given the strong impression that being wet and dirty was the worst possible thing for a young girl to be, especially when going out in public. So my plan was to jump into the river, because after that they wouldn't be able to send me anywhere.

They'd have to wash my clothes, dry them, iron them and, by then, I'd have convinced them that I needed Nanny to keep me respectable.

I was standing on the muddy bank, my new brown leather shoes already slipping towards the swollen river, when Frank yelled at me. I was so surprised I sat down in the mud, looking around for the shouting boy.

But there was no one in the garden. It was drizzling and the bluebells were out under the trees. I remember because, being only six, I thought it was a fairy talking to me from the flowers. Nanny loved stories about flower fairies. But I'd assumed a fairy would have a sweet melodious voice not a loud, bossy boy's voice like you'd hear arguing about a ball in the park.

He convinced me, in the end, to stay away from the river, go back inside and get on with it. Going to boarding school didn't do him any harm, he said. Lots of fun to be had in school. Games, practical jokes, snowball fights. Besides, he would come with me.

But I'd better not do anything as stupid as trying to dunk myself in the river ever again. What a ninny.

Never having had any brothers or sisters, I found this surprising and rather nice. Although I was soon to realise how demanding and destructive he could be. *No one is perfect*, as Nanny used to say. And when you have no living friends, *beggars can't be choosers*, which was another of her favourite sayings.

I hope you're interested in what's happened to me since you left. I'm very interested in what happened to you. Particularly after the one postcard you sent on the 12th of May, 1922 from Port Said, before going through the Suez Canal and on to the Arabian Sea. In it you told me how much you loved and missed me, and asked if I knew there were camels in Egypt? The postcard had a camel and a pyramid on the front, in case you've forgotten.

I still have that postcard, although it is practically falling apart. I keep it inside my copy of *Our Wonderful World: Peeps at the British Empire*, a book full of maps and illustrations. I've hidden the postcard between the pages about India, and I've brought it with me.

After that postcard, there were no more. Then after several months, Grandfather told me that you would never write to me again as you'd died of fever, or shipwreck, or snake bite, or tiger attack. He didn't actually tell me, a four-year-old, how you died, and so I have simply invented all these things.

He lied to me. It was easier to do so without details.

Nanny stroked my forehead until I stopped crying and fell asleep. And after that, no one would talk about you, ever. If I asked, they would simply ignore me. Now I'm on a ship, steaming through the Mediterranean Sea, on the same route you took in 1922.

Hilda and John Pendleton are also going to Port Said, but not through the canal. Instead they are going up the Nile to the city built by the rebel Pharaoh Akhenaten, to direct that excavation. Then they are coming to Crete, as Mr Pendleton is the new 'curator' of the site of Knossos. Sir Arthur Everett appointed him. But Mr Pendleton doesn't seem very impressed by Sir Arthur, whom he calls 'Little Arthur'. Uncle Leonard, on the other hand, worships Sir Arthur, who has stacks of money and can do anything he wants with it. Uncle Leonard is obviously hoping to keep on his good side, but Mr Pendleton doesn't seem to care a jot about that.

You can tell I've been doing more eavesdropping – but also Hilda Pendleton and I have been on deck together a few times, and she always answers my questions. So I know something about Knossos and the Minoan people who lived there. They loved bulls, acrobatics and, bizarrely, snakes. Seems odd to me.

Mrs Pendleton thinks it's wonderful that women were important in Minoan religion, holding great power, leaping over bulls, charming snakes and going around with fantastic flouncy dresses that left their bosoms exposed! It's hot in

Crete, she explains. But still, that's not something I can imagine Uncle Leonard being comfortable with.

Hilda Pendleton also points out sights of interest along the journey, such as ports and coastlines. She's told me stories about Gibraltar and its Barbary apes, about Cadiz and its kings, about Tunisia and the Roman armies marching up and down making roads, theatres and mosaics.

She obviously used to be a teacher, but I don't hold that against her. She's an archaeologist now, working alongside her husband. Did I mention that John Pendleton has a glass eye? It's very realistic. He played a practical joke on Uncle Leonard with it, involving soup. Uncle Leonard nearly choked. He was still coughing half an hour later.

I suspect he's not best pleased to have to work with Mr Pendleton at Knossos. In fact I'm quite sure Uncle Leonard dislikes people generally and just puts up with them as an unfortunate necessity.

In all this information I'm not telling you the most important thing which is that I've now got an excellent plan to find you. I've already smuggled a letter to you into the postbag on the ship. But that's just a backup in case my main plan fails.

I am going to fake my own death.

If they can lie about your death to me, I can do it to them.

When the ship arrives at the port of Piraeus near Athens where Uncle Leonard is to disembark, I'll have disappeared. I've kept out of his way as much as possible, so he's used to my absence. He won't miss me until it's time to leave. I'll place my hat near a railing, so it looks as if I've gone overboard. Then I'll hide under the canvas of the lifeboat until we reach Port Said, which is apparently only two days further on from Athens.

I'll be a stowaway! I've read all about that in a newspaper. Billy Gawronski, a boy from New York, dived into a river and climbed aboard a ship sailing for Antarctica, just for an adventure. I don't know what happened to him in the end. He might've been frozen solid. But my reason for stowing away is much more important than mere adventure, and luckily I don't eat much, unlike boys. I've been hoarding bread rolls from breakfast for two days. Also a piece of cheese. And the Mediterranean is not as cold as the Southern Ocean, even in January.

Frank doesn't think much of my plan, but then he never does.

If I can't make it through Port Said undetected, I'll have to convince Mrs Pendleton to claim me as her ward for a while. My plan after Port Said is vague, but I do know that the ship is definitely going all the way to Bombay. When I arrive, I can ask about you, using the photograph. I'll keep showing it to people until someone recognises you. This will only work if you made it as far as Bombay, so I very much hope you did.

People are swarming on the deck now. We're coming into a port that Hilda Pendleton is very excited about – Syracuse on the island of Sicily. She told me all about Archimedes the great inventor who lived and died there in 212 B.C. He was a genius and helped defend the city against the Romans by making massive catapults that could sink their boats. Hilda (she insists I call her by her first name) also knows about Roman lavatories, Vestal Virgins, death rites and hasn't attempted to tell me about pottery sequences once. She does, however, ask me a lot of personal questions. I haven't told her about you – or anything else. I'm good at evasion.

After a night in Syracuse, it's only one more day's travel to Piraeus where I'll be putting my plan into action. While I'm travelling through Egypt, I'll find out how to undo the curse on Uncle Leonard. There are bound to be priests or scribes who can help me. Or maybe Mr Pendleton can. He's an expert in hieroglyphs, I think. But I'm not sure I can trust him with my secrets. He's different to his wife. Thinks only about his work, his achievements, his interests, and his jokes. I'll have to wait and see.

In the meantime, Sicily is almost on our bow. I wish I could get off the ship and find a Roman lavatory to try out.

## Chapter 6
18th January, 1930
Piraeus, Greece

My plan failed. I won't be coming to find you in Bombay. Not yet, anyway.

I have only myself to blame I suppose, but it is very hard not to blame Uncle Leonard, who's been absolutely beastly!

I was sure that, if I stayed quiet, they wouldn't bother with me after a cursory look round. I enjoyed listening to the panicked searching, safe under the canvas, although it wasn't at all comfortable lying on the boards of that wooden lifeboat. And I probably shouldn't have taken the blanket from my bunk with me because I heard Uncle Leonard say *Who falls overboard with their blanket?* But really Uncle Leonard had his own safety on his mind more than mine.

The Egyptian curse I wrote began: *if you abandon this young girl and she comes to harm . . .*

They searched the entire ship for hours. Eventually it was Mr Pendleton who found me in the lifeboat after we'd been in dock for quite some time. Hilda Pendleton cried with relief that I hadn't drowned in the cruel sea, but Mr Pendleton was less charitable. And Uncle Leonard was incandescent with rage.

I like that phrase, although I didn't enjoy experiencing it. He didn't hit me – but he did haul me out of the lifeboat by the collar of my coat, shake me and shout at me for what seemed like hours.

After being scolded by the ship's captain and hugged by Hilda Pendleton, in my case, and slapped on the back by Mr Pendleton, in Uncle Leonard's case, we eventually walk down the gangway onto the dusty landing and stand next to his lonely trunk. Uncle Leonard's palm is sweaty; he grips my hand hard. It hurts. My suitcase is heavy, and I can't swap hands. The sun is bright and blinding.

Most of the passengers left hours before, so there isn't a single taxicab, just a mule and cart. Uncle Leonard drags me over to it. The driver stops smoking and eyes us.

What follows is a swift conversation in a language completely unknown to me, which must be Greek. There's some negotiation, probably about the price, which the mule driver seems to enjoy. I'm able to stroke the mule's soft nose and muzzle while Uncle Leonard is distracted.

They finish the transaction with plenty of hand-shaking. The man easily lifts the trunk and both our cases into the cart and offers me a hand up. There's a little bench just behind the driver's seat. We're riding more or less on top of the luggage. Uncle Leonard is muttering under his breath. Swearing, I think. His knees are up around his ears, and his expression is furious. The driver cracks a whip high over the mule's head, and we lurch forward.

'Where are we going?'

'We are going to Athens, and you,' he pauses and wipes his forehead, 'are going to stay where I can see you at all times and do as you're told.'

I should be meek and just nod as if I'd learnt my lesson, but I'm tired and angry too. I want to be back on the ship on my way to Bombay, not stuck with him.

'You should have left me – then I wouldn't be so much trouble for you. I could've stayed on the ship and gone to Bombay to find Mother. You'd never have had to see me again.'

He barks a laugh.

'So that was your game.' He sounds bitter. 'I've been told you're a clever girl, but you don't seem to be able to understand the simplest facts. Your mother is not in Bombay. She died years ago.'

'That's not true.'

He turns away from me and watches an overburdened cart going in the opposite direction.

'Just like doubting Thomas. Until you see the body you won't believe,' he mutters and pulls the brim of his hat down so it nearly covers his eyes.

'If it *is* true, tell me what happened! Tell me everything! No one will ever talk to me about it! How did she die?'

'I will not be screamed at by a rude little girl,' he hisses.

I start crying. It's the disappointment – and having to listen to him lie about you again.

Uncle Leonard lets me cry.

The mule driver starts asking questions in Greek. Perhaps 'Why is the girl unhappy? Would she like a toffee? Or a decent family?'

I'm sure Uncle Leonard answers him with lies, as usual. The driver listens, nods and is silent.

The mule cart is clopping down a dirt road. Occasionally a car roars past, covering us in fine dust, but otherwise there's only the sound of the wheels on the rough, stoney ground and the mule's huffing breathing.

Uncle Leonard has his head in his hands. I can't see under his hat, so it's a surprise when his voice emerges.

'Your mother wasn't happy in England. She was going to India to start a new life. But she caught malaria when she arrived in Bombay and died quickly of fever. She's buried in a British cemetery in the city, and that's the whole story. I'm sorry you don't believe me, but that is what happened.'

I don't answer.

We're passing groves of trees with small, elongated silvery leaves. The sun is briefly covered by cloud, and I wipe my eyes on my sleeve. I decide to pretend that I believe him. It's a better cover for my plans than continuing to argue with him. If he thinks I've accepted his lies, he'll let his guard down, and I'll be able to find another way to escape.

It's difficult, but I try to sound as if I'm taken in.

'What's malaria?'

Uncle Leonard takes off his hat and wipes his forehead with a hankie.

'It's spread by mosquitoes. When they bite, they inject the disease into your blood and in some cases it is fatal.'

'Isn't there a cure?'

'Sometimes quinine helps prevent it, but not always.'

I pause for a moment.

'And who is my father?'

Uncle Leonard coughs in surprise and looks angry again.

'I should not have to deal with this,' he whispers. 'I'm a bachelor.' He stares at the increasingly busy roadside lined with shops, keeping his face averted as he answers me. 'Lily,

I will never talk to you about this again. Your father was a soldier. Rosetta met him during the Great War. Then he died on duty.'

'Were they married?'

He shakes his head.

'It was a dreadful mistake. Long ago. The best thing is to forget it.'

'What was his name?'

Uncle Leonard shivers, as if someone had walked over his grave. He shuts his eyes.

'I believe his name was Douglas Buchanan.'

'Douglas Buchanan?' There is silence between us, but the city noises become louder. 'Where was he from?'

'Scotland.' He grips his hands tight between his legs. 'There's no point questioning me further. I've told you all I know.'

*Douglas Buchanan.*

*You* could tell me a lot about him. And you will when I find you.

My head swirls with questions: How did you meet? What was he like? Do you have a photograph of him? How did he die?

I'm half-Scottish. I've never been to Scotland. Did he give me this strangeness, this weird sense of what's happened in the past, this door in my head that allows disembodied people to talk to me? Or did you?

If he's really dead, can *I* talk to *him*?

I find myself wanting to speak to Frank. I have so much to tell him – and to ask. But I'll have to wait. Going into a trance on a mule cart next to my uncle would be the nail in some kind of coffin.

It turns out our destination is The British School at Athens, a small boarding school for adults who study archaeology and the classics, it seems. It's much more bright and cheerful than any boarding school I've ever been to.

When we arrive, I'm given some fruit juice and a plate of bread and cheese, shown the bathroom and sent to bed, although it's only three o'clock in the afternoon. Uncle Leonard locks the door from the outside. He treats me like a criminal. My room on the first floor has a single bed, a sink, a desk with a lamp and a small window. I check if I'll fit through it, but the drop is too high for escape. I'd probably break my ankle.

I sleep for a couple of hours, although I don't want to – until Frank wakes me up. He keeps saying he told me so about the stowaway plan. And he doesn't seem very interested in what I've found out. But he *is* impressed that my father was a soldier and starts speculating about how he died. I change the topic.

'Frank, why did you start talking to me all those years ago?'

*You were about to kill yourself jumping into that river, silly. I had to stop you.*

'But why were you there by the river?'

*I just used to be around there, so I noticed you.*

'Where are you now?'

*Next to you!*

'No, I mean where are you when you're not with me?'

*I don't know. Why are you asking me such stupid questions?*

'Did you know my mother?'

*What is this, an interrogation? I'm not interested in women. I had a dog called Buster. Now he was terrific fun.* I can hardly hear him; his voice is so faint. *You're so far away; I'm stretched out like elastic. You should have run away in England while you had a chance.*

I try to hold on to him, but he trickles away like water through cupped hands.

'Please don't go, Frank. I'll be in England again soon. Stay near me. Without you, I'll only have Uncle Leonard for company!'

There's no reply. Just a high-pitched buzzing in my ears. He's gone.

At least if Frank is feeling weak, he can't break things in a spectacular way and cause havoc. But I'm worried. If he leaves me, will something or someone else take his place?

# Chapter 7
## 19<sup>th</sup> January, 1930
## Athens

When Uncle Leonard eventually lets me out in the morning, he looks exhausted. That's probably due to the shouting I heard from his room, right next to mine, last night. He fought in the Great War (which was only great because of the number of dead. In every other way it was truly terrible). Uncle Leonard was hit by shrapnel in his right arm, luckily survived the infection and was invalided out of the army. All his friends died. I suppose that might explain why he's strange, grumpy, doesn't like talking and has nightmares all the time. Mrs Jones certainly thought so.

At breakfast he reads a book while I watch a large bird on the lawn outside the dining room. As it comes nearer, I see its long, curved beak. An ibis, the bird of *Thoth*. It's poking around near the garden pool, but its glossy eye catches mine. When I move my chair to get up, Uncle Leonard jolts out of his study of ancient tombs and frowns at me.

'*Where* are you going?'

'Into the garden.'

'No time for that. Get your coat. We're going out.' Uncle Leonard lays the book down, wipes his mouth carefully with a napkin and gets to his feet. 'I'll wait for you by the door.'

I glance back at the inviting garden. The bird is gone.

'Can we visit the Akropolis?'

'This is not a sightseeing holiday, Lily. I'm here to work, and because I can't trust you, you'll have to come with me wherever I go. It's your own fault,' he says, pushing his chair under the table.

I walk slowly to the stairs. Whatever Uncle Leonard has to do, it's bound to be boring. Outside, the air is clear, and the garden of the British School is full of birdsong. I'd love to roam around by myself. I'm usually good at not being noticed and sneaking into useful places without being seen. But it's going to be a while before Uncle Leonard lets his guard down with me, and I can't afford to raise his suspicion again. I must pretend to be obedient.

I brush my teeth and pull on my coat. The curse paper is still in the pocket – a silly place to keep it. It might easily fall when I take out my hankie. I smooth it on the desk. Maybe if I add some hieroglyphs to undo the curse and appease *Thoth*, it will be cancelled. Or if I cut out certain symbols, like a used train ticket being punched.

But would that make it worse? I've already called up powers I don't understand. I should've brought the hieroglyph book with me and tried to work out a counter-spell. For now, I hide the curse paper amongst the Egypt pages of *Our Wonderful World* and lock the bedroom door.

Downstairs, Uncle Leonard is standing opposite the front door, as promised, looking at his pocket watch.

'Give me the key.'

I place it in his palm reluctantly. He puts it in his breast pocket and opens the door. We walk onto a bright stone walkway with pots of flowering plants at each column. He marches towards the gate at the end. I decide to try to establish a better relationship with Uncle Leonard. All this hostility is very tiring.

'What are those trees, Uncle?'

'Olive trees. You'll see them everywhere. And taste them.' He stops at the gate. There are cars rumbling along the road outside. A church bell rings; the deep notes echo off the wall. 'Now listen carefully,' he commands, turning to face me. 'I will not hold your hand, but you are to walk beside me *at all times*. Do not speak unless you are spoken to, and do NOT go anywhere without me. Is that quite clear?'

I look up at his pale, frowning face.

'Yes, Uncle.'

'Good. Watch out for the trams.'

And we walk out onto the streets of the Greek capital.

Athens is nothing like London. It's cold but sunny, has broad streets and lots of cafés where people sit outside, in the open air, smoking and drinking coffee. I don't see a single pub. They have shops piled high with all kinds of pastry, but I know better than to annoy Uncle Leonard by asking for one. Sadly, they look too sticky to sneak into my pocket.

I don't steal often, just sometimes, if I'm hungry, or if I need something that adults refuse to get for me. Only ever from a shop, never from a person. You would have given me these things yourself if you hadn't gone away, Mother.

I know you understand and wouldn't want me to suffer from hunger. Would you?

Maybe you should've thought of that before you left, because since then I've often been hungry and sad.

But this morning I'm too excited by Athens to be either. Many of the men have large moustaches and thick, dark hair. Many older women are dressed from head to toe in black, but younger women wear the same fashions as they do in London. The stone buildings are large and have balconies. The sky is bright and cloudless. In spite of everything, I feel lighter. Possibly even happy.

Then, abruptly, Uncle Leonard stops in front of a blue door next to a shadowy shop window. I peer past the reflections. At the back are boards with paintings of bulls and beautiful women in bright dresses, and in front are golden masks and large decorated vases marked with swirls and tentacles. The sign above reads *É. Girardon – Athènes*

'Don't touch anything,' Uncle Leonard says, ringing the bell beside the door.

We wait for several slow moments. Eventually a woman answers, wearing high heels and a dress with many flounces. She looks a bit like the paintings. Her dark hair is piled on top of her head in an elaborate mountain of curls, but her thick makeup doesn't quite conceal the wrinkles squeezing the centre of her forehead and pulling down her mouth.

'Yes?'

'Leonard Ash to see Monsieur Girardon. He's expecting me.'

She looks us over, unimpressed, and gestures us inside. 'Wait here, please.'

I cannot place her heavy accent. Her heels strike the marble floor as she walks to the back of the shop and knocks on a closed door.

I sidle away from Uncle Leonard to look at some of the things on the table in the middle of the shop. Most of the objects on display are ceramic pots decorated with designs of fish or bulls. Uncle Leonard has his back to me and is gazing into one of the glass cases by the wall. I put my finger on a pot decorated with a curling snake. There's no vibration of time, no image in my mind of the maker or user. It's just a reproduction, although it looks old.

A man comes out of the office and greets Uncle Leonard. Short, smartly dressed, with a goatee beard and thick moustache that curls like wings below his cheeks. Dark eyes. He doesn't smile or frown at all as he and Uncle Leonard make their introductions and shake hands.

'And who is this?' The man gestures at me.

'My ward, Lily. She will not touch anything. I have warned her.'

'But she *must* touch. See what she'd like to take. A small souvenir from our atelier? A piece of ancient history. *N'est-ce pas*? You cannot visit us and leave empty-handed.' Despite his words, the man's expression is quite blank.

I look at Uncle Leonard. He doesn't like to be contradicted, but pretends to be grateful.

'That is kind. Lily, be very careful with all the things here.' He gives me a meaningful look.

'My wife will help her. You come, and we will discuss Sir Arthur's plans for this restoration. Ernestina!'

The woman turns, failing to disguise her impatience, as Uncle Leonard follows Monsieur Girardon into the office. She walks towards me in her high black shoes.

'So, what you like? We have small things to fit your pocket.' She gestures me over to the central table to look at small clay figurines and discs imprinted with human figures, animals, birds and flowers.

I pick them up one by one, and, to please her, choose a tiny dolphin disc painted in grey and blue. It reminds me of Hilda Pendleton. But it's a lifeless object, another reproduction. Around the shop, there are real objects from a distant time, beating out a vibration in my head. Their call is strong, strange – irresistible.

'Thank you,' I say as she wraps the dolphin in some dull brown paper and pushes it towards me over the counter. I slip it into my coat pocket. 'May I look at the things in the cabinets?'

She clicks her tongue and looks impatiently at the office door.

'Only if you promise to be careful. Some of these are real objects from Knossos which the master is going to copy. Some are copies going to very important museums for their displays. You must stand very still. Like a dead person.' She looks severely down her straight nose.

I shiver and nod silently.

The glass cabinets contain miniature sculptures and sealstones engraved with symbols and animals. I peer in. I'm sure I'll be able to touch such tiny objects without them affecting me too much.

'You want a real one?' The woman unlocks the door with a shiny little key.

I nod. It'll be the first time I've held an object from Crete. I wonder if I'll see the women with snakes. I'll be able to control the visions if I only hold it for a moment, and, with this impatient woman, that's all I'll have.

She reaches in with long fingers and selects a purple, lozenge-shaped stone.

'Open your hand.'

She places it on my palm.

'Hold it at an angle so the light shows the design.'

But I'm already seeing a herd of goats with long curved horns climbing a mountain, white with snow and crumbling stone. An old man watches them from the doorway of a low stone building. He is happy they have returned. He opens his calloused palm and stares down at the reddish-purple stone catching the sunlight.

'Here, give it back to me. Are you sleeping?'

Madame Girardon snatches the little goat stone out of my hand.

'No, I just have a headache,' I manage, my throat tight. 'It's beautiful.'

'Yes, it was found at Knossos and will go to the museum in Heraklion after we have made some impressions and a reproduction for Sir Arthur. The stone is porphyry. Very hard, imported from Egypt.'

'It's lovely. So perfect.'

She replaces it on its small cushion in the cabinet. 'Just one more. I have work to do.'

'Another real artefact, please.'

'Very well.'

Madame Girardon reaches up to the top shelf and carefully removes something small and golden.

'This is the best, so be very careful.' She holds it in her manicured hand. 'It's from a tomb near Knossos, and we have the task of making a copy for the largest museum in France. It's entirely unique.'

She places the tiny gold deer into my hand. The beautifully carved head and ears fold back on its sleek body, as if its mother had just left it behind, and it was waiting quietly so as not to attract the attention of any predators.

But it has no past. I turn it in my fingers, this way and that. It's as dead as a newly made brick, and my disappointment makes me reckless. I put it back in her outstretched hand.

'Are you sure it is a real, ancient artefact?'

'What do you mean? You don't like it?'

'No, no, I think it's beautiful, but I just wondered if you were mistaken and it's new because –'

I can't tell her why, of course, and she's staring at me furiously.

'What lies! This is the genuine one! Did your uncle tell you to say that?' She takes a step towards me, holding the deer high as if she'll hit me with it.

I step back fast, bumping into the other cabinet behind me.

'*Attenzione!*' Madame Girardon drops the deer and grabs the teetering cabinet. The objects slide about in disarray. The golden deer rocks to and fro on the marble floor.

The woman glares at me.

'Stupid girl! Look what you have done to a priceless work of art! Go and sit down over there!' She points to a chair against the wall and gathers up the fake deer, making a great show of checking it all over for damage before putting it back on the top shelf and locking the cabinet door.

I sit on the chair and stare at my hands while she makes sure all the objects in the second cabinet are back in their right places, muttering angrily in a language I can't, and don't want to, understand. As she locks it with a turn of her wiry wrist, the office door opens and Uncle Leonard and Monsieur Girardon re-enter the room.

# Chapter 8

Monsieur Girardon can't wait to get rid of us. He ushers us through the door while his wife continues complaining loudly in several languages. I think they're about to have an almighty row.

Perhaps he doesn't want her letting children handle his precious, faked objects. Perhaps Uncle Leonard put him in a bad mood, just as he always does me. Perhaps she thinks she's above dealing with children. I'm glad I don't have to watch the fight.

Madame Ernestina does not help my cause by telling Uncle Leonard that I'm a *clumsy, dishonest little girl*. I can think of a few choice words for her too, but I keep my mouth shut. No more damage is required.

Uncle Leonard questions me as soon as we turn the corner of Skoufa Street. I try to explain, without mentioning that I see the past. Instead, I tell him how frightening Madame Girardon was and how she was the one who dropped the artefact. Of course he doesn't believe me.

There are some very beautiful buildings and parks in Athens, but I'm not allowed to stop and look at anything. He marches me straight back to the British School, holding my forearm in an iron grip, and locks me in my room again.

Tomorrow we are sailing to Crete, and Uncle Leonard doesn't want me ruining the timetable with *one of my little tricks*.

I think it must be about six o'clock now. Uncle Leonard is downstairs having a drink with some of the other archaeologists. I can hear their chatter through my window. I've eaten a strange pastry with spinach and a very salty cheese and a cup of sweet tea, but in fact, I'm a prisoner.

I'd like to point out that I never asked for this ability. Other people have perfect pitch or understand complicated equations about the universe. I hear spirits of dead people and read the past through objects. At least that's what I think is happening. I've never found anyone who could explain it to me.

When I first saw a vision of the past, around the age of seven, I told a teacher. She'd brought in an ancient flint arrowhead to show us. It was passed around the class. When I talked about how it was made, she told me I had a *vivid imagination*. But when I persisted in explaining that the man who'd made the arrowhead had used it to shoot a giant deer with enormous antlers, she became enraged and hit my palm with a ruler.

Did I inherit this gift from you, Mother, along with my straight blond hair?

If not, perhaps it came from my father, Douglas Buchanan. Or from no one. Just a freak.

I wish I could ask you if Uncle Leonard told me the truth. I need to talk to someone, and the only 'person' available to me is Frank. Not that he's a good listener. Do you know many ten-year-old boys who are? But sometimes he does surprise me with useful insights.

I must concentrate very hard when I call him. I sit cross-legged, shut my eyes and try to open a door in my mind, one that seems to be located in the centre of my forehead. Then it feels as if a ribbon of energy is being pulled out of my head towards a point in the distance. My entire body tingles, not gentle tingles – strong like the worst pins and needles. There's a heavy feeling of pressure inside my head, as if I've just entered a narrow, deep cave. And then I fall faster and faster into blackness until Frank finds me.

*What do you want?*

'I need your help.'

*I'm weak here. I can't help you. Why don't you come home, then we can have fun.*

'You mean the kind of fun that gets me in trouble – the breaking vases and windows kind of fun?'

*It's better than being locked up on the other side of the world, isn't it?*

'I didn't know Uncle Leonard was going to take me to Greece and keep me prisoner! I didn't want this to happen.'

*You've done it all wrong – you should have lost him in London when you had a chance and gone back home from there.*

'But then I wouldn't have gone on the ship, and that was my chance to find Mother.'

*Do you have any idea how many people there are in India?*

I don't answer.

*Millions. Millions and millions of people. And all you've got is a photograph. And no money.*

'I do have money.'

*How much?*

'I'm not telling *you*.'

Frank makes his usual rude noise. But it's fainter than before.

'How do you know so much about India, Frank?'

*I don't remember.*

My attempts to find out about Frank's life are usually blocked. I once tried to ask him how he died, and he became so angry it left me with a headache for days. I'm getting that feeling now.

'Well, forget about India. What do you think I should do now to escape?'

*What have you got with you? List your weapons and tools.*

'Umm, I have the curse paper, a photograph of my mother, a book about the world with maps, my clothes, a pair of boots, some money and some hair elastics and ribbons.'

*You need a slingshot.*

'I don't have anything like that.'

*Make one. Use your hair elastic.*

There's a sound at the door, as if someone is turning the handle. I try to ignore it.

'What should I use it for?'

*Write a message, wrap it round a stone and sling it over the wall. Say you're being held hostage by your uncle.*

'But I can't write in Greek.'

*Someone in the police will read English, you idiot. Stop making excuses.*

The handle is properly rattling.

'Frank, I have to go! Someone's at the door.'

There's a long pause.

*Someone else is coming. Shut the door! Don't let them in!*

I force my eyes open, feeling giddy from Frank's sudden exit. The room is empty. The harsh light of the bare bulb overhead makes me blink. The door handle shakes violently.

'Who is it?' My voice is hoarse.

There's no answer.

The handle continues to jerk as if it's a trapped animal.

I kneel and inch towards the door, shivering. The floor is freezing cold. There's a spirit in the threshold, and it's trying to come through.

*Someone else is coming to you.*

This resident spirit is stronger than Frank. Older. The door is nearly off its hinges. It's banging the catch against the lock. The whole frame is shaking.

I must close my mind. The best way is distraction, happiness, activity, but I've got nothing inside the narrow room. The new spirit pulls and pulls, and the keyhole gets bigger and bigger.

He is desperate. Determined. He's been waiting a long time for a mind to speak to. He has plans for me.

'No!' I push myself to my feet and start running back and forth across the room. 'No!' I shout out loud again. I need to stay alert and away from the door, but I can't keep going all night by myself.

Eventually the spirit will get in.

I start singing *Good-bye-ee*, holding my eyelids open. I try to fill my mind with memories of you, the kind man in the museum, the toffee.

Behind me the door slams open.

'Lily! Stop shouting at once!'

I'm even relieved to see Uncle Leonard, although he looks more furious than concerned.

'There was –' I stop. 'I had a nightmare.'

'Were you asleep already?'

I nod, trembling all over.

'You look terrible. What's happened to your arms?'

There are scratches along my forearms, just beading with blood. He looks at a complete loss.

'Perhaps I could have a cup of tea?'

'I see,' he says, pushing his hair back across his temple. 'Yes. Tea.' He's looking around the room as if it's a battleground. 'I thought I heard you shouting at someone.'

'It was just my nightmare.' I edge towards the door.

He looks frightened himself – probably because of the curse. I'm showing signs of being hurt, and he's worried about being eaten alive, even though he's not in Egypt or anywhere near a river.

And he should be.

'I see.' He presses his hair to his scalp again. 'I'll take you to the kitchen. But we have to be up very early. We mustn't miss our ship.'

I nod and follow him, meekly enough, down the stairs. I'm cold, exhausted and my head aches. Even if the front door was wide open, I wouldn't be able to run away.

We walk through the dining room, past young students talking loudly in Greek, leaning on a table crowded with bottles and glasses. We stop by a door at the back of the room, and Uncle Leonard taps on it with his knuckles.

The door opens.

'*Kalispéra?*'

Uncle Leonard says a few words in Greek, grimacing awkwardly, and the woman opens the door wider.

She's not much taller than me, dressed in black, her grey hair almost completely hidden by a white scarf tied at the back of her neck. Her expression is warm, her dark eyes creased with wrinkles. Like a grandmother – but a kind one. A bit like Nanny, only more lively.

'Go with Kyria Sofia,' he says. 'She'll give you a warm drink.'

I follow her and sit by the fire on a stool she pulls out for me.

The woman speaks and I smile, understanding nothing. She picks up a pan and pours milk into it from a jug, then puts it on a grate over the fire to heat. I watch the flames while she keeps up a soft chatter, and the cold begins to lessen.

She's pressing something into my hand. A little plate holding a pastry in a puddle of syrup. No, it's honey. Delicious, flowery and rich. The milk's ready, and she tips it into a cup, adding more honey by the spoonful.

Uncle Leonard is at the door again. I turn away from him, hoping he isn't going to take me away. The thought of returning to my cold bedroom alone is terrifying. But the woman shoos him away and begins humming a tune as she washes and dries the pan.

I finish the drink and the pastry. It feels as if no time has passed. Maybe I've drifted off to sleep. I lick my fingers to keep awake.

Kyria Sofia wipes the blood from my arms, strokes my hair and asks me a question.

I shake my head and frown regretfully.

She laughs and points behind me to a corner of the kitchen where a large woven cloth with a zigzag design hangs on the wall. She takes my hand and leads me towards it. The bed in the alcove behind the woven rug is warm from the kitchen, and a tabby cat is sleeping on the pillow. Kyria Sofia pulls down the blue blanket for me to climb under.

'Thank you,' I say, knowing I'll be safe from the new spirit here, and that's all I care about. The cat gets up when I slip under the coverlet, stretches and yawns showing its sharp white teeth and rough pink tongue. Then it turns a circle and lies at my waist on the bed, purring a little before quickly falling asleep again.

I can hear Kyria Sofia muttering and the chink of cups and plates. Maybe she's laying out things for breakfast on a tray. Some light seeps into the alcove. I can see intricate designs painted on the ceiling – like a path that angles around itself. A kind of maze.

Once more I hear Uncle Leonard's voice. Kyria Sofia replies, he objects, she insists firmly. Finally, he leaves.

I'm already asleep when the cook gets into the bed beside me, but when I wake up in the night having dreamt about you drowning in a deep well, she's there, her strong arm holding me, anchoring me to the reality of honey, cats and kindness.

In the morning, she's already preparing breakfast when Uncle Leonard comes to the kitchen door to reclaim me.

# Chapter 9
## 21ˢᵗ January, 1930
## The Villa Ariadne
## Knossos, Crete

We arrived late last night after an eighteen-hour journey over rough seas in an old fishing vessel, during which I was sick as a dog. I was shown to my room and fell asleep straight away in my clothes, so I had no idea what I'd wake up to on my birthday morning.

It's the best room I've ever had. This floor is below the main reception rooms, so at first it seems as if I'm in the cellar. But when I push the creaking shutters open, I see the beautiful front garden. There's even a window seat! I'm small enough to climb through the window straight outside onto a path that goes all the way around the Villa.

Bright sun, clear air, new birds – even lizards! There's a brown one with tiny legs on a sunny wall. It's about the length of a kitchen knife, but much thicker, with light brown, spotted skin. I watch it for several minutes and only its eyelid moves.

The morning is chilly so the lizard has to warm up in the sun before it can hunt for prey. Same with other cold-blooded animals like snakes. I remember that from a winter science lesson long ago, when the thought of sunshine felt like an impossible dream.

It's not as cold as England here – it feels like early spring. However, it *is* winter so most of the flowers are dead, but the garden has a lovely smell, a bit like scented soap.

I'm called to breakfast by Kosti the cook. He speaks good English and teaches me this: *proino gevma*, 'breakfast', and here that means thick creamy milk called *yaourti* served with honey and round rolls topped with currants. I eat everything. I'm famished.

Uncle Leonard does not say 'Happy Birthday'. I'm sure he's never known, or cared, when it is. I keep the fact to myself in case I need to blackmail him into doing something later. We are the only non-Greek people here. It's very early in the season apparently. Most foreigners will not arrive until March, like the Pendletons. And Sir Arthur himself isn't due until sometime after that.

I've never asked Uncle Leonard what his job is in Knossos. We've yet to have a civil conversation. But I can hear his voice from where I'm sitting, just below the open window of the dining room. He has a visitor.

'Kyrie Ash, I am the foreman of the Knossos excavations – Emmanuel Angelakis. Sir Arthur and the other English archaeologists call me Manolaki.'

I notice a slight clearing of the throat whenever Uncle Leonard has to talk to a stranger.

'Pleased to meet you. I hear from Sir Arthur that your work is excellent, and you are the very best person for identifying pottery and finding tombs.'

'You honour me. I have worked here many years, and Sir Arthur has taught me everything.'

I like the foreman's voice. It's deep and strong, but very warm and unhurried.

'This is my son, Michalis. He is known as Micky. If you want to find me, he will know where I am. He works as a messenger on site. His English is very good. You also have a child?'

Uncle Leonard has to properly cough this time.

'My niece, Lily. I'll tell her to stay away from the new excavations. She's too young to be trusted.'

I feel myself bristling. If anyone is too young, it's Frank. But I always get the blame.

'It will be good for her to see the Palace and where you work. Then she understands where she can go and what she should avoid. Michalis will show her.'

'Very well. If you think that is necessary.' Uncle Leonard sounds less than convinced. 'I don't want to take Micky away from his important duties. Lily doesn't require amusement.'

'It is good that she knows where things are, and you can do Sir Arthur's work without worry. Where is she now?'

'I suspect she's in the garden.'

'Mikis will find her,' Kyrie Angelakis says calmly, followed by a few quiet words of Greek.

I am both intrigued and horrified. I've only just got my freedom and now I'm to have a minder, a Greek boy, telling me where and where not to go, keeping an eye on me. He might not speak proper English. I hesitate for only a moment, then run as fast as I can. I'm good at hiding, and I have a head start, although not a big one.

But I don't know the garden well, and beyond it I know nothing at all. I start by climbing a tree. Trees provide a good viewpoint, and most people don't look for girls in trees. The one I've scrambled up has very scratchy bark and rather sparse leaves. Not the best choice, but I'm pressed for time.

I hear the boy before I see him.

'Miss Ash, Miss Ash!' Although his accent makes it sound like 'Meees Ass', which makes me want to giggle.

He's taller than me, but not by much. He wears a short-peaked, blue cap over dark hair, a woollen jacket, baggy black cotton trousers and there's something on his shoulder that's certainly moving. I can't see his face properly under the cap.

'Miss Ash, I must show you Knossos!' He has climbed the steps up to the veranda and is looking out over the garden as if he owns it. I suppose he has more right to it than I do, but because I've only just got my freedom and it's such a beautiful place, I've already become its ruler in my heart. I don't want to share.

He walks down the steps onto the gravel path, unhurried, looking carefully around. I just want him to conclude that I'm not there and go away, giving me a bit more time to myself. So I sit very still in the tree.

Maybe you think at the age of twelve I shouldn't be so childish. But I haven't had a mother to help me, so, in fact, it's your fault that I am who I am. And maybe you're good at hiding too, and that's why I can't find you.

This boy is not one to give up, however. It's a big garden, and he keeps calling and looking, until eventually I get very uncomfortable and have to shift position. He happens to be looking at the tree at that very moment. Our eyes meet. I slide to the ground ungracefully.

'What is that on your shoulder?' I ask so that I don't have to explain why I've been hiding from him.

He looks me up and down and shakes his head, bemused.

'It's a spiny mouse.' He holds out his arm and the mouse runs down onto his palm. The creature is very quick, with big black eyes and fur that sticks out like soft spines.

I put a finger out to it. 'Does it bite?'

'Only if you are a beetle.'

The mouse sniffs the tip of my finger and runs back up to sit on the boy's shoulder.

'Does it nest in your cap?'

'What?'

'Does it sleep on your head under your cap?'

'No – why would I let a mouse sleep on my head? I would get mess in my hair. It sleeps here.' He holds open the large pocket of his wool coat. Inside there's straw and bits of cotton. The mouse races down the sleeve and jumps into the pocket, turning round until it's hidden by the straw. The boy gently lets go of the flap of fabric and looks at me thoughtfully. 'Now I found you, we need to –'

'Actually, I found you,' I say. I don't know why I'm being so contrary. I think it's because I'm tired of being told what to do.

He tilts his head at me as if he's misheard and tries again.

'Miss Ash, I must show you Knossos.'

'Call me Lily,' I retort. 'What is your name?' Although I already know.

'Michalis,' he says. 'Mikis to my family.' I can see his expression under his cap now, and he looks somewhat annoyed whilst making an effort to hide it. 'All the English archaeologists call me Micky.'

'I'll call you Micky then. What's the name of your mouse?'

He hesitates a moment. This isn't going the way he expected. 'Her name is Margarita.'

'Why?'

He shakes his head.

'You ask a lot of questions, like my little brother. Here, come this way.' He starts walking down the gravel path away from the Villa. 'I found her under the Margarita.'

'What's that?'

'A flower. A small one, with a yellow centre. White petals.'

'A daisy?'

'Daisy. Maybe.'

'Will she come out again?' I'm following him down the path away from the Villa Ariadne and into part of the garden I haven't yet explored.

'Later. She is sleeping.'

I don't want to be like his baby brother, so I stop asking questions, although I do want to know more about how to get a pet mouse. I've never been allowed animals.

'Here – we must climb. Which will not be hard for you,' he says, giving me a sideways glance. We've reached the boundary of the garden, a steep bank dotted with pine trees. The ground is covered with their dropped needles.

It shouldn't be difficult, but the pine needles are slippery and my new shoes have smooth soles. After a while, I accept his offered hand, and he pulls me up to the top. I'm sure my face is turning red.

'From here you can see almost the whole Palace, and so later you will not get lost.'

I don't like people assuming I'm going to lose my way, but I keep my mouth shut this time because the view is quite amazing.

Mountains loom in the far distance below a very blue sky. Just beyond the road, there's a jumble of terraces, pavements, steps, walls, columns, some plain stone, some painted. The site is much larger than I was expecting and less flat. Most ancient sites in Britain are rather boring to look at. Just a few stone walls here and there. But Knossos is more like a small city, half-ruined, full of different corridors, levels and staircases, tumbling down the valley.

'You see, there are many different areas, so I explain a little,' Micky begins.

I can't pay much attention to him because I'm beginning to feel strange. Maybe it's all the travel catching up with me. I wonder if it's Frank, but the sensation is different. My head aches with pressure. The ruins are swimming before my eyes.

'Over there is the Theatral area below the North Portico, and the Royal Road goes that way.' Micky's hand traces the distant stones.

I sit down abruptly, turn away and close my eyes.

'Lily?' Micky takes off his cap and begins waving it in front of my face. 'Are you fainting?'

'No.' I open my eyes, shake my head and concentrate hard on a red and black ant climbing over the pine needles. 'I just don't feel very well.'

'You need a drink. The Greek sun is strong. It happens to many English people. We will find Kosti. Come.'

He assists me down the slope, and I start to feel better as soon as I'm out of sight of the ruins. I'm completely well even before I drink the glass of lemon mixed with honey and cool water provided by Kosti in his kitchen at the back of the Villa.

Micky has some too. He and the cook talk about me in Greek together, but I pretend not to care. My main concern is how I'm going to manage in Knossos if I'm on the verge of collapse every time I look at the ruins.

I haven't met Micky's glance or said a word since we got to the kitchen. Kosti has returned to his work by the sink. Getting up from his chair, Micky calmly declares that the tour of the Palace of Knossos will wait. He'll call for me in a day or two.

'I hope you feel better,' he says, walking to the door.

'It's my birthday,' I blurt out, immediately regretting it, my cheeks burning.

He's taken aback, but not for long. With that same thoughtful look, he pauses in the doorway for a moment. Then he reaches into his pocket.

'You may hold Margarita if it is your birthday. Put your hands together.'

He places her on my cupped palms, and I feel the vibration of her whole body through her feet. She puts one little paw down, then another on the end of my finger.

Micky sprinkles some seed from his pocket on my palm. Margarita snuffles at my hand, tickling me. I have to bounce from one foot to another to bear the sensation. She nibbles one seed at a time with great concentration.

It's the best birthday present I've ever had. I hope he lets me hold her again tomorrow.

## Chapter 10
### 24th January, 1930
### The Villa Ariadne

Do you know the story of the labyrinth in Crete? There are some rather gruesome bits. I'm only warning you in case you're as delicate as Grandmother. But I suspect you're not.

Many centuries ago, in Crete there was a king called Minos. He was very powerful, but, it seems, not very bright. He offended the God of the Sea, Poseidon, by refusing to sacrifice a bull to him. It was a special bull that Poseidon had provided for him, not just any old cow. So Poseidon took revenge on King Minos in a disgusting way. He made Minos's wife, Pasiphäe, fall in love with the bull. And then she had a son by him. I told you it was horrible, but a complete fantasy of course. Anyway, this son was called the Minotaur – which means half-Minos, half-bull.

Minos, Pasiphäe and all the rest of the family didn't like this monster son one bit, but they couldn't kill him because that would have made Poseidon even angrier. So they asked the clever architect, Daedalus, to make a lair for the Minotaur under the Palace of Knossos – a prison from which it would be impossible to escape.

Then there was the problem of what to feed him, because obviously, being half-man, he couldn't just eat grass.

They made the peculiar decision to provide seven young men and women from Athens for his dinner as part of a peace treaty. The hero of this story is Theseus, Prince of Athens. He went along as part of the sacrificial group, planning to kill the Minotaur. Of course, one of Minos's daughters fell in love with him. Myths are full of falling in love and killing, I've noticed.

Her name was Ariadne, and that's who this Villa is named after. She gave Theseus a ball of thread to help him find his way back out of the labyrinth. In case you haven't followed the complicated family relations, the poor Minotaur was Ariadne's half-brother.

Theseus did it all. He killed the Minotaur, saved the Athenians and sailed off with Ariadne. But then he abandoned her on a lonely island. So the question in my mind is: why do we think he's a hero? If you abandoned me, I wouldn't think you were a heroine.

Maybe you did, maybe you didn't. Perhaps you'll tell me what happened one day.

So that's where the story of the labyrinth came from – a maze to hold a monster. And Micky tells me that the corridors and storerooms of Knossos Palace reminded the archaeologists of this legend, alongside the images of bulls and people leaping over them. So Sir Arthur decided to call the people who lived here Minoans, after King Minos and his monster. If you ask me, which you haven't, I think they are jumping to conclusions, not just over bulls. And teachers have always told me not to do that.

In any event, I went with Micky for the tour of the site yesterday, and it did have a strange atmosphere, even more than the museums I've visited. I took great care to keep my mind focused elsewhere and not touch anything. All the workmen on site think I'm the most well-behaved girl, when actually I just know that if I accidentally touch something, like a throne, an altar or even a piece of pottery, I might go into a trance and see what the Palace was really like thousands of years ago. And be taken for a lunatic.

If I was on my own, I'd let myself enter the past and gradually return to consciousness. That might be fine. But there are people all over the Palace. Not many tourists at this time of year, but plenty of workmen and experts from Heraklion. If you are from Crete, you do not pronounce the 'H'. It's actually *Irákleion*. However you say or spell it, it's the main city of Crete and the port where we arrived.

Kosti, Micky and Kyria Maria, the housekeeper, are all trying to teach me Greek. They think my pronunciation is very funny. They are always asking me: *Tha ithéles lígo tsái?* which means 'Would you like some tea?' They find English tea-drinking very amusing too.

They've been telling me stories about Sir Arthur, who is a 'Little King' according to Micky. He's very short, even compared to most Cretan men who are not overly tall, generally speaking. He imports English food and will only drink French wine, never local wine. I think this rather offends Kosti's Cretan pride.

Maria tells me that he insists on having the best of everything. He had a big copper bath installed in a room next to mine at the bottom of the Villa. I'm not allowed in there, obviously. She warns me that one should never cross

Sir Arthur because he has a short, sharp temper and is used to getting his way in all things.

I wonder how Uncle Leonard will like being obedient – as he expects me to be.

Today Micky is taking me to his house in the village to meet his brothers, sisters and mother who, he says, have not stopped asking about me since I arrived. His father has agreed to the visit because the digging season hasn't truly begun yet, so Micky isn't needed as a messenger. Micky stopped going to school when he turned twelve. He works on the site to earn money for his family.

Kyrie Angelakis is a nice man, but that doesn't mean I'm in a hurry to meet the rest of Micky's family so they can laugh at my attempts to speak Greek. I'm walking slowly, kicking a stone along the dirt path behind Micky when I feel the pull in the centre of my forehead. The familiar demand.

Frank has not visited me since Athens. I can't refuse to speak to him now. I claim to need the lavatory urgently and run back in the direction of the Villa, veering off behind a stone wall where the workmen dump the soil from the excavation.

Frank's voice is very faint but has the same tone as ever.

*What took you so long?*

'I was with someone, but I'm alone now. I thought you'd gone, Frank. I'm so glad you found me!'

*You're the one who's been gone! I've been trying to get through, but you're so far. And there are others here, stopping me. Guarding their land. I've been trying to warn you.*

'What? What about?'

*The other spirits, great powers. I told you last time, you have to keep them out. They will eat you alive.* His voice is slow and serious. It chills me. *They are very old. I can't keep them away. This is their territory.*

He sounds weak. So unlike himself.

'I don't know what you mean, Frank! What do you want me to do?'

There's a long silence.

*He's coming. Close the door now!*

My body shivers. I try to concentrate – to close the channel between us. But the new presence arrives while the door to Frank is still open a chink. Frank is gone and the other spirit is pushing into my mind.

'Let me speak to Frank,' I cry. 'I don't want anyone else!'

*The boy is not strong enough to guard you. You are here for me.*

'No!' I must shout this very loudly because I feel my eyes flash open, although I can't yet see what's there. Only the rushing colours of the world beyond ours. 'I don't want you!'

The feeling is not what I'm expecting.

This spirit isn't the cold, hungry presence in that narrow room in Athens. This spirit has huge strength and power, different from Frank's childish tantrums. An immense presence, like a mountain or a charging bull. I'm with him, on the bull's back, riding.

There's no way to resist, but I mustn't let him into my soul, I can't let him consume me.

'Lily!' My shoulders are being shaken. 'Lily!'

I gasp out of the trance. Micky is kneeling over me, looking terrified. Somehow I've fallen on my back.

'I'm okay,' I croak.

'You had a fit. I should get the doctor.'

'No, I'm fine.' I push myself up. 'Absolutely fine.' I feel as if I'm still floating in mid-air, but my hands are covered in soil, my dress and hair too. I must have thrashed around on the ground. My head is throbbing.

Micky looks on wordlessly as I brush off the worst.

'Does this happen a lot?'

I shake my head.

'Once a week maybe,' I mutter.

'You should see a doctor. You might be hurt. People bite their tongues, or worse.'

'No – I don't get hurt.' But I feel as weak as a kitten. Or a mouse.

Margarita has climbed out of Micky's pocket and onto his shoulder. I hold out my hand.

'Not now,' he says. 'Your hand is shaking.'

He reaches up to get the mouse, but she jumps off his shoulder onto the ground. In that split-second, there's a flash of movement by the stone wall. A light brown snake with patches of red and black whips out of a hole and speeds after Margarita down the path.

Micky is running after them, a stone in his hand. It all seems to happen in slow motion, but also too quickly for me to move. The mouse dashes for cover. The snake's head is raised to strike.

Another spirit fills my mind, surging with new power. Entirely different. Like a wave crashing and breaking through the still-open chink. Without any conscious decision, my arm jolts out straight, and the snake's whole body is thrown sideways, as if the ground underneath has picked it up and jerked it towards the scrubby bushes. The snake lies motionless except for the end of its tail, twitching from side to side.

Micky glances at me, at the snake, but barely slows down. He's running after the mouse, gasping words I can't understand. He crouches down in the dirt, holds out his hand and begins singing. Finally Margarita runs towards him.

Micky picks her up, strokes her, murmurs softly, and lowers her into his pocket. Then he turns and stands ready to throw his stone.

The snake shivers all over, flicks out its tongue, and slithers into the undergrowth. Micky is silent for a long time, staring after the snake, holding the stone. My breathing is shallow, so I put my head down, try to calm my racing heart and close my mind completely.

When I finally look up, Micky is staring at me. His face is pale under his cap. He kneels on his haunches a few feet away, looking at my arm, which lies motionless at my side.

There's a scratch on it, like the scrape of a fang.

'You and I, we must talk.'

# Chapter 11

We are walking down the south side of the Palace, outside the perimeter. It's uneven ground. I have to step over piles of loose rock. I'm tired and thirsty. The effort of keeping going is almost too much.

'Where are you taking me?'

'Where no one can see or hear.'

Eventually Micky stops in the shade of a copse of trees. I sink to the ground. He lets me get my breath back before he starts the inquisition.

'How did you do that?'

Perhaps if I was less tired, I'd try to pretend that he'd imagined it all. But I'm sick of lying, and, although I met Micky only a few days ago, I feel I can trust him. He has an aura of genuine friendship. That sounds sentimental, but it's true.

I sigh, only because it's going to be so hard to explain.

'I'll tell you if you take me straight back to the Villa for some of Kosti's lemon drink afterwards.'

He nods.

'I didn't do it – it was one of the spirits who try to communicate with me.'

'What?' Micky cocks his head.

'I know it sounds crazy, but that's what happens. Spirits, probably dead people, talk to me. They can also make real things move. Vases lift up and smash, things fall off walls, snakes are swept aside.' I pause. He's staring at me open-mouthed. 'Well, you saw it! I didn't touch the snake, did I? There was still a door open in my mind after you interrupted my trance. A spirit acted through me. Luckily for Margarita.'

'But, *who* speaks to you?'

I look him in the eye. Micky is taking me seriously, not laughing and not panicking.

'There was a man. An ancient spirit. I don't know who he was – who he is. It was the first time he spoke to me.'

'What did he say?'

'That he had a task for me.'

'What is it?'

I shrug. I feel incredibly tired, but there's no chance of that being enough information to satisfy Micky, and if I tell him what the first spirit actually showed me, he'll most certainly think I'm insane.

'I didn't ask. I was too surprised.' I don't want to try to explain the other presence who'd overwhelmed my mind like a huge wave and had actually controlled the snake. That female spirit came and went so fast, all I knew was her vast strength and the taste of salt on my tongue.

'Maybe the spirit used your thoughts to save Margarita?'

Micky is taking all this fantastical information in his stride and thinking it through.

'Mmmm. Maybe.'

'Why is there blood on your arm?'

'If the spirit moves something, there's always a sign on my body. Usually on my arms. It doesn't really hurt. For every action there must be a reaction.'

Micky tilts his head and squints at me.

'We can find a bandage,' he says eventually.

'It's stopped bleeding already. I'll wash it when we get back. Is Margarita alright?'

Micky lifts the flap of his pocket.

'She's sleeping. I think she is shocked.'

'I know the feeling.'

He glances at me with a half-smile which disappears quickly. Worry lines crease his forehead.

'So, when you have a fit, that is what is happening? You are talking to a spirit?'

'Normally it's just a trance. I've spoken to one particular spirit for many years, and it's usually peaceful if I don't ignore him. But he's weak here and was pushed aside by this new spirit. I was fighting him for control, which is why it looked like a fit, I suppose.'

Micky chews his lip. I can see he's trying to understand, to believe, but he's afraid that I'm making fun of him.

'My uncle has epilepsy. He was burnt falling in the fire.' Micky shakes his head. 'But that is not helpful for you.'

'I think most people would have decided I was mad by now. But you haven't.'

Micky picks up a broken piece of pottery and weighs it in his hand.

'There is more to the world than we see and hear. Anyone who listens in church knows this.'

'That's certainly true.'

'Animals sense things we don't.' Micky looks up at the sky. 'Like dogs being able to smell who is bad and birds flying north.'

'Well, I'm glad you don't want to take me to the lunatic asylum like my family did.'

He looks baffled.

'The what?'

'The place people are sent who've lost their minds.' I tap the side of my head.

Micky looks horrified.

'Sending people away makes them worse!'

'Don't you have lunatic asylums in Crete?'

'I don't know one.'

'Good. I'm safe here.' I throw a pebble into his lap. 'Micky, I know you're curious, but please can we go back to the Villa now, and I'll answer your questions tomorrow? I'm so tired.'

Micky gets up and offers me his hand.

'Of course. Tomorrow. We will find a better place to talk.' He straightens his shoulders and frowns. 'You need someone to help if this happens again.'

'It probably won't,' I lie. 'And Micky, don't tell anyone about this, please. I haven't spoken about it to anyone else, not even my uncle.'

He hesitates a moment, then nods.

'I will not tell.'

'You'll have to think of an excuse for your mother. Say I'm ill.'

'She will give you horrible medicine if I say that.'

'I can pour it down the drain.' We're walking carefully up the slope. 'What kind of snake was that?'

'Leopard snake. Our neighbour keeps one. They eat mice. Tourists shout at them – and at the whip snakes. But they don't harm people.'

'You know a lot about animals.'

'I did not have many toys when I was young, so I played with animals.' He pulls on my arm. 'This way. Not into the Palace. There's a big tour group from America today. They always want my picture.' He mimes someone holding a camera.

I can't help but snort. 'You're famous in America!'

We're walking under the shade of pine trees towards the Villa. A figure is coming down the path towards us. A man. In the shadow and bright patches of sun, I can't make out who it is.

When he's just twenty feet away, I recognise Monsieur Girardon from Athens. He looks very out of place in his smart suit and useless walking stick. And he looks about as pleased to see me as I am to see him.

I stand behind Micky who greets him in Greek. He replies in English.

'Isn't that Mademoiselle Lily behind you? Destroyer of worlds. You still have the dolphin seal we gave you?'

'Yes, thank you, Monsieur Girardon.'

'They bring good luck, you know. Which you will need. I hope you like it better than the golden deer. What very high standards you must have to be unsatisfied by the best artefacts from Knossos.' His voice is high and edgy.

'I am sorry for upsetting –'

'Not at all, Mademoiselle, I am merely, how do you say, teasing you.' He waves the stick in my direction. 'Madame Girardon is not here to scold you. Don't look so worried. I see you and Micky have become friends.' He directs his stick at Micky next. 'Don't let a mysterious foreign girl distract you from your duties, boy. The excavation will fall apart without you.' There's definitely a sarcastic tone to his voice.

'Yes, Kyrie Girardon. When digging starts, I am alert.'

Monsieur Girardon taps his stick on the dusty path.

'Now, where is your father, Micky? I have instructions for him.'

Micky begins to explain where his father is surveying.

'No, no. You lead me there. That's why you get your money, isn't it, Micky?'

Micky closes his mouth and glances at me.

'I'll be fine. I know how to get back to the Villa,' I say softly.

'Is young Lily not well? Greek sun not agreeing with you? Or is it the food? It's always one or the other with the English. Lead on, Micky.'

I watch them leave the shade, heading down the bright stone path towards the site. How long is Monsieur Girardon going to be here? Is he going to sleep at the Villa? I hope I don't have to endure many more of these condescending little talks. I don't trust him, and the feeling is obviously mutual. I must ask Micky what exactly Monsieur Girardon does for Sir Arthur, and then I can work out how to avoid him as much as possible.

By the time I've dragged myself up the slope to the Villa, it's lunchtime, and Kosti hovers around me, making me wash my hands, examining the scratch and insisting I eat. But I don't want a heavy meal, just a drink and plenty of sugar or honey. I convince him to let me have sweet tea and the dessert they call *baklava*, which is sweet, crisp pastry with nuts. He wants me to eat lamb stew as well, but I excuse myself and go to my room.

I shut the door, sorry that it doesn't lock. I'd like some uninterrupted time to myself to think about what just happened. The bull spirit was overwhelming. I wasn't at all prepared for his power. I think he must have been a king long ago. He began to give me his orders, but then the other one arrived – the female spirit who moved the snake and protected Margarita. It all happened so fast.

Maybe these spirits can protect me from other terrifying ones, like that cold screamer in Athens. They are older, more impressive than Frank. Maybe they can overwhelm the crocodile daemon, *Ammut*, and undo the curse. I hope, at least, they'll tell me more about the world beyond. Frank only understands as much as a ten-year-old boy and hates answering questions. Sometimes I wonder if he actually realises that he's dead.

I feel rather disloyal to Frank, but having said he would stay with me, what has he actually done to help? Has he ever used his physical power to do good, rather than just breaking things when he's cross?

The new spirits are very strong, but next time I'll be prepared. I'll stay in control.

## Chapter 12
### Villa Ariadne

I've slept for several hours, and it's nearly sunset. I hate the groggy feeling after spirit conversations. I imagine this is how people who drink too much whisky feel the next morning.

Evening at the Villa Ariadne is full of noises. Unfamiliar bird calls from the garden, music and shouts from the village drifting through the clear air, goats bleating on the hillside. Sitting on the edge of my bed, I can see the front garden through the window.

My uncle is pacing there, back and forth, back and forth, as if he's waiting for someone to arrive. He doesn't smoke cigarettes, instead he drinks gin and plucks at his thinning hair when he's worried. He can't see me because my room is dark.

Uncle Leonard is supposedly my only family, so I should probably feel some affection for him. But I don't. However, I do feel a bit sorry for him. He's obviously an unhappy man. His father was a bully. His mother was weak and fearful. He went to war and had to watch most of his fellow soldiers die. His only sister vanished. Now he is responsible for a girl who listens to the dead and sees the past.

And he has an ancient Egyptian curse on him.

Maybe if we remain here long enough, the curse will expire. Curses can't last for ever, can they? I don't even know how long we are staying in Crete, that's how little we have spoken to one another.

I'm going into the garden to have a proper conversation with him. Or at least try to apologise for cursing him and explain what happened. It can't make things any worse, surely.

I'm sitting on the window seat tying my shoes when I see someone walking up the drive towards Uncle Leonard. A person smoking a thin cigar. Even in the low light, it's obvious straight away that it's Monsieur Girardon from the profile of his elaborate winged moustache. I freeze for a moment. The man doesn't exactly frighten me, but he does cause a feeling of nausea, as if he's a swirling picture I can't focus on.

Whatever I feel about Monsieur Girardon, I very much want to hear the conversation between him and Uncle Leonard. They have their backs to me, looking out over the shadowy garden and the hills beyond. I very carefully lift the latch and push the upper pane of window glass out, securing it on the pin. Then I stand half-hidden behind the shutter, my ear as close as possible to the gap in the window.

They're still in the pleasantry stage of their conversation, and, not surprisingly, Monsieur Girardon is doing most of the talking.

'Of course, there is still plenty to do: repair of important walls, the area to the south needs attention and proper display of the frescoes in the other rooms.'

'But Sir Arthur was quite specific that he wanted to find the burial area for Knossos this season, so his focus will be away from the central Palace,' Uncle Leonard counters.

Monsieur Girardon blows out a long, thin stream of smoke.

'I know he is hungry for more treasure, but unless we think seriously about what the visitors want, the tourists will stop coming on their cruise ships, stop buying the souvenirs.' He picks a bit of tobacco off his lip. 'The neglect since the Great War makes Knossos less attractive. We require tourist money to keep our jobs, don't we, Monsieur Ash, now that Sir Arthur has sold the site?' Monsieur Girardon flicks his cigar ash into the undergrowth. 'Or maybe you do not agree? Maybe you would rather be a treasure hunter too? I thought you were a serious archaeologist trained at Oxford and here to ensure the oversight and quality expected of the British School at Athens?'

I don't think Uncle Leonard is accustomed to being spoken to in this manner, but he eventually rallies after much clearing of the throat.

'Of course, Monsieur Girardon. I'm here to work with Sir Arthur and to carry out surveys for the British School. But without Sir Arthur none of this would be possible. We mustn't antagonise him.'

'Oh, I would never do that. I only ever do as he tells me.' Girardon's sarcastic tone is back. 'We must be obedient to the new King of Knossos.'

Uncle Leonard says nothing, but he takes a big gulp of his drink. Then another.

'Did Sir Arthur approve of bringing your niece to the site? I know he sponsors the Boy Scouts, but he wouldn't want a clumsy girl wandering around his precious ruins.'

Uncle Leonard drains his glass this time.

'Sir Arthur is pleased to accommodate her.' His tone is icy. At least Uncle Leonard isn't accepting Monsieur Girardon's criticism of me.

'Well, we must just keep her away from anything precious or breakable, and all will be well.' Girardon puffs out a great cloud of smoke, and Uncle Leonard coughs. He was exposed to gas in the war and has a delicate chest.

'Apologies, Monsieur, I forgot your weakness,' Girardon says, with fake sympathy.

'The air in Crete is good for me,' Uncle Leonard says stiffly.

'Why was it necessary for Mademoiselle Lily to come to Crete? Was there no boarding school in Britain that could house her?'

The horrible man is like a cat sniffing around for a mouse.

'Unfortunately not. I'll make sure she does not damage any of your work, Monsieur Girardon. And once again, let me apologise for the upset at your atelier.'

'Not at all. Not at all,' Girardon puffs. 'You must have affection for the waif to bring her all this way. I understand that some children are a bit careless at that age.'

Uncle Leonard makes a noncommittal noise. There's a moment of uncomfortable silence.

'Do you ever do any work on Egyptian antiquities, Monsieur Girardon?'

'Egyptian? Sometimes, but very rarely. Why? Are you enquiring on behalf of Monsieur Pendleton, the new Pharaoh of Amarna? I hear he's a very energetic man.'

'Indeed. Yes, he is. I met him and his wife on the ship.' Uncle Leonard takes a wheezy breath. 'What kind of Egyptian objects have you worked on?'

'Statues, necklaces, sometimes gold objects.'

'Do you understand hieroglyphs?'

'Are you interviewing me for a job, Monsieur Ash? Might you have a commission for me?'

'Perhaps. There might be Egyptian objects found here. There was plenty of trade between the two civilisations.'

'I see,' Girardon says. 'Yes. Well, if anything turns up and you need to understand script, you will have to wait for Pendleton. I know nothing of the meaning of hieroglyphs, although I can carve them easily enough.'

'Ah, so if you had a set of hieroglyphs to copy in stone, you would be able to?'

'Of course. I carve hard and soft stone, and I challenge you to find any differences between mine and the original. My work is of the highest quality, *bien sûr*.'

'Your reputation precedes you, Monsieur. I've heard only sincere praise for your reproductions. I may have a little commission for you, but it will have to wait until next month.'

There's a short pause.

'I offer credit,' Monsieur Girardon says, knowingly.

Uncle Leonard sounds as if he's choking. Eventually he stops coughing.

'No need. I have the wherewithal. It must simply wait for Mr Pendleton.'

'But how intriguing. I look forward to knowing more, Monsieur Ash.' Girardon grinds the cigar under his heel. The dinner bell sounds at that moment, and he gestures Uncle Leonard through the door ahead of him.

So, if you heard that conversation, what would you conclude? I'll tell you what I think before I go to the kitchen for my supper. I think Uncle Leonard is trying to counteract the curse. If he wants to write something in hieroglyphs in stone, he obviously believes there is a form of symbols that can break the power of what I wrote. Or perhaps he wants to rebound the curse on the one who wrote it.

I must tell him that I want to destroy the curse too, that I might be able to help even though I don't have the book of translation here.

If only he'll trust me.

I suspect he's made up his mind that I'm bad, and, even if he doesn't quite echo Monsieur Girardon's damnation of me, he probably won't believe that my gift isn't always under my control.

Seemingly to prove that point, I feel the tell-tale pulling at my mind, and the tingling down my neck. I sit on the side of the bed and shut my eyes.

*Lily.*

'Frank! I can barely hear you. Speak louder!'

*I'm trying, but you're too far away.*

'You said you'd stay with me, Frank.'

*I didn't know this would happen. I thought I'd always be strong. Now you're across all that water, and it's so hard to get through.*

His voice is fading.

'I'll be back soon. You can wait a little while, can't you?'

*I don't know. It's never felt like this before. I don't know where I am any more. But I need to tell you about the danger!*

'What danger? What are you talking about?'

*A great power. Different. Deeper. I'll try to warn you.* There's a pause. *I'm being pushed out!*

He gasps, as if he's short of breath.

And I feel it too – that strong, insistent presence, coming towards me like a thundercloud. Not as powerful as when I was sitting amongst the ruins of Knossos, but still, the Bull King dwarfs Frank.

*Shut the door, Lily! Shut the door! I can't hold him off!*

Twice in one day is too much. I try to whisper the words of the *Good-bye-ee* song, hoping it will help. Finally, I concentrate so hard that I manage to close my mind, although it feels like I'm pushing against a charging bull, as if I've run a hundred miles.

It's clear that whenever Frank tries to speak to me, the Bull King spirit will attempt to get in and take over. So I mustn't speak to Frank unless I'm feeling very strong, and I'm a long way from the Palace of Knossos.

Poor Frank. He sounded so lost.

I wish you were here, Mother. You might be no help with spirits, but at least you could feed me, because I'm too tired to go to the kitchen and too hungry not to.

# Chapter 13
### 6<sup>th</sup> February, 1930
### Villa Ariadne

I've been ill.

When I was eight, I had measles at school. I was so poorly they thought I would die. This time wasn't as bad, but I had a very high temperature for over a week. Maria and Kosti looked after me. The lemon drink was the only thing I could keep down for some time. Uncle Leonard hovered in the doorway occasionally, no doubt mainly worried about becoming a crocodile's dinner. Micky tells me that he tried to get in to see me, but they wouldn't let him anywhere near me in case he caught the bug.

I believe him.

Now, two weeks later, I'm very weak, but the worst is over. I wonder if this is the danger that Frank was telling me about. If so, he did a bad job of protecting me. All the spirit visits weakened me, and the sickness took advantage.

There were many frightening bulls in my dreams, but the cat from the cook's bed in Athens chased them away. No point wasting time describing silly dreams. Anyway someone is at the door – the real door, not the one that's inside my head!

It's Kosti letting in Micky – giving him strict instructions that I'm allowed to go into the garden for no more than half an hour. I'm glad to stay near my room, as it's only the second day I've been out of bed. But I will not be held by the arm like an old lady, so we walk very slowly to the back of the garden, past the tree I climbed when I first met Micky. That feels a very long time ago.

Micky is carrying a small cardboard box tied with string. He won't tell me what's inside. But when we sit down below one of the palm trees, he puts it in my lap.

'I found it yesterday,' he says proudly.

'They've started excavating already?'

'A test pit. I go down first to see inside the tomb, because I'm small. They want to do some work before Mr Pendleton arrives.'

'Who do you mean? Uncle Leonard or Girardon?'

'Your uncle. He wants to find a rich tomb and impress Sir Arthur. Monsieur Girardon has gone back to Athens. He does reconstruction, not excavation.'

I'm hugely relieved.

The box is lighter than I expect. I give it a gentle shake.

'Be careful. I will be in trouble if you break it,' Micky warns. I give him the look he deserves.

'You don't believe those stories about me, do you?'

Margarita chooses this moment to break the tension by jumping out of her pocket nest, running up Micky's arm and nibbling the collar of his shirt. While he's busy finding her a seed to eat, I begin untying the string. My fingers are weak and clumsy, but eventually I pull the knot apart and lift the lid of the box.

All I can see is the bowl of a small cup, black and rather dusty. But I'm not fooled by its uninteresting interior.

'Take it out. Look at the sides,' Micky says. He's sitting on his haunches watching me eagerly. 'It's very beautiful – and all in one piece!'

I hold the box out to him.

'I can't.'

'Don't worry, I know you will not break it. Take it out.' He pushes the box back at me.

'I can't, Micky. You take it out and show me.' I hold out the box again.

He looks at me with his head cocked for a moment.

'Why can't you?' he says, taking the box carefully.

I really don't want to tell him. I'm afraid that he, like every other friend I've nearly had, will decide I'm too strange to be with. But some explanation is required, and so far Micky's been more understanding than most people.

'If I touch an old object like that, I might go into another trance, and I'm too weak at the moment.'

Micky opens his mouth and slowly shuts it again. He looks down into the box and lifts out the cup very carefully, cradling it in both palms. He holds it out towards me. He's right, it is pretty. White and yellow decoration on a dark background with bands, dots and flowers that might be crocuses. Very delicate. The edge of the cup is thin and finely made. Amazing that it's survived thousands of years in the ground.

Micky pulls the cup back and places it in his lap.

'What would happen in the trance? Would a spirit talk to you?'

'Probably not, but I would see things from the past – things that happened when this cup was used or when it was made. It happens more with objects that were important to a person. Things they used often, like a cup that touches the lips. But a big jar, like the ones in the Palace storerooms, might not because they are only used to hold olive oil or wine.' I stare down at my empty hands. I've never tried to explain this before. There'll certainly be more questions.

But Micky is silent, staring at the cup and not really looking at it. I stretch my legs out in front of me and pull my skirt over my knees. It's not fair that, just when I'm getting well again, I have to confess to another bizarre ability.

'I wish *I* could do that,' Micky says, upending the cup and looking at the base. 'I wish I could see what happened in old Knossos, when it was alive and full of people and animals. You are lucky.'

I snort at that.

'Trust me, I'm definitely not lucky.'

'But you know more about people in the past than archaeologists do by digging in the ground.'

'Not really. I just see images, feel some emotions. I can't tell you about who was king or which country was trading what or when. I just see inside a mind, like listening to a snatch of song that comes on the wireless radio when you're tuning in to something else.'

'But to see the real past –' Micky looks up at the sky. 'It's amazing!'

I've never considered it much of a benefit before.

'Sometimes I can't come out of the memory when I want to. I get stuck in an eddy – a time spiral.'

'When you are feeling better, will you try it and tell me what you see? I will stay with you. I was able to get you out of the trance before.'

A spotty brown lizard moves across a sunny patch on a nearby stone. It notices us and freezes in place. If I move, it will race away from what it considers to be danger.

I feel like that lizard. Warm in a patch of sunlight in the friendship of Micky, but knowing there are dangers in the dark beyond that warm safe place – spirits that could invade while I'm in a trance. Maybe he won't be my friend if I keep saying no.

'I can try,' I say.

Micky puts the cup back in the box and ties down the lid again.

'Safe now.' He puts the box on the ground. 'When did it happen first?'

I consider telling him about the time I held the arrowhead in the classroom and was caned, but decide against it. Honestly, I wish I could share a normal memory, like when he tells me about his younger brothers and sisters fighting and making him laugh.

'When I was about seven years old.'

'So it has happened for five years.' His eyes are bright and excited, as if he'd just uncovered a piece of gold in the dirt.

'Not that often. I usually avoid touching things.' A vivid image of the Egyptian girl in the tomb, *Menka*, enters my mind. I cradle my head in my hands. It was foolish to promise to restore her hieroglyphs when I have no idea how to go about it.

'Are you feeling ill? Do you need to lie down?'

'No. I just did something stupid, and I'll have to figure out a way of making it right. But that's not important now. It's the wrong country.'

Micky looks thoroughly confused.

'Can I help?'

I force a laugh.

'Just let me hold Margarita. She always makes me feel better.'

She runs around on my skirt for a while and then sits on my shoulder where she eats a nut. She has good table manners and carefully washes her face with her front paws afterwards.

Kosti calls from the Villa, sounding anxious.

'I think our time is up.'

Micky puts his hand on my shoulder, and Margarita runs up his arm, stopping by his neck to nibble her favourite part of his collar again. He gets to his feet and holds out a hand for me. For once, I take it without hesitation. Just standing up is tiring at the moment.

'Tomorrow I will teach you more Greek,' he says as we walk back to the kitchen. 'You should learn while you are here.'

'And tomorrow, I'll be just as bad at remembering it as ever,' I promise in return.

'Phyllia can help. She will make it fun.'

The thought of finally meeting Micky's famously brave, silly, six-year-old sister does cheer me up.

'How did you learn such good English?'

'My father learnt as a boy when he started the work for Sir Arthur, washing pot sherds. Then he taught me every day. And I listen to the English archaeologists when I carry messages. It's the golden key to better work. That is what Father says.'

'Do you want to be an archaeologist when you grow up?'

'Maybe. Or something that helps living people. I save my money to go back to school. But Sir Arthur has given us something to be proud of in Knossos. Without him, my father would still be living in the Amari Valley, growing cherries.'

'That doesn't sound bad.'

Micky taps his forehead. 'It is if you have a busy mind.'

We reach the kitchen, and Micky is quickly dismissed. Kosti gives me milk with honey and ushers me back to bed. I'm better looked after here on Crete than I've ever been since you left. I hope we don't have to leave too soon.

# Chapter 14
## 13<sup>th</sup> February, 1930
## Villa Ariadne

## The Greek Alphabet

| | |
|---|---|
| Alpha | A α |
| Beta | B β |
| Gamma | Γ γ |
| Delta | Δ δ |
| Epsilon | E ε |
| Zeta | Z ζ |
| Eta | H η |
| Theta | Θ θ |
| Iota | I ι |
| Kappa | K κ |
| Lambda | Λ λ |
| Mu | M μ |

| | |
|---|---|
| Nu | N ν |
| Xi | Ξ ξ |
| Omicron | O o |
| Pi | Π π |
| Rho | P ρ |
| Sigma | Σ σ |
| Tau | T τ |
| Upsilon | Υ υ |
| Phi | Φ φ |
| Chi | X χ |
| Psi | Ψ ψ |
| Omega | Ω ω |

The Greek language has twenty-four letters, and the trouble is that some look different to English letters. I don't know how I'm ever going to be able to speak Greek, never mind read it. But Micky and Phyllia have taught me my first Greek joke. It's very old, from about one thousand five hundred years ago, and I don't think it's funny at all. I'll tell you in English.

*An intellectual fell ill with a fever. He called the doctor and received treatment. He promised to pay the doctor if he recovered. The intellectual then started drinking lots of wine, and his wife scolded him for drinking when he was sick. But he said: 'Do you want me to get better and have to pay the doctor?'*

There, I told you it wasn't very funny. They found it hilarious last week when I asked to go with them to the river to look for snails. It was Micky's way of saying 'No, you'll make yourself worse', even though I've never drunk wine in my life.

But today I am officially well enough to go out on an expedition. Uncle Leonard has consulted with Kosti and Maria. He called me to his table after breakfast and gave me a list of conditions as long as my arm, about not getting too much sun, not bathing in the river, only drinking boiled water. Honestly, it's ridiculous. But I nodded and agreed because I'm going to stay at Micky's house in the village after we've been to see the new site his father discovered – the tomb where the cup came from.

I think Micky suggested it because he wants me to go into a trance and tell him about the past. But for whatever reason, I'm leaving the Villa Ariadne for the first time in ages, and it's a fine day. It's not too cold or hot, and the wind has stopped for now. Perfect walking weather.

I've been going stir-crazy indoors, especially trying to keep my mind open in case Frank makes contact, but closed to other spirits. I miss Frank's conversations, but I'm relieved he can't make any of these precious ancient pots smash. That would be a true disaster, and I'd probably be buried alive in one of the tombs by Girardon or my uncle.

I'm glad Micky's father doesn't know about what happened in Girardon's atelier. Manolaki cares for the site and its artefacts as if they're his newborn babies. He's very calm. I've never seen him hurry anywhere. He couldn't be more different from Uncle Leonard.

That said, my uncle does seem different here. Perhaps being away from Glascott Manor has allowed him to relax a bit. I saw him smile the day before yesterday.

I have to get ready to go now. I can hear Micky in the garden.

I follow Micky down the Villa drive, walking in a direction I've not been before. The house by the gate used to be a taverna, but it's now a guesthouse and Maria has a room there. She waves from the garden.

Soon we are walking along a dusty, rocky path, only wide enough for single file. I'm following Micky, who has barely spoken to me since we left. There's definitely something wrong. Maybe he's concluded that I'm a liar, I really just have epilepsy like his uncle, I'm clumsy, like Girardon said, I'm not so interesting after all and he'd rather spend time with the boys from the village. Or maybe he wants me to go into a trance so that he can watch and make fun of me.

See how many bad thoughts are going through my head on our long walk to the river?

Micky doesn't have anything with him except our lunch in a small woven haversack that hangs over both shoulders. No cardboard box containing dangerous pottery. We halt for a drink of water under an olive tree, and Margarita comes out to play.

'How old is she?' I ask, trying to distract myself from my worries.

'I found her last year, close to Easter. She was very small.'

'Was she an orphan?'

'Maybe. I found her near the back door. Maybe our cat ate her mother.'

'How do you keep Margarita safe from the cat?'

'She stays with me always, even at night. I put her in a little cage. The cat is in the storeroom. Don't worry, I won't let her be eaten.'

Micky says something in Greek that I don't understand. I shake my head. He guides Margarita into his pocket and says something else as he gets to his feet.

'Don't you remember, Lily? It means *Are you ready to go?*'

'No. Sorry.' I stand up. 'Yes, let's go.'

My shoes are covered in dust and my legs ache. Although I agreed to the expedition, the journey is harder than I'd anticipated.

Micky stares at me, his head on one side.

'Are you tired?'

'No. I'm fine. Let's go.'

'Your uncle will be angry if –'

'I don't care about my uncle, and anyway I'm fine.'

Micky shrugs and begins the descent to the river path. I practically have to go down on my bottom, it's that steep. I suppose I'll have to climb up it when we go back to his house, and that's not going to be easy.

The river is narrow but strong and fast-flowing.

We walk down the uneven path towards an old mill. The big water wheel is no longer turning. In fact the roof of the building has collapsed. After we pass the ruined mill, Micky follows a goat track going across the hillside. I try to keep up. He hasn't gone far when he stops abruptly.

'Here it is.'

A narrow, stone-lined path leads diagonally into a black hole in the ground.

'This tunnel is the *dromos*. The tomb – *thalamos* – is at the end.' Micky points at the darkness. 'There are no bodies. They took all the bones and offerings last week. The ceiling is high, like a beehive.' He makes the domed shape with his hands.

I have to force myself to follow him a few paces down the open tunnel. The area near the tomb is causing severe tingling down my neck and arms. The problem isn't whether there are bodies in the tomb, the problem is the voices, just like in the cellar at the Manor. The spirits who've been here for centuries, for millennia, will begin speaking as soon as I enter.

I put my hand on the side of the tunnel. It's a sunny day, but the stone is ice-cold to touch.

'I need to sit down. Please.'

'Here?'

'No, no.' I stumble away from the entrance and drop onto the crumbly ground nearby, next to a stunted bush.

Micky follows and sits opposite me. I keep my head down because I don't want to see the concern, or pity, or amusement in his expression.

'What is wrong, Lily?'

'I can't go into that tomb. Sorry.'

'Is it the dark? I brought a candle.' He takes it out of the haversack.

I shake my head. If only a candle could solve the problem.

'It's hard to explain.'

'Try.'

I take a deep breath.

'The voices of the dead will still speak to me in there. I might be taken over for a while. It's not pleasant.'

He takes off his cap and scratches the back of his head.

'But there are no bodies. That doesn't make sense!' He frowns. 'Why don't I feel anything?' He sounds annoyed.

'Be glad you don't.'

'I am not glad. You tell me about these,' he waves his arms in the air, 'pictures of the past, but I do not see them or hear them. And you won't show me.'

'I'll hold something old for you and tell you what I see, I promise. Just not in that tomb.'

'You are not trying to fool me?'

I shake my head. He stares at me with his dark eyes until I start to fidget.

'I have brought something here. Don't tell your uncle! I took it from the site storeroom.'

Micky reaches into his shirt pocket and brings out a small object wound in black cloth. He unwraps it in his lap, and my heart begins to race.

He holds it up to the light. It's a small stone like the ones at Monsieur Girardon's workshop, no bigger than the last joint of my index finger. A beautiful orange stone, curved on one side, flat on the other. A hole has been drilled through it, and the flat side carved with symbols.

'It came from this tomb. It will be drawn for Sir Arthur before it goes to the museum in Irákleion. The carving shows a dolphin and an octopus. The Minoans wore sealstones on their skin. It should work. Here.'

Micky holds it out to me between his finger and his thumb, challenge in his eyes.

There's something different. It isn't only Micky speaking.

'Micky, have you been talking about me to anyone else?'

He shakes his head earnestly.

'Only in confession to Papa Persakis, but he has to keep everything he hears secret.'

'Why did you talk to a priest about me? I told you not to tell anyone!' My voice is shaking badly now.

'Priests do not count. I wanted to know if your abilities were from the Devil or were God-given like other talents.'

'The Devil?'

Micky shrugs.

'I thought I should make sure.'

'And what did the priest say?'

'He told me you probably lied about the spirits.' Micky looks uncomfortable. 'And he asked where you come from and if you attend church. Don't worry, I did not tell him your name.'

'When was this?'

Micky chews his lip.

'Some days ago. He only gave me short prayers to say every day. That means it isn't very bad.'

'You're testing me? Either I'm a fraud, or I'm from the Devil?' I feel so angry that the tiredness and fear leave me. 'Fine! I'll show you what happens.' I snatch the sealstone out of his hand and hold it flat in my palm without even looking at its carving. It's searingly cold.

An image comes straight away. It's a boat – long, thin, made of tied reeds – with a prow like a seahorse. The boat is low in the water. Its cargo is a woman in a bright flounced skirt. Her dark, curling hair lifts in the wind. Her face is radiant. Dolphins leap alongside the boat, flashing in the sunshine. Flying fish jump out of the sea.

Behind everything, there is a voice – beautiful, liquid, melodic, insistent. Becoming louder, stronger. Like the waves of the sea pounding on my mind.

*Come to me!*

*Swim to me!*

*Down to me!*

My whole body stiffens, resisting. I mustn't go under the water, although it feels soft and warm on my skin. Although it would be so comfortable, so peaceful. I have to pull back. The blackness of unconsciousness is creeping inwards.

Before I lose the vision, I hear another very familiar voice calling faintly.

*Shut the door, Lily! You bloody idiot! Shut the door!*

# Chapter 15
## 14th February, 1930
## Knossos Village

It's probably after midnight now. I'm in the Angelakis house on a little slatted bed with a wool mattress. Everyone else is asleep. The bed is behind a hanging tapestry that separates this girls' alcove on the upper floor from the one for Micky and Alexi. I can hear Phyllia and Theonymphae breathing deeply, fast asleep. Their parents are downstairs. Someone is snoring. I might tease Micky about that in the morning. Or maybe not. I need to think of something that will repair our friendship, not make it worse.

All I remember is waking up lying on my back on the ground with water spilling over my face and Micky above me, holding the water bottle, looking terrified. I did my best to pretend that I was fine, despite shaking all over. I couldn't even hold the bottle to take a drink. Apparently I'd flung the sealstone out of my hand quite quickly. It took Micky a long time to comb through the scrub and find it. He was covered in sweat, and I was wet and shivering by the time we left. We made quite a pair.

He barely spoke to me all the way back to his house and let everyone else do the talking during the evening meal.

I explained my wetness to the family by claiming I'd slipped crossing the river, and they all laughed. Micky didn't defend me, which I thought was bad form considering he'd flung the water all over me.

I need to find out what happened while I was inside the vision, because if it's what I suspect, Micky's behaviour is completely understandable. He might've heard me speaking with the voice of the powerful spirit before I managed to close the door. That's enough to frighten anyone.

It will be the end of our friendship. He'll definitely tell the priest I'm possessed by the Devil and never want to speak to me again.

What if I am? I've never known how to explain what happens to me. Maybe that's it. Maybe I should visit the priest myself and submit to an exorcism.

As if in response, Frank pulls at my mind, sudden and strong, as he used to in England. It feels like a whip lash.

*Lily – the danger I warned you about is coming! Get out of that house, quick!*

'What danger? I'm in bed surrounded by people. You're the one putting me in danger by letting the other spirits in!'

*I told you! It's down deep. The deep earth. It's coming. Get out now – move!*

He's gone, leaving me in silence except for the heavy throbbing in my head.

I can't just run away from the house and leave the whole Angelakis family in some unknown danger, and I can't ignore what Frank is saying. His fear for me was genuine.

But what if Frank is wrong, and I wake the whole family for nothing?

I grip my hands in tight fists, thinking.

*Deep earth.*

It's only when I press my palms beside me on the trembling bed frame that I understand and dash across the narrow upstairs balcony.

Micky's bed is in an alcove covered by a thick hanging. I can barely see.

'Micky! Micky!'

A muffled cry, as if he's covered his mouth. I sit down next to him and fumble for his hand.

'We're in danger. We have to leave right now!'

Micky's hand is shaking – he's afraid of me.

'I won't hurt you! I'm trying to save you and your family! Listen! My old spirit has warned me. He's saved me before. He said we have to get out of here. It's an earthquake. Wake up your family, quick or they'll be crushed!'

The floorboards vibrate under my bare feet.

'Can you feel that? Come on, we have to wake them!'

I make out the gleam of his eyes as he launches out of bed, pushing past me to pick up his baby brother.

'You get the girls!'

I run back to the little bedroom and shake them awake. They're stunned and sleepy, but the shutters are already rattling and there is no time to explain. I pull Phyllia out of bed and push her down the ladder after her sister. I hear Micky waking his parents. With a girl in each hand, I run to the front door. But it won't open. I keep tugging at the latch. I can barely see. The floor is shuddering under us.

'Out of the way!' Micky cries, pushing me aside, snatching at the latch pin, flinging the door open and pushing us through as one of the ladders crashes down behind us. We tumble onto the path and struggle to our feet, only to be thrown down by the earth heaving under the road. Kyria Angelaki lurches out of the door, her hands over her head.

'Emmanuel!' She turns round to reach out for her husband, but there is no sign of him.

Micky thrusts Alexi at Theonymphae and runs back to the house.

'No!' I run after him, trying to grab his arm. But before I can reach him, his father stumbles across the threshold holding a wooden box to his chest just as the roof collapses inside the walls, and we're all thrown to the ground.

Dust rises into the clear night sky.

We sit up, and Manolaki leads us, crawling and coughing, away from the crumbling house. Screams and shouts come from down the road, cracking wood and crushing stone.

'We go to the church! It's safe,' Micky shouts at me, pointing.

We're crawling on our hands and knees. Every time we get to our feet, we're whipped by the force of the moving ground. The rocks bellow and groan as they grind against each other.

We give up and lie down a safe distance from any tree or building. I'm next to Phyllia and Micky, my arms over my head, eyes tight shut. It feels as if someone is tossing us up and down in a blanket made of stone.

I have no idea how long it lasts. After a while, the shaking lessens. I sit up. The girls are huddled next to their mother, who is also cradling Alexi. But Micky and Manolaki are gone.

I get up. Feel nauseous. In fact, I'm sick behind a bush.

The Angelakis house is closest to the road to the Palace. There's enough moonlight to see that the village is hard hit. Houses have turned into piles of plaster and wood. Men and women digging through debris to release trapped people. That's where Micky and his father will be. And I will be of no use.

I need to know if Uncle Leonard is alive. If Kosti and Maria –

I can't afford to start crying. I start up the road towards the Villa. But it's no longer a road, more a series of lumps and cracks, large rocks and deep holes. If I continue in the dark, I'll break my ankle or cut my bare feet at the very least.

So I turn back to the terrible wreck of the village, find the huddle of children and sit down next to Phyllia, who's clinging to her mother's long nightdress. It's very cold. Kyria Angelaki is chanting under her breath. Maybe it's a prayer.

We stay there until the sky finally lightens. It's possible to see the road, or what's left of it. So I move Phyllia off my lap and get up, shaking my limbs to get rid of the pins and needles. I begin picking my way towards the Villa Ariadne again.

A few minutes later, Micky catches up with me.

'You should not go by yourself!'

I keep walking.

'You have your family to look after. Don't worry about me.'

'My father sent me. He wants to know what happened at the Villa too.'

I don't reply. It's hard enough finding a path through the rocks.

'No, not that way.' Micky's voice sounds hoarse. 'It's safer here.' I follow him. He knows the place better than I do.

The sun is above the horizon when we reach the Villa. There's a crack running through the road in front of the gate, like a wound. We skirt round it and climb over fallen branches. Some of the trees lean at new angles.

'The walls are standing.' Micky runs a hand through his dust-stiffened hair. 'Four years ago, there was an earthquake. Sir Arthur was in his bedroom and was not hurt.'

I nod, but, now that I'm in front of the Villa, I don't want to go any nearer. I stare at the upended paving stones outside my shuttered bedroom window.

'Kyrie Ash,' Micky calls. 'Kyrie Kosti! Kyria Maria!'

There's no answer. Not even the birds in the garden are singing. Micky's dusty face is as white as a ghost, and his fingers are bleeding from moving stone and rubble.

I begin to cry. I can't help myself – it's the shock. I don't want any more disaster and loss. I don't want to have to leave the Villa Ariadne and Crete. I don't want to be without any relations in the whole world.

Micky takes my hand and we pick our way towards Uncle Leonard's bedroom window. The shutters are hanging crookedly. We push them to one side.

Uncle Leonard's gaunt face is just visible behind the shards of glass.

'Lily! Micky!' he cries, looking happier than I've ever seen him before. 'You're alive!' He reaches through a gap in the broken glass for my hand. 'Thank God, you're alive!'

## Chapter 16

Uncle Leonard is trapped in his bedroom because the ceiling squashed his door closed, and he can't fit through the buckled frame of the smashed window. He's wearing a shirt and trousers, so obviously found time to change out of his pyjamas while trapped inside. That's the army training, I suppose.

'I thought you were dead, Lily. You too, Micky, and I was frantic, not being able to get out. I was pushing and scraping. Look at my hands!'

His hands are rather scratched, but nothing compared to Micky's.

Oddly enough, he seems elated. I suppose it's been a terrible shock to his system. He can't stop talking, and normally it's a job to get him started.

'Are your parents alive? What happened in the village?'

'All the family are safe, thanks to Lily.' Micky glances at me quickly.

'That's wonderful news! I'm so relieved. How did you save them, Lily?'

I look at Micky, who raises an eyebrow at me.

'I was awake and felt the first tremor.'

'What great luck! And what about your house? The village?' Uncle Leonard's voice peters out when he sees Micky's expression.

'Our house and some others are ruins. Many people are injured. I know two who are dead.'

Uncle Leonard lowers his head.

'What a terrible power Poseidon wields,' he mutters. 'Heraklion will be the same. The Museum. The Palace. All damaged. I can't think of it now. You are alive and that's what matters!'

He reaches through the pane for my hand again, but I pretend not to notice. This character change is unnerving me.

'Where are Kosti and Maria?' I ask.

'They went to find help to get me out, but I don't know where. They are both fine. The Taverna wasn't so badly hit, they said.' His eyes are swimming. 'Thank God, you are safe, Lily! I was so frightened, and I couldn't do anything!'

Uncle Leonard keeps on talking emotionally until Micky can't stand it any more and excuses himself to return to the village where he can be more useful. I promise Uncle Leonard I'll be back and turn to follow Micky. It's alarming seeing my uncle looking so vulnerable, with tracks of tears running through the dust on his cheeks.

I catch up with Micky as he reaches the Villa gate.

'Wait!' I call. But when he turns round, I don't know what to say. I just stand there, and we both look down at the ruined drive and our scratched, bare feet.

'I'm sorry for what happened yesterday. I'm sorry I'm so strange, and talk to dead people, and have fits. But please believe me, it's not the Devil or anything like that!' I wrap my hands in the folds of my nightie. 'Can we be friends again?'

Micky shakes his head.

'I should apologise to you. You told me not to talk about it, and I did. I was scared, so I did something stupid. But there are bad things happening to you, Lily. Voices coming through you. They want your life! You need help from someone – someone brave that knows about these things.' He looks away for a moment. 'I don't know who. But I'll help, if I can, to thank you for saving my family. If you didn't warn us –' He shakes his head again.

I don't know what to say. I'm about to ask to hold Margarita when I remember. She won't be in his pocket because she stays in a cage overnight, and that cage is still in the ruined house.

I start crying. I can't help it. That mouse is the way we found to be friends.

Micky pats my shoulder awkwardly. I take a deep breath.

'Go and find Margarita. She might have survived – the cage might've saved her.'

Micky sniffs and wipes his nose. Then he nods and walks out of the gate towards the village.

I go back to Uncle Leonard. There's nowhere else to go.

He's standing at the window, looking anxious. I've almost reached him when an aftershock hits. The house groans and shifts.

'Get down, Lily!'

I know enough not to try to run anywhere, so I curl up by the retaining wall of the path.

'Stay down, cover your head!' my uncle shouts.

Watching the walls shake is terrifying. I screw my eyes closed. Other images come instead. What's happening to Micky, exposed on the road with no shelter? He could be swallowed up by the ground and crushed.

I've never trusted anyone before, never had a friend in this world. I can't bear the thought of losing him.

'Don't take him, Poseidon. If you have the power. Please, please, spare him.' I draw a deep breath. Hold it. Concentrate.

The shaking quickens. The path shivers, and little cracks run under my hands. Foolish to think a prayer to the God of the Sea would stop the vast slabs of earth clashing, making mountains and islands. Micky and I are no more than ants.

But I'll try anything.

Above the din, I hear Uncle Leonard calling me – a new, frantic tone in his voice.

'Lily, come here quickly! I must tell you something. I can't die without you knowing!'

So I push myself up and half-crawl back to the window, even though I'm sure I'm in much more danger than he is. I cling to the window ledge. Plaster dust falls around us. Uncle Leonard's face is twisted with fear or desperation.

'You have to understand that Father made me promise. He said it would kill Mother if I told you.' He's staring into my eyes, and I wonder if he's sustained a knock to the head or been pushed into some kind of mania by the danger.

'I understand,' I shout, although I don't.

A tree branch crashes onto the Villa roof. It's hard to stay upright. I meet his fevered gaze.

'Tell me now, Uncle, before it's too late!'

Out of nowhere, Kosti lurches up to the window carrying a crowbar on his shoulder.

'Get back, Kyrie! Get back, Lily!'

Uncle Leonard retreats into his room. I scramble out of the way. Kosti breaks the window glass and fits the crowbar into the window ledge. With the strength of two men and a terrible shattering sound, he levers the window frame, in pieces, out of the wall.

'Come out now!' Kosti yells through the dusty ruin of the window.

Uncle Leonard pushes himself out and crouches on the buckled, shaking path.

'Come with me, both of you. There's a shelter. Maria is there.' Kosti is holding out his hands.

But we have to wait for that aftershock to end because Uncle Leonard can't move. He's clinging to the low wall, watching the violently swaying trees, his face completely white, his teeth chattering.

When it's over, Kosti takes him by the arm, and we run to one of the Palace rooms rebuilt in concrete. Maria and many of the other female workers are huddled there together. Kosti finds us a place to sit and goes out again into the chaos like a warrior.

Someone passes us a jug of water. It tastes better than anything I've ever drunk, my mouth and throat are so parched.

Uncle Leonard is looking around at the women as if just waking up.

'I shouldn't be here. I must go and help.'

'There are lots of helpers in the village. Stay here and tell me what you were going to say before Kosti came!'

But he looks at me strangely, gets to his feet, brushes off his trousers and marches out into the unnatural, dust-filled sunshine.

I consider running after him, but decide against it. He doesn't seem quite right in the head. Of course he'd been in the war, with all the shelling and explosions. He's probably convinced he's back in a battle. The earthquake has awakened awful memories, and he's going out into the danger even though he's terrified, because the worst possible thing that could happen would be to be branded a coward. I feel sorry for him. I hope he'll make it back and return to his senses – and tell me the secret.

Maria sees me looking out of the doorway and pulls me down next to her, patting my shoulder to make me sit. Her English is not as good as Kosti's, but she gives me some bread and more water, and that's what I need. I think I sleep on her shoulder for a while.

When I wake up, all the other women are gone.

I have no idea what time of day it is, or even what day. The sun is high and the wind is blowing. There's dust flying everywhere.

Maria guides me up the road, but we don't go down to the Villa. She pulls me into the Taverna instead. Other than minor damage to the windows and some furnishings, it's amazingly untouched. She gives me more bread and some cheese. While I'm eating, a marmalade cat comes through the door, miaowing loudly.

Maria is ecstatic. She strokes it, hugs it and gives it a saucer of milk. I think of Micky – whether he made it back to his house and what he might've found in the rubble.

So I finish the food and go out. Maria tries to call me back, but I wave and keep walking down the road. There are two people I need to talk to. One is obviously Uncle Leonard, who has an important secret to tell me. He may decide not to, now that the immediate danger of death is over. But I'm going to try to get it out of him, *come hell or high water*, as Nanny used to say.

The other is Micky.

I nearly make it to the village before Kosti catches up with me.

'You will see bad things there, and it is not good for a young girl. Micky and his family are safe in the church. I promise. You come with me now, Miss Lily.'

And that is that. I have to go back to the Taverna and sit in the kitchen with Maria and her cat. Eventually as the sun sets, Kosti comes to get me. He's holding my shoes.

'The Villa is safe. We have checked your room, and it has no serious damage.'

'What about Uncle Leonard?'

'He went to check the whole Palace and is very tired. But he had a drink and sleeps now.'

'Is he himself?'

'Himself? I don't know what you mean, Miss Lily,' Kosti says diplomatically, as he places the shoes in front of each of my feet.

So I leave it there and follow him. I'll try to talk to Uncle Leonard tomorrow. Now I need to sleep, although I keep thinking about Micky, Margarita and the whole Angelakis family. It must be terrible to watch your house and all your belongings being destroyed.

Since you left, Mother, I've never felt like I've had a real home. But I can see that losing the home you love might be much worse.

# Chapter 17
### 17th February, 1930

Maybe everyone has times like this, when you've assumed that life will go on as it has been, and then the ground is, literally in this case, pulled from under your feet. Perhaps you'd point out that life was already different for me, leaving England and the Manor, and that's true. But I'd never truly felt close to death before. I'd never worried for my friend's life too.

Three people died in the village and many more have been taken to the hospital in Heraklion. Others are lying on the school floor with broken bones, unable to help with the relief effort.

Micky told me this when I found him digging out the rubble from their house. The lower walls are stable, but the falling roof destroyed the upper storey and all their furniture. Around the house is a collection of broken chairs, beds, tables and pots. The only thing rescued was the family chest which contained all their saved money. There's no sign of Margarita's cage.

Kyria Angelaki has gone with the younger children to her sister's house in Heraklion. Micky's aunt was one of the lucky ones in the town. Many buildings were damaged, but her house was untouched.

Meanwhile, my uncle is still behaving strangely – barely speaking, barely eating. Kosti keeps an eye on him as he wanders around the Villa Ariadne and the Palace, doing no work but constantly in motion and alert.

I mention the war to Kosti, and he nods sympathetically.

'It will fade,' he says, 'and he will return. In time.'

I hope so. Because he needs to tell me the secret that his father forbade him to reveal. I'm sure it's about you. And I'm not going to let Uncle Leonard forget, even though he looks at me as if I'm a stranger and walks away whenever I try to talk to him.

I want to do something useful to help the people who've lost their homes, so I'm spending time in the Taverna kitchen with Maria, chopping vegetables for stews that she carries to the village. No one is thinking about archaeology except the Ephor of Crete. He's the overseer of archaeological work here. The Heraklion Museum building has been damaged, several vases and other objects have been destroyed, and he's worried about the Palace. So he's come to Knossos this morning to see for himself.

Luckily the Palace is more or less intact, unlike Uncle Leonard's mind. Uncle Leonard manages to shake his hand, but when the Ephor starts asking him, in English, about the earthquake, he nods at him, turns round and marches out of the Villa by the front door.

The Ephor and Kosti have a brief conversation in Greek afterwards. I pester Kosti until he tells me that the Ephor has decided to write to Sir Arthur to tell him about the damage to the site, as Uncle Leonard is clearly not able to.

This doesn't bode well for Uncle Leonard's continued employment by Sir Arthur. I hope he recovers quickly, or he'll lose his job and we'll have to leave Crete.

You'd think I'd be glad to leave a country where I nearly died in an earthquake, but it's quite the opposite. I love the owls that call at night outside the Villa, the bright sunshine in the day, the mountains and sea in the distance, the flowers, the fragrant honey, and the friendly people who have been so kind to me. Except for Girardon of course. But he's Swiss, not Cretan.

There's only another hour or two of sunlight left. Maria has gone to the village. I'm not tired or hungry. So I'm going to look round the site, see what has happened there for myself and try to talk to Uncle Leonard about it. It might help bring him back to the present.

I'm determined not to be afraid. Determined that, if I'm given any visions or voices, I'll use them and control them myself. I should be able to decide what happens in my own head.

It's quiet. As far as I can tell, no one else is about. The only sound is nightingales singing in the early evening. After so much fear and worry, it seems peaceful, as if the earth is sleeping deeply after a nightmare. The wind has dropped. I can hear my own footsteps on the stones of the ancient Royal Road leading to the Palace.

I run my fingers along the wall beside it, keeping moving, like a blind person reading braille, not allowing any particular memory to take hold. Eventually I reach the wide Theatral Area – broad rising steps on two sides and a platform where the powerful people of the court would sit. I take off my shoes.

I've stopped thinking. My eyes are half-shut. A dance rhythm comes through the soles of my feet, so different to the juddering movements of the earthquake. It's a complex pattern, and I find the spirals of it on the stones, with the dancers of the past in their swirling skirts, their long, curling hair, decked in gold and blue strands of beads and garlands of flowers, swaying and crossing as they move around a bull tethered to a post in the centre.

Perhaps I should stop and pull myself back to the present, but I've become part of the women around me, the beat of their dancing, the stamping of their feet in unison. The Bull King speaks through the bull at the centre of the dance, the one about to be used for sport. His voice is deep, insistent.

I keep moving in the pattern, observing, shielding myself among the women. Although I understand his meaning, the Bull King's words are in a strange tongue. This is part of his funeral ritual, but his tomb was robbed, leaving his spirit unquiet and adrift.

The Bull King's bones and offerings are scattered. He will never rest until he's properly buried with his treasure. I must do this for him.

He will make me do it.

But I am with the women and girls dancing, keeping him at a distance, keeping time to the chant and the drum beat, and keeping my place in the present world by holding on to a memory: my arms around your neck and you smiling, throwing me upwards to make me laugh.

I'm your four-year-old daughter again. I bring you into my mind, and we shut the door together.

When I open my eyes, I'm sitting in the centre of the Theatral Area. The sun has set. The night is covered in stars, and a full moon rises over the western hills. The stones are cool. I've been gone a long time, and my mind still hears the rhythm of the dance.

I've seen Ariadne's dancing-place where the female spirit who saved Margarita holds power. The one I saw when I held the sealstone. Lady of the beautiful tresses. Lady of the Sea. The Bull King does not command this part of the Palace. I feel stretched, as if I'm floating above the site. I barely understand my own thoughts.

A figure moves on the periphery of my vision, emerging from the North Portico passage, below the painting of the great bull.

'What are you doing?' A man in a long black robe and hat is approaching. 'What sorcery are you practising in this place?' His voice is high, his accent heavy.

He has a bright gold crucifix hanging round his neck.

I scramble to my feet to face him.

'I was just looking around to see what's damaged.'

'No.' He shakes his head and moves towards me, his sandals slapping on the stone. 'You are dancing; you make unnatural sounds. You do bad things here.'

I take a step back and put on my most innocent expression.

'I'm sorry, Father. I was just playing. I know I shouldn't in the Palace, but I was just pretending.'

He's about two strides away from me, and I can see his face in the moonlight. It's thin, bearded, with a high forehead under the black hat worn by all Greek priests.

His mouth twists.

'No, you lie. I hear about you. You do some black magic here. You call up evil. Come with me.'

'No!'

I must have shouted, because my voice echoes off the Palace walls and comes back again. There's a moment of silence, and then his sandals slap on the stone, coming towards me again.

'You bring forth bad spirits. Now, in the name of God, they will be banished.'

He reaches out for me, but I turn and run up the ramp into the Palace. My feet are still bare, and it's dark. There's no way I can outrun him along the narrow Royal Road. I have to hide somewhere in the many rooms of the Palace, but I mustn't let myself be trapped in a dead end.

Up and down, in and out of the corridors, the slap of his flat sandals and his wheezing breath are close behind me. He may be faster, but I'm more agile and smaller. I can stay in the shadows made by moonlight. I can hide in places he can't enter.

But it's disorienting. I must've taken a wrong turn. I need to find my way to the Central Court, and then to an exit on the west side.

I stop running. Hide behind a pillar. My heart is racing, but I hold my breath until I hear his footsteps going down a side passageway, then I sprint, gasping, into the Central Court and begin to inch along the darkness cast by the pillars and the rebuilt walls. I must try to reach the trees and slip back to the Villa under their shadow.

I hear the priest before I see him. He's come out through the Throne Room on the west side. There's no escape that way. He's rushing straight for me.

I backtrack, find a flight of stairs going down to the eastern side, dash along a low wall, pass a corridor full of looming shadows, giant wide-mouthed jars. It's the room of giant pithoi, all much taller than me. All full of darkness. I have no choice. I choose one in the middle and shin up the side, using the clay handles as footholds. Clinging to the rim, I climb down the inside as quietly as possible.

I crouch, trying to slow my breathing so I can listen for his footsteps slapping on the stone.

'Where are you, English girl? The bad spirits will try to hide you, will try to take you. Come with me and we will exorcise them.' His high voice bounces off the sides of the great jars. He starts hitting each one, probably with a stick, working his way down the row towards me. The sound makes me flinch, but I stay still in the centre, not touching the sides of the jar.

Something is moving at my feet, disturbed by the noise. I don't want to feel what it is. I can guess. It slips around and between my bare feet.

I'm sharing my hiding-place with a snake.

I hope it's the same kind that Micky said was harmless to people. It's so dark inside the jar, I can't tell. I don't dare move a muscle.

The priest reaches my jar and hits it hard. The snake hisses loudly and begins circling the base of the pot around my legs. The priest is standing on the other side of the pot wall, listening.

'Snakes. More things of evil,' he mutters and moves on to the next pithos. Down the row of pots he goes like a demented drummer in a terrifying band.

'What on earth do you think you are doing?' It's my uncle's voice, full of his most privileged Oxford authority. 'Stop abusing this ancient site at once, or I'll call the police to arrest you!'

# Chapter 18
## The Palace of Knossos

'That girl is doing evil. I must stop her.'

'What are you raving about? Get away from those pithoi with that stick, and come out here where I can see you.'

A shaft of light is moving above the jars. Uncle Leonard has a torch, and his voice has all the authority of a sergeant major. Or a schoolmaster.

'I have the right. This is my parish. I must keep it safe from evil.'

'What the blazes? I thought you were a robber! What's a priest doing here abusing the artefacts?'

'I told you!' The priest's high, wheedling voice sounds very aggrieved. 'I saw your child here doing bad things, and I must correct her.'

'What a load of tosh. You're imagining things in the moonlight. Lily is in the Taverna kitchen with Maria. And whether you are a man of the cloth or not, you will be taken to the police if you damage this site. Hasn't it suffered enough from the earthquake? Go and comfort your parishioners.'

'She brought on the earthquake by talking to spirits in the stones. The girl is dangerous. She brings death on us.'

'That's enough! I told you she's in the Taverna. Whatever you think you saw, it was not her. Do you want me to report this to Sir Arthur?'

'He doesn't own the site. It belongs to the Cretan people, not the godless English,' the priest says, defiant.

'It's looked after by the British School at Athens, on behalf of the Cretan people, and if you want me to alert the Ephor to your activities here, I will. Go back to your church, Father. Immediately!'

I don't know if Uncle Leonard still thinks he's at war, but he certainly sounds as if he's commanding a troop of soldiers.

'You are a visitor to Crete. You do not understand.'

'I understand that you are trespassing on this monument at night when your flock needs you elsewhere.'

The priest says nothing more that I can hear. The implied insult about his service to his parishioners has done the trick. His footsteps move quickly away down the line of pithoi, but I wouldn't put it past him to be hiding in the shadows just outside, waiting for me. I have to get out now, with Uncle Leonard, or wait like this, a statue in a giant jar with a snake at my feet, until morning.

'Lily!' It's just a whisper – but one that carries in the still air. At this point I don't care if he scolds me. Anything to escape from the fear of being trapped and bitten.

'I'm here!'

His footsteps stop beside my pithos.

'How on earth did you get in there?' he whispers.

'There's a snake,' I manage.

Uncle Leonard swears under his breath.

'Has it bitten you?'

'No. It's between my feet. I don't have any shoes.'

'I know. I found them at the Theatral Area.'

So he knew I was here and lied to the priest to protect me.

'I'm sorry. I didn't mean for this to happen.' There's a catch in my voice.

'Later for the explanations. First, we get you out.'

He sounds different. More confident. Perhaps he's faced his war terrors and defeated them.

'I'm going to check that the priest has gone and then get something to stand on so I can reach you. Don't move. I'll return soon.'

Maybe it's ten minutes, but it feels like hours. The snake has stopped moving, but I can feel its cool scales against my heel.

Footsteps approach. Not the flap of sandals, it's the clip-clop of well-soled shoes.

'Lily!'

'I'm still here.'

'I've got a stool.' There's the sound of wood on stone, then the torch illuminates the inside of the jar, and I have to shade my eyes. The snake rears up and hisses at the light.

Uncle Leonard curses again.

'This must be one of the reconstructed jars that has sherds missing. That's how it got inside to make its nest. The snake is not big, and it's not venomous, but it might bite you.' I can see the blur of Uncle Leonard's head against the light but not his expression. 'It will only hurt like a needle hurts. No harm will come of it.' He speaks calmly. 'I'm going to put the torch away and let the snake calm down. Then I'll lift you out.'

There's a moment or two of complete darkness and quiet, then the creak of the stool as he shifts his weight.

'Can you see my hands, Lily? Reach up and try to grab them.'

I slowly push onto my toes as high as I can. Uncle Leonard's dry fingers grip tight.

'Now try not to move at all as I lift you, and I'll get your torso over the lip of the jar.'

It's a good thing I'm not big, because lifting any weight vertically while reaching down is very difficult. I feel the snake circling as my feet rise from the sand at the bottom of the jar. I'm holding my breath and gripping Uncle Leonard's hands as hard as I can when it strikes my heel, and I have to stifle a cry.

Uncle Leonard pulls me over the edge of the jar, steps down from the stool and lifts me under my shoulders, placing me on the ground. I clap my hand over my mouth because I can feel myself wanting to scream.

'Did it bite you?' Uncle Leonard puts me on the stool and lifts my feet one by one. 'It's just a small scratch. I'll take you back to the Taverna, and Manolaki will see to it.'

'Manolaki is at the Taverna?' I sniff.

'Yes – and Micky. When they arrived and found you gone, they came to tell me. Manolaki knows all about Cretan animals. He'll know what to do.'

Uncle Leonard carries me silently all the way, wrapped in his coat, my shoes in each of its pockets.

By the time we reach the Taverna, my foot is throbbing, and Uncle Leonard is sweating and panting. He calls at the kitchen door. Maria opens it, shouting behind her for Manolaki.

I really don't like being the centre of attention, but I seem to get myself into situations where people gather around me looking worried.

I'm blinking in the bright light of the kitchen lamps, and Maria is bustling about, heating water. Manolaki Angelakis is sitting on a chair opposite me, holding my foot in his lap. Micky is leaning over his Father's shoulder, and Uncle Leonard is wiping his forehead with a white hankie.

'What kind of snake?' Manolaki peers at the smear of blood on the side of my heel.

'Long and thin. Orange red pattern on a pale brown background, black bands along the head, about a metre long,' Uncle Leonard says, breathing hard.

'We have nothing to worry about.' Manolaki turns my foot to the side. 'We will get the alcohol and clean it out.'

'No venom?' Uncle Leonard asks. He'd pretended to know before so as not to panic me.

'No. Didn't you hear? Heracles chased all the venomous animals off the island as part of his Seventh Labour, when he was catching the Cretan Bull. Not a dangerous spider or snake on Crete. The other Greek islands have the viper, but we have the beautiful and sacred leopard snake.'

'What a blessed island,' Uncle Leonard mutters.

'What were you doing out there, Lily?' Micky asks.

'Don't start the inquisition yet,' Uncle Leonard interjects. 'She's in shock.'

'Not now, Mikis,' Manolaki agrees, then says something in Greek, and Micky goes to the pantry.

'You both need some brandy, and we'll also pour alcohol over the wound.' He turns my ankle to the side. 'See, it's just a small hole. In two days, you will not feel anything.'

It's wrong that they're making such a fuss over me, considering all the people who've died, or been injured and lost their homes.

'I'm sorry to cause this trouble.'

Manolaki raises his eyebrows.

'You don't seek it out. It finds you. We know. But also you saved us from being crushed in our beds. Mikis told me. So no saying sorry, please.'

And that's how it is. I keep quiet. Manolaki washes the puncture wound and binds it in a soft bandage. Maria gives me warm milk with a dash of brandy. The men drink it neat. Micky has a sip and screws up his face.

When Maria finishes serving, she sits down at the table and starts speaking agitatedly in Greek.

Manolaki replies, gesturing. I look at Micky for an explanation, but he won't meet my eyes.

Maria takes out a lace-edged hankie and dabs her eyes.

Manolaki looks at me appraisingly.

'Kyria Maria is upset because she was looking after you today, but you went to the Palace when she was out, and she blames herself that you came to harm. She says she is very sorry.'

Of course I have to tell everyone it's not her fault. I'd just gone out for a little walk but got so lost in the various rooms of the Palace, like in a labyrinth, that I wasn't sure how to get out.

At times like these, it's useful to look young for my age.

Micky's not fooled. I can tell from his expression. Uncle Leonard saves me from having to explain any further.

'Time for us to return to the Villa and let Kyria Maria get some rest.'

Manolaki stands up and holds out his hand.

'I'm glad you are feeling better, Kyrie Ash.'

'And I'm glad you were here to reassure us that Lily has escaped serious harm. Again.' The men shake hands.

'She does seem to have luck on her side.' Manolaki gives me a knowing look as I slip my shoe on over the bandage.

'Are you sleeping here?' I ask Micky.

'Yes, so Father can be near the site if there are more aftershocks. The rest of the family are safe in Irákleion. That house is strong.'

'Have you found Margarita?' I whisper.

He shakes his head.

'But I have something else to show you. I'll come in the morning,' he promises.


There's a thick silence as we walk down the uneven drive towards the Villa in the light of Uncle Leonard's torch. He's holding my hand, more to make sure I don't hare off into the dark again, I suspect, than out of any camaraderie.

I can tell he's wondering how to begin talking to me.

'Thank you for helping me, Uncle. I don't know how I would've escaped if you hadn't come.'

He doesn't say anything for a few strides.

'I'm glad I found you. There's enough natural danger around without adding strangely obsessed members of the clergy.'

I wonder if this is his idea of a joke.

'I'll try not to get in trouble again.'

'If you *would* try, I'd be much obliged, especially as our fates have been intertwined somewhat.' Again the dry tone.

'I didn't really want to curse you,' I say quickly. 'I just didn't want to be sent to an orphanage. But when I put the hieroglyphs next to the stone, something happened I wasn't expecting.' The impossibility of explaining stops me there.

'Something unexpected is always happening to you, Lily.' We have reached the gate to the Villa. He lets go of my hand. 'And something always will, I suspect. So, it's time we understood one another better. I've not been well since the earthquake, but this incident has brought me back to my senses. In the morning, we will have the talk we should've had years ago.' He switches off the torch and walks towards the door. 'If you could possibly stay within the Villa and avoid being bitten by reptiles until then, I'd be grateful.'

He looks down at me as he opens the door, and there's a half-smile under his moustache. For the first time in my life I meet his gaze properly – and nod.

# Chapter 19
## 18<sup>th</sup> February, 1930
## Villa Ariadne

You'd think I'd sleep like the dead after all that excitement. But I can't. My ankle is aching, and so's my head. I want to talk to Uncle Leonard, and, at the same time, I dread it. He's going to reveal something, and it will change my life. I know that much.

It's nearly dawn when I finally drop off to sleep, and nearly lunchtime when I wake up. Half the day's already gone. I wash and dress quickly then begin searching for Uncle Leonard. He's not in the Villa. Kosti tells me he left at about 11 a.m. So that's it for the day. He's working, and I'll have to wait until evening to hear whatever he has to say.

Micky appears as I'm eating at the kitchen table. He's not wearing his cap, which must have been ruined when the house collapsed. I can see the worry lines creasing his broad forehead.

'What's wrong?' I ask, around a mouthful of sweet bread.

He shakes his head and points at Kosti's back. Something he doesn't want overheard.

'How is your foot?' He pulls up a stool. 'Shall I look?'

'No, leave it bandaged, otherwise I'll have to find someone to do it again. It's fine. I can walk on it well enough,' I say, although it's actually quite painful.

Micky nods impatiently. There are obviously things he wants to talk about, so I hurry through a bowl of *yaourti* and honey, wipe my mouth, shout thanks to Kosti and follow Micky into the garden.

The day is warm and very still. It feels almost like spring. We sit down in a sunny patch behind a bank of shrubs.

'What's the matter? Is it your priest?'

'How did you know?' Micky looks shocked.

'He tried to catch me in the Palace last night. I was in a trance, and he saw me. He wants to exorcise me.' I shiver, remembering his intense stare and high voice.

Micky's eyes widen.

'That's why he woke me up at dawn! He took me to the church and asked me questions for more than an hour.'

'What did he want to know?'

'Everything. What you do when you are in a trance, who you talk to, how you know that artefacts are real or not.'

'What?'

'He said that you must get information from bad spirits.'

'But what did he actually say? I don't mean in Greek because I won't understand it. Did he say that I can tell real artefacts from fake ones?'

Micky shades his eyes to see me better.

'Can you?'

'Yes, but how did he know?' I demand. 'You didn't tell him, did you?'

Micky shakes his head.

'I didn't know! And I didn't tell him anything.' He bites his lip. 'Although he threatened to excommunicate me.' Micky rubs his eyes hard. 'It is my fault. I should not have told him about you. He has always been strange.'

I remember the priest's expression, his staring eyes. It would be hard to refuse him.

'Have you told your father about any of this?'

Micky shakes his head.

'He has gone to look at the far buildings of the Palace with your uncle. I don't know how much to say. Father has always gone to church every week.' His voice trails off.

At this moment I decide that secrets are absolutely no good between friends. I tell Micky everything about my visit to the atelier in Athens, and how Monsieur Girardon has been suspicious of me ever since.

Micky looks even more worried.

'Then Kyrie Girardon has been talking to Papa Persakis,' he whispers. 'He arrived in Irákleion yesterday. He is staying in the town, near the museum, but he will come to Knossos today or tomorrow, my father said. Why would he talk about fakes to the priest?'

'I don't know, but I need to stay out of their way.' I shift my sore foot. 'Whatever they're doing together, they don't like me knowing what I know. And I'm not sure that my uncle is strong enough to stand up to them. He's so new to Crete. He wouldn't want to fall out with Girardon. He has to keep his job with Sir Arthur.'

'Maybe you could stay with my aunt in Irákleion as well?' But Micky doesn't look hopeful.

'She already has plenty of people to look after. Don't worry. Maybe I'll pretend to be sick. Then he'll have to leave me alone.'

'No! They might call the priest to pray for you,' Micky exclaims. 'And you won't be able to get away. He can pray for hours!'

We both start giggling – more out of nerves than because it's actually funny.

'We will think of something,' Micky says. 'Come on, I promised to introduce you, if you can walk as far as the Taverna?'

We don't have to go inside. Round the back of the Taverna, tied to the trunk of a tree, is a dog. Light brown, alert pointy ears, big black nose. Its two front legs are white up to its ankles. It holds one of its back legs off the ground. Nonetheless its curled tail wags furiously. There's a patch of mottled white fur on its chest. It wriggles and squirms as Micky approaches it, then falls over on its back and displays a soft belly to be rubbed.

'This is Kaltsóni. He's only a few months old.'

I bend down. The dog scrambles onto his three legs and licks my hands, then starts on my face.

I stand up and back away.

'What happened to his leg?'

'The earthquake. I found him in one of the ruined houses, trapped under a fallen bed. I don't think it's broken but –' He shrugs. 'I'm keeping him tied up so he can rest it. Look, it's the same injured foot as yours.'

'Except he's got twice as many feet! Whose dog is he?'

Micky pushes the hair back from his face.

'His master is dead. Father said I should look after him.'

I kneel down again, and Kaltsóni licks my hands enthusiastically.

'Poor dog.'

'He has found the honey from your breakfast,' Micky says, fondling the dog's soft ears.

'Still no sign of Margarita?'

He keeps his face averted.

'I put out some food for her near the house.' Micky's voice is unsteady.

'She'll come back,' I say.

'Do you ever hear animals when you talk to the dead?'

I have to stop myself from laughing because the idea is so strange.

'No. I'm sorry. I wouldn't know what they were saying if they did come through.'

'Of course,' Micky says. 'Yes. I see.' He scratches Kaltsóni's chest. 'I hope his leg isn't broken. He wants to run and play.'

'He's lucky to have you to look after him. What does his name mean?'

'Stockings. Because of his legs.'

I snort. Micky smiles briefly.

'Oh, I nearly forgot. I heard other news.'

'From your family?'

'No. They are all fine. The repair of the houses will start when the equipment comes from Irákleion. The news was something else.' He looks around. 'Something to keep between us. Come over here.'

We walk further away from the Taverna window and sit on an old wall at the back of the yard.

'What's happened?'

'Yesterday, one of the boys from the vineyards told me he found something special. He knows I work with Sir Arthur. The boy wants him to see it. I asked what it was, and he said a gold ring with an ancient design. He found it after the earthquake in his father's vineyard. Hanging from a low branch. Maybe it was pushed out of the soil by the earthquake.'

'Did he show it to you?'

'No. He said his father is keeping it safe until Sir Arthur arrives. I think they want to sell it to him, but that is not allowed. They have to take it to the museum. So I told him that, and he was not happy.' Micky rocks on his hands. 'I really want to see it. Maybe – you could touch it?'

Micky has a hopeful gleam in his eye, but I feel too exposed and exhausted to start handling Minoan gold.

'Better to leave it alone now that the priest is keeping an eye on us. Can you come with me back to the Villa? I'm not feeling very well.'

'Really – or are you pretending?'

I give him my worst frown.

'My head is aching. Really.'

Micky follows me to the gate. Kaltsóni whines and pulls on the rope. Micky speaks to the puppy in Greek, and Kaltsóni tilts his head as if understanding. He lies down, his head between his paws, eyes watching us as we walk away.

'I'm sorry,' I say. 'I know it's an exciting discovery. But I'm just worried about doing anything that's going to draw the priest's attention.'

'How would he know about it?'

'Priests are able to talk to anyone, and people tell them all kinds of things because they think they can trust them.'

'Mmmm. Maybe. See you tomorrow,' Micky says as we reach the Villa steps.

I'm always having to disappoint him, but I'm surrounded by men who don't wish me well. It's not a comfortable feeling. I'm going to get an aspirin from Kosti.


Two hours later, Uncle Leonard returns. I try not to pounce on him as soon as he comes through the door, but I've been waiting to continue a real conversation with him all day – not one full of evasion and lies.

He delays whilst unwrapping my foot and applying iodine and a fresh bandage. I suppose he learnt his bandaging skills in the war, so I don't comment. Then he fixes himself a large gin and tonic from the dining room sideboard and beckons me. We go into Sir Arthur's office, also used for displaying finds from the excavation, and he locks the door. Then he checks the window is shut, and finally turns to look at me.

'Sit down, Lily.' He sits behind Sir Arthur's desk. I think he needs it for support. He looks nervous.

'I'm very sorry about the curse, Uncle,' I say, just to break the ice.

He shakes his head.

'That can wait. Let me begin. There are things that must be said.' He clears his throat and takes a gulp of his drink. I wonder if the pressure of telling me will send him doolally again.

'I think you should know the truth although it's terrible. Lies just poison us. Poison everything. I told you some of the truth but not the most important part. Your father was Douglas Buchanan. He was from the Highlands in Scotland. Rosetta met him when she was nursing the injured during the war. They fell in love.' Uncle Leonard stops and folds his hands in front of him. 'But Father would not hear of her marrying him. Douglas was poor.' There's a long pause. 'Before he went back to the front, they made vows of their own to each other. You were conceived.'

Time has slowed down. Motes of dust fall through sunlight. Bubbles rise in his glass. His mouth moves. I hear the words, understand them, but it feels unreal.

'When you were born, Douglas was alive. But Father would not accept Rosetta, or him, or you. He threw her out – refused to see Douglas or even hear his name. She lived in a flat with you in London. Then your father died in August 1918 – an accident on his troop ship. So close to the end of the war.'

'Where?'

'What?' Uncle Leonard looks surprised, as if he's forgotten I'm listening.

'Where did he die?'

'In Egypt, at Port Said, I believe.' He wipes his damp forehead although it's not warm in the room. 'Then your mother had no one. They weren't married in the eyes of the law. She had no money. She went back to Father for your sake, so that you wouldn't suffer hunger or want.'

He takes a long gulp of his drink.

'Father arranged for her to go to India, to find a husband. Many men in government service there are in need of wives. In the colonies, they aren't as –' he pauses, thinking of how to put it – '*particular* about a woman's past as they are in

152

Britain. Father promised that, when she was married, you would be sent out to join her. He promised your grandmother that too. He sent Rosetta out to Bombay on a ship.'

'Did it sink?'

Uncle Leonard shakes his head.

'She arrived in Bombay.'

I'm holding my breath.

'Later that year, she met a man and was engaged. She asked that you be sent over immediately. Said that her fiancé was happy to adopt you. But the man she was engaged to was not English. He was Indian. Father refused. Father disowned her again.'

Uncle Leonard is sweating profusely now. He downs the rest of his drink.

'He made us promise that we would never communicate with her and never tell you that she was alive. I think it killed Mother in the end. Especially after what happened to Francis.' Uncle Leonard covers his face with his hands for a moment.

'But I must tell you only what you need to know. Rosetta is still alive. And I have to tell you about your father. I met him once.'

I'm having trouble following what he's saying. It's too much. I'm light-headed. I've never heard of a Francis. But there's more important information to extract.

'You met my father? What was he like?'

Uncle Leonard raises his head slowly.

'You're very similar to him, Lily.' He fingers his empty glass. 'Rosetta told me he had second sight.' Uncle Leonard glances at me, then drops his eyes to the table. 'That was the other reason why Father would not have him in the family, other than his poverty. Douglas frightened him, just as you did. That's why he treated you so badly. Why we all did.'

It feels as if my head is exploding – as if I might faint.

'My mother is still in India? Where?'

There's a loud knock that makes us both jump.

'Monsieur Ash!' It's the voice of Girardon.

He's right outside the office door.

# Chapter 20
## 26<sup>th</sup> February, 1930
## Villa Ariadne

I hope you've missed me. I've certainly missed you. For a very long time. And I'm still angry. I'm furious, in fact.

Why haven't you ever come to get me? That's what I want to know. Why are you still in India, with your new husband, and why did you leave me with your bully of a father for all these years? In all those cold, harsh schools? Why haven't you even written to me?

Whatever it is that you are doing, I just want you to know that you should be doing it with me. I suppose you have other children now. They take up all your time. They take up all your love.

And *horrible* Grandfather behind it all. Lying and lying and lying!

I have tried looking for him in the spirit world. It wasn't a good idea, and, luckily, Frank stopped me before anything worse arrived. I just wanted my grandfather to know that he ruined my life for his rules, his expectations, his reputation! Who knows where his spirit has gone. Sunk deep in the mud of the Underworld for only ever caring about himself.

Uncle Leonard went along with the lie for all those years, making it look as if I was a bad girl, when he knew I'd inherited my gift from my father. I'm so angry, I'm afraid I'll hurt someone, namely him. So it's better not to see or speak to Uncle Leonard until the feeling subsides. He has slipped notes under my door but not tried to speak to me – yet.

I've been in my room for a week.

As soon as Uncle Leonard unlocked the office door, I sprinted out past Monsieur Girardon and barricaded myself in my bedroom, pushing the bookshelf and the desk against the door. I didn't trust myself not to smash everything in Sir Arthur's office, all the precious pots, the windows, the lot!

A whole week.

That's how long Girardon has been here – staying in the room next to mine. I've been on edge, trying not to think about him and yet listening out for him all the time. Someone has been patrolling outside my door and my window – walking, stopping, listening. I know it's Girardon spying on me. I keep the shutters closed so he can't look at me from the front garden. I've only spoken to Micky through the window, and Kosti has supplied plates of food. I suppose I'm lucky I don't have to starve.

Just now, when he brought my breakfast, Kosti told me that Monsieur Girardon left yesterday evening. Finally! I'm so tired of darkness. I need to see the sun, feel the breeze.

I'll walk to the Taverna first in case Micky is there. I've wrapped up some bread and put it in my coat pocket. I'm heading for the sea. The coast is visible from the hill behind the Palace. It can't be that far away. It's the same sea that washes on the shores of Egypt, where my father died. It's the same sea that you travelled on, and the sea I'll have to navigate to find you.

I hope you don't think I'm going to swim across the Mediterranean and all those other seas to find you. I'm not stupid. I know I'll need to work out a proper plan and get on a ship. I only want to escape from the people who are suspicious of me for a little while. Have time to think on my own.

The Taverna doors are locked. Only Kaltsóni is there, tied to an olive tree. He starts barking at me, but when he gets my scent he tries to lick my face. Then he rolls over, and I scratch his belly. He's putting weight on his foot normally and seems desperate to escape.

I sympathise. I too want to find the person who, I hope, loves me, but I've been stuck, kept in chains, for years. Soon I'll break free.

Without thinking, I untie the dog and start walking down the road. He trots alongside me, panting, an expression of what could be joy on his face. My vague plan is to head north over the fields away from the Villa. But as soon as I set off, it's as if people are lying in wait for me. Farmers ask where I'm going, children follow me, Kaltsóni starts barking at them.

I have to turn round and head south, a route I know better, skirting around the eastern side of the Palace site. If we climb up one of the distant hills, at least I'll have a good view of the area. Kaltsóni pulls on the rope, but I won't let him go and risk losing Micky's dog as well as his mouse.

The southern part of the Palace is where things tumble down the hill towards a Minoan viaduct and a long, low building called the Caravanserai, near where Micky took me all those weeks ago after I first heard the Bull King. The Caravanserai is not as exotic as it sounds; it's only walls, rubble and dust, but they think this is where travellers to Knossos would have arrived and washed their feet.

It's quiet and cool. Olive trees line the old road, and we keep in their shadow. I don't want to be questioned by any of the workers I see in the vineyards on the pale hillside. Kaltsóni has stopped pulling and is walking right next to my leg. He looks up at me and whines softly.

I feel him too, tugging at my mind – the Bull King.

My feet leave the road, heading into a sloping field of stone slabs and scrub. The dog is whining more loudly, but I don't stop. The connection is growing stronger. The Bull King's tomb is near, destroyed and desecrated. This is the place which must be restored, where his burial goods must be returned.

It's just a field scattered with rocks, but in the past sacrifices were made, blood was poured down into the basin around his pillar. His spirit was fed by these rituals. Then the thieves came, took the gold, the gems, the embroideries from his coffin. Leaving his soul stripped and unanchored. It's as clear as day in my mind, scene after scene, as I sit against one of the stones, my eyes closed, Kaltsóni's head on my lap.

I don't know how long I've been in a trance when the dog starts licking my face. I push his muzzle away, and he starts barking, nosing my hand, licking me again. It takes an enormous effort to close the door of my mind to the Bull King. I'm sweating. Kaltsóni is panting. Then he turns and shows his teeth.

A young boy is standing beside me, his mouth moving. I put my hand on Kaltsóni's collar and give my head a shake. The boy is wearing a ragged shirt, waistcoat and baggy trousers, just like the Cretan men. His face is sun-weathered. One of his front teeth is broken. I sit up properly and try to concentrate.

I can't understand a word he's saying. He's speaking Greek very fast, and all the while looking behind him as if he's afraid of someone. I stroke Kaltsóni's head, and he stops growling at the boy.

'*Kaló apógevma,*' I croak. My throat is so dry. The boy looks as if I've just hit him on the head, whereas all I've said is *Good afternoon.* Again he starts a stream of words.

'English,' I say. 'Do you speak English?'

He stares at me and slowly shakes his head.

I put my finger to my lips.

'Don't tell anyone I'm here, please.' I shake my head and put my finger to my lips again. He looks at me curiously, then at the dog.

In the following quieter stream of Greek I recognise 'Angelakis'.

'Michalis Angelakis?' I ask.

He smiles, nods, starts talking nineteen to the dozen again. I gesture for him to slow down and trot out some of the few words I remember.

'*Eínai fílos mou o Michalis.*'

His smile practically splits his face in half. Then he starts laughing. I suppose he finds my accent very funny. I thought I'd remembered the word for 'friend' quite well. I get up, and Kaltsóni almost pulls the lead out of my hand, heading for the road. I start picking my way over the stones.

The boy scampers after us, still talking. I'm tired of it by this point. He's showing me his thumb, miming putting a ring on it. I remember how excited Micky was that a young boy found a gold ring near a vineyard. We're walking past vines right now. The leaves are just beginning to show after the winter.

'*Pos se léne?*'

'*Nikos. Nikos Papadakis!*' He's jogging to keep up with us. Kaltsóni growls again.

'*Efcharistó. Antío, Nikos.*'

He looks crestfallen but still follows. Even Kaltsóni's bark doesn't deter him. There's a shout from behind us, and he flinches.

'*Geia,*' he mumbles and runs down the field towards a man waving a stick in the air by a ramshackle cottage. I don't look back. I need to talk to Micky, but I'm sure this is the boy who found the gold ring thrown up by the earthquake, or perhaps dropped by robbers thousands of years ago. It was probably part of the grave goods of the Bull King.

I trudge up the hill to the eastern side of the site, Kaltsóni panting and trotting by my side. I'm extremely thirsty. My legs ache. They haven't had any exercise for a week, and I've been climbing over uneven ground.

Where's the ring now? In that run-down cottage guarded by that angry man? Unlikely. Perhaps they buried it in the ground again, to keep it safe. The crumbly, rocky, pale ground, where landmarks are constantly moving.

I need to talk to Micky.

And get his dog back before he starts to worry.

## Chapter 21
### 28<sup>th</sup> February, 1930
### The Taverna

Whatever you thought of me when I was a four-year-old girl unable to tie my own shoes, still needing help to brush my teeth and cut up my food, you'd surely be more impressed by me now. I've figured out a system to get messages to Micky so I don't have to look all over Knossos for him and risk bumping into that priest, or Girardon if he turns up again.

It involves climbing trees and displaying different designed flags, which are just pieces of paper I've salvaged from around the Villa. I've told Micky to meet me in the Taverna garden where I'm petting Kaltsóni. But he hasn't come alone.

The other person is Nikos Papadakis. He *is* the boy who found the ring, as Micky confirmed yesterday. Micky has him by the elbow. I'm not sure if Nikos has been forced to come, but when he sees me he immediately looks worried.

Most of the conversation is in Greek, which leaves me trying to read the story through their facial expressions. The boy is definitely nervous, and at one point Micky looks shocked. I'm sitting on my haunches next to Kaltsóni, scratching him behind the ear, trying not to look as uncomfortable as I feel. Nikos saw me while I was in a trance, and I don't like the way he's glaring at me.

The conversation ends abruptly with Micky speaking to him sternly and waving him away. Nikos looks as if he might say something to me, but then thinks better of it and dashes across the yard and down the road, his ragged clothes flapping.

Micky swears under his breath. I know that much Greek from spending time in his company for the past five weeks.

'What did he say? What's wrong?'

More whispered curses. Kaltsóni goes over and licks him. He's a bright dog who knows how people are feeling.

'His father sold the ring for 20,000 drachmas!'

'How much is that in pounds? It sounds like a lot.'

Micky wipes his forehead.

'I don't know – but a drachma isn't worth very much compared to a pound. Maybe it would be £70?'

'That's a lot of money.'

'Not for an ancient gold ring. It would be priceless!' He shakes his head. 'But that's not the worst thing. He sold it to Papa Persakis – the priest!'

A shiver runs down my spine.

'Has Nikos been talking to the priest about me?'

Micky doesn't meet my eye.

'I think so.'

I was in the field where the ring was found, in a trance, and the priest has the ring that belongs to the dead ruler who wants it back. How to explain that without sounding completely barmy? Kaltsóni lies down between us, legs in the air, and Micky scratches his soft tummy.

'Nikos is happy because he will get a new pair of shoes. But he said some bad things about you.'

I shift position and cross my legs.

'I'm sure the priest has told him I'm evil, conjuring bad spirits, a danger to others.'

'What was happening when you two met?'

'I was in a trance, communicating with a Minoan ruler whose tomb is nearby.'

Micky begins to laugh then notices my expression.

'You're not making a joke?'

'I think it's his ring.'

Micky stands up and starts pacing around the yard. I take over scratching Kaltsóni to give me something to do with my shaking hands.

'Do you want me to prove it to you?'

He looks surprised.

'How can you?' He pauses. 'No. I don't need proof. I believe you.' He looks at me speculatively. 'What about the people who died here in the earthquake. Could you talk to them?'

I hug my arms, covered in goosebumps. The dog rolls over and presses his warm body against my leg.

'I would need to be in their place, hold their possessions. They could be confused, unhappy. They might damage things.'

'Has that happened before?'

So I tell him about Frank.

'Who is he? You must have some idea.'

He's right. I should know who Frank is. But he quickly became my problem as well as my friend, and one I didn't want to provoke.

'I don't know. The dead keep secrets, just like the living. He won't speak about how he died. None of them do. I get the impression it's very bad manners to ask.'

I start telling Micky about my father having second sight, and his eyes nearly pop out of his head.

'That is where you got it from. There are people in Crete who have that special sight too. Have you heard about the *Drosoulites* at Frangokastello?'

'The what?'

He says it more slowly, but it doesn't help.

'A ghost army. Many people see them. They are called "Dew Shadows" because they appear in the morning when the sea is calm and the air is wet. You can watch them from a distance, walking or riding horses. It's from a battle more than one hundred years ago against the Venetians. Many Greek soldiers died.' Micky gestures at two points in the air. 'They go from the monastery to the castle.'

There's a moment of silence

'They must have died for that soil, for that place. They made a strong connection,' I suggest.

Micky nods eagerly. 'Cretans know that there is more than just this life. That spirits can remain in an area, and some people have the gift to see them. Others don't.'

He looks sad. Kaltsóni gets to his feet and noses Micky's hand.

'It is not a blessing, you know,' I say. 'Imagine having a disease like epilepsy. Having no control and, at the same time, having an ability like perfect pitch. Knowing things others don't – knowing too much. It's complicated.'

I sound weary as usual. There just aren't the words to describe it.

I can see Micky is unsure what to say next. He decides to change tack.

'Why were you so upset after the snake bite? You weren't ill. I know you don't trust Girardon, but why did you stay in your bedroom for a whole week?'

Friends are friends. I explain what Uncle Leonard told me. I can see it for what it is: a sad story about a man who thought his family was only there to reflect his own status. A man who brought up children without caring about their happiness.

Micky finds the story hard to believe. But then, his father is completely different to my grandfather. All his children respect and love him because he lets them be who they are.

'Your mother lives in India?'

I nod and hold his gaze.

'With an Indian husband. And I'm going to find her.'

Micky strokes Kaltsóni thoughtfully.

'It is a long way. Do you have a map?'

'Yes.'

'That reminds me! Good news. The Pendletons will arrive soon. Girardon told me.'

Two different feelings arrive simultaneously: gladness that I'll see Hilda Pendleton again – and anxiety.

'I thought Girardon left for Athens.'

Micky shakes his head.

'He stays in Irákleion and works at the museum. The Pendletons are coming early because Mr Pendleton heard about the earthquake and wants to see the damage to the Palace.'

'Good,' I say. But my mind is spinning.

Girardon still in Crete, making objects he passes off as genuine. The golden ring in the possession of the priest, his associate. A disturbed but unexcavated tomb.

Whether I like it or not, I'll have to speak to Uncle Leonard. He needs to know there are many things tangled around Knossos – and people serving their own interests working at the heart of it.

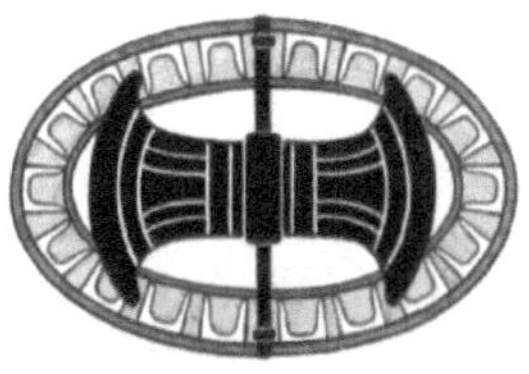

## Chapter 22
### 2nd March, 1930
### Villa Ariadne

Before I can find him, Uncle Leonard disappears for two days to Heraklion to organise things for the arrival of the Pendletons. When he gets back in the late morning, I'm up a tree in the Villa garden. As he walks towards the front door with his head down and arms linked behind his back, I take my opportunity.

'Uncle.'

He jumps like a rabbit and looks around comically, which is satisfying. Then he looks up. I haven't seen him for ten days, and he seems to have aged twenty years. I feel guilty, but the man who's really to blame, my grandfather, is dead. Uncle Leonard is his victim too.

I shin down the tree and stand in front of him. We walk a little way into the garden without talking. Gravel crunches under our feet.

'Lily. You have a right to be upset, but let me tell you the rest.'

He takes a few more moments to collect himself.

'You must understand that the war changed everything. So many dead. Injured everywhere. So few men left.'

Uncle Leonard looks up and takes a deep breath.

'Father had Rosetta's best interests at heart when he sent her to India to find a husband. But he would never accept her marrying an Indian. Rosetta must have suspected what Father would do after his refusal of Douglas.'

'You are making excuses for Grandfather – for what he did? You're blaming my mother?' My voice is shaking with anger.

'No, not excuses, explanations. If you can understand why it happened maybe you can forgive –'

'What he did was cruel. He was a horrible man. I hated him when he was alive. Now I hate him more.'

Uncle Leonard grimaces. It's as if all he suffered at his father's hands gathered into a fist and forced him to stick up for that bully.

'Lily, please. At the time it seemed the right thing to do to protect you.'

'You didn't protect me. You neglected me. If my mother asked for me, you should've sent me to her. She would've looked after me properly. Just because she married an Indian doesn't make her a bad person or a bad mother!'

'It put her outside of good society. You must see that, surely?'

'If my grandfather's an example of good society, I don't want anything to do with it.'

I have to get away from Uncle Leonard and his prejudice, so I run off and end up in a tree again. I stay there until lunchtime.

He made me so angry that I forgot to tell him about Papa Persakis and Monsieur Girardon, the ring and the tomb.

Did you know that marrying an Indian man would put you out of good society and separate you from your child, Mother?

Well? Did you?

I don't know about love, never having fallen in or out of it, but I would've thought you have some choice in the matter. But anyway, why should one man be better than another just because of the country he's born in or the colour of his skin? Grandfather, for example, was from a 'good family', but he was a terrible human being with stupid ideas.

Luckily, some nice people have arrived at Knossos. The Pendletons look sunbaked and happy, although they had a horrid boat ride on very rough seas from Egypt.

Nothing seems to worry Mr Pendleton. He's already taking charge – chatting to the crowd of site workers in Greek, tossing his glass eye at unsuspecting children and telling jokes, I presume, because they're all laughing with him. Hilda Pendleton also speaks Greek. She's swapped the red wool beret for a broad straw hat with a blue silk scarf tied around the crown. She comes over and gives me a hug when she spots me at the back of the crowd.

'You've grown about a foot, Lily Ash!'

I suppose she's right. The food here is so much better than what I've been used to in all those boarding schools, and the weather is so sunny. My dresses and vests are starting to feel tight and uncomfortable.

'You must come to the Taverna and tell me everything,' she says.

I'm going there later on this afternoon, once they've settled in and unpacked. The Taverna is going to be their home while they are working here. But I certainly won't be telling her everything, no matter how nice she is. I don't want her to think I'm mad.

I wonder what you'll think of me when I find you, and what your husband will think. I suppose all the letters you sent from India were burnt by Grandfather to destroy the evidence that you were alive. I wonder when you gave up trying.

I'm on the way to the Taverna, a walk of five minutes at the most, when Papa Persakis jumps out at me. He must've been lying in wait for me at the point where you can't be seen from either the Taverna or the Villa Ariadne.

I know I can't outrun him, and anyway I'm tired of running. This man is frightening, but is he really that powerful? I don't think so. He stands in front of me, breathing fast, although he's only popped out from behind a tree. It's rather funny really. A priest, supposedly the most respected man in the district, hiding behind a tree like a spy or a thief.

'What do you want with me?' I try to use my loudest voice, but it cracks with the fear that won't quite go away. He looks up and down the road, leaps forward, grabs my arm and squeezes it hard.

'You use evil spirits to see things. I will catch you if you go down by the vineyard again. You stay away from the Papadakis family. Stay out of this business, or you will regret it!'

He's bending over me, and little bits of spittle are flying out of his mouth. His breath stinks of alcohol. A sudden wave of rage overwhelms me. I stamp on his sandalled foot as hard as I can and wrench my arm out of his grip. He shouts a string of Greek words and raises his hand to hit me, but I've already dodged past him.

'Keep away from *me*,' I gasp. 'You stay away, or *you'll* regret it!'

'You threaten a man of God?'

There is fury on his thin, contorted face.

'Attacking a young girl is *not* how a man of God should behave. If you want to talk to me, then do it in front of my uncle.'

I meet his eyes and summon up the most intimidating stare I can manage. Time ticks by in birdsong. Suddenly, he spits on the ground and limps away towards the village on his sore foot.


When I reach the Taverna, I'm not looking quite as well as before, which Hilda Pendleton notices with her piercing gaze. Maria is making something in the kitchen, so Hilda asks her to bring me a drink and takes me to sit in the garden with her. I'm still feeling shocked but also buzzing with the excitement of having stood up to the priest. My hand shakes as I raise the glass to my lips.

'What's happened, Lily? You seem upset.'

Hilda leans forward and puts a hand on my arm. The hand of an archaeologist – strong and calloused.

'I'm fine, thank you, Mrs Pendleton. I'm just recovering from being ill.'

'Oh dear. These early spring bugs can be nasty. I hope you've been looked after?'

It goes on for a bit like that until I ask about Egypt. As you know, I have reasons to be interested.

She tells me about the buildings they uncovered and a few of the more interesting artefacts, including a necklace of great beauty that her husband John decided to wear for a photograph. This made her laugh.

'Isn't he afraid to use it for a joke in case there is a curse on it?'

She stops smiling and looks at me closely.

'You know that the tomb curses aren't true, don't you, Lily? The story about the curse of the Pharaoh Tutankhamun was just cooked up by the press to sell more newspapers. There's nothing to worry about on that front.' She takes my hand and rubs it between her warm palms. 'I think you must have had a fright. Why don't you tell me what happened? Did you have a very bad experience in the earthquake? It must have been terrifying.'

'It was, but I'm grateful to have survived. Did you feel the quake in Egypt?'

She shakes her head.

'No, we were quite far down the Nile in Amarna. But they felt it at Port Said.'

'Have you excavated any children's tombs in Egypt?'

'You are a brave girl to think about that! Yes, one or two. It's always very sad to find a child mummy, to know that they died before they'd lived out a long life.'

She looks thoughtful.

'Would you like to come to Egypt with your uncle and see the city of Amarna? You seem to have a real interest in archaeology, and women are certainly needed in the profession. We have a valuable perspective to bring to interpretation.' She is launching on a favourite topic, I suspect.

'Yes, I'm very interested in Egypt. Do you read hieroglyphs?'

'A little, but John is much better than me. Do you want me to spell your name in hieroglyphs? I can just about manage that, and it's always fun to do.'

I don't think that's wise, considering what happened the last time I wrote my name in hieroglyphs. But she's getting up from her chair, I suppose to find pencil and paper.

'I'm sorry, I have to go. I said I'd help Micky with his dog.' I head for the gate. 'See you tomorrow, maybe. Thank you for the drink.'

At that precise moment, Micky, wearing a new cap, comes into the garden with Kaltsóni at his heel. John Pendleton follows, grinning under his own broad hat.

'Hilda, I've just heard some very exciting news! A large Minoan gold ring has been found. New iconography, new find site. Perhaps a new tomb. What a magnificent country!' He pulls Hilda to her feet and starts dancing her around the yard until his hat falls off.

Micky looks rather astonished.

'Let's go,' I whisper. 'I need to talk to you!'

# Chapter 23
## Villa Ariadne

'Why did you tell Mr Pendleton about the ring? He's so enthusiastic, he'll tell everyone!'

Micky stops walking and raises his eyebrows at me. Kaltsóni cocks his head.

'That is a good thing. There will be attention on where the ring came from, and how the priest got it, and what he does with it.'

'Speaking of the priest, he's still after me.'

I describe our encounter.

'Trying to hit you! He is crazy.' Micky shakes his head. 'He has many children. They run around like kittens. I don't think he pays attention to them, just to his other interests.'

'I tried to frighten him away, but I don't think it worked.'

'It could make things worse!' Micky looks over his shoulder towards the Taverna. 'But when Sir Arthur arrives, he will take control. He is in Athens now, giving a lecture about Minoan religion.'

'Really? How can he possibly know about that?' I remember the rituals I've seen in my trances – the dances, the offerings, the vision of the woman in the boat.

'There is always a sign in the remains,' Micky says cryptically. I think it's something he heard from his father.

'Well, I'll show you something you should know about. But we must go when there isn't anyone around, especially not that priest, or Nikos who can't keep his stupid mouth shut.'

Something, maybe my fight with the priest, is making me uncharacteristically rude. Micky casts me a sideways glance and sucks his teeth.

'What is it?'

'The tomb where the Bull King was buried. He's the spirit who keeps talking to me. It's above the vineyard where Nikos lives. The only way the Bull King will rest is if his bones and grave goods are brought together and the funeral rites happen again.'

'That is not going to be easy.'

I stifle the angry reply on the tip of my tongue and take a deep breath.

'The best chance is for the site to be excavated, and done properly, so his bones are at least in one place. Then we can try to do the rest secretly.' Getting hold of the ring will be the most secret part.

Micky looks dubious.

'Why do *we* have to do this? It isn't our problem.'

'But it has to happen! The tomb can't stay ruined and desecrated!' My voice is loud and furious. I put a hand over my mouth. I have to convince Micky, but these angry words won't help.

Micky frowns and scratches under his cap.

'Lily, you can't –'

I interrupt before he can tell me how barmy I am.

'If we get Uncle Leonard and John Pendleton to start an excavation, and we stay involved through your father, I'll know what to do when the time comes.'

He sighs and looks up through olive leaves to the cloudless sky.

'The only time those vineyards are empty will be tomorrow morning, Sunday, when everyone is at church. But I must go also.'

'Can't you miss it this once?'

Micky grimaces.

'It will be noticed. I will be questioned by the priest.' He looks very uncomfortable.

'What if you pretend to be ill?'

He shakes his head.

'I don't want to do that. Father can always tell when I am lying.'

I guess he doesn't like deceiving his family because they actually care about him, whereas that's how I've survived all these years. I have to swallow my anger. Micky doesn't realise how important the tomb is, but I don't want to fall out with him and lose such a good friend.

'You'll think of something,' I say, trying to sound normal. 'When is Sir Arthur coming to Knossos?'

'Soon. Maybe next week.'

So I definitely need to visit the tomb and get prepared.

'Does your father trust Mr Pendleton as the curator of the Palace?' I'm thinking of him trying on the Egyptian necklace. That behaviour will not please the Bull King.

'I don't know. His other visits to Knossos were short. But he speaks good Greek, so he's probably a good man.'

He gives me a significant look.

'I know I should practise! But just think how well your English is coming on because you have to speak it to me all the time.'

Micky shakes his head, half-smiling.

'You have an answer for everything.' He checks the position of the sun. 'It is late. I have to go to Irákleion on the bus to see my mother. Will you look after Kaltsóni for me?'

'Are you coming back today?'

'Maybe. But I might tell my father that I am staying overnight and walk back so I can come with you to the tomb in the morning.'

I can't help grinning with relief. 'Isn't it a long way?'

'Not for me. Maybe two hours if I stay off the road so I'm not noticed. Meet at the pine trees at nine a.m. Everyone will be in church, and the roads will be quiet by then. We can both keep out of sight.'

I can see he's excited in spite of his doubts.

'Thank you, Micky. I'll look after Kaltsóni. Find you a delicious supper, shall we, boy?'

'Leave him at the Taverna in the morning. He will give us away if he barks.'

I rub Kaltsóni's ears to distract him while Micky walks up the road to find his father. He stares at me with his amber brown eyes. I kneel down and scratch the lovely soft white fur on his chest. His back paw taps on the ground in time with my scratching.

I've never looked after a dog before, but I know he'll need supper soon, so we go back to the Villa and I get some food from Kosti. After that, and a little constitutional around the garden, I manage to sneak him down to my room. We're both tired, and, with him beside me on the bed, I have the best night's sleep I've had for ages.

I skip breakfast. I don't want to run into my uncle or anyone else and have to explain where I'm going. Kaltsóni's ears go back when I tie him up at the Taverna, and he whines softly. I give him a pat and a bone I saved from the kitchen. I have to force myself not to look back when I walk away. Soon Hilda and John Pendleton will be up, and they'll distract him, I hope.

Back at the Villa, I reach the trees at the end of the garden without being noticed. Church bells are ringing across the valley. I sit down with my back against a trunk. At the corner of my eye, a shadow detaches from a bush and moves towards me.

My heart lurches, but it's just Micky. He looks tired. Wordlessly, he pulls his haversack off his back, pulls it open and brings out a paper bag. He takes half the sticky pastry and hands the rest to me.

Standing together, looking over the sunlit Palace, eating sweet pastry, I'm so glad to have a friend I can trust. But Micky's on edge.

'The tomb is below the Caravanserai?' he asks, brushing flecks of pastry off his dusty shirt.

I nod, my mouth full.

'We need to keep off the road and go through the Palace to keep out of sight.' Micky pulls the haversack over his shoulders and tugs his cap low over his eyes. 'Let's go. The Divine Liturgy has started.'

We scramble off the hill, cross the road, and head down the track into the ruins.

'What do you know about the people who used to live here?' I ask to distract him from his worries.

As we clamber around the ruined walls, he tells me how the Minoans made beautiful fabrics and purple dye from sea shells, and how they had lots of ships and traded all over the Mediterranean.

'People think the Palace is part of the old myth about the Minotaur and the labyrinth, but Sir Arthur thinks that is wrong. You see the double axe symbol on these stones?' Micky stops to trace the outline on the dusty block by the entrance to a ruined room. 'They found many scratched in the stone and real axes made of metal. *Labrys* is the ancient name for a double axe, and Sir Arthur thinks that's where the word labyrinth came from: *The House of the Double Axe*. Nothing to do with a maze.'

But it's still a maze to me. I'm blindly following Micky as we head down a long corridor to the west of the great court, when I stop. There's a turning into a dark passage on my left. Something is calling me. There's desperation and command. I go down the passage, my hands running along either side of the walls, and I come to another turning left.

'Not *that* way, Lily!' Micky stands on the threshold behind me, his face shadowed by his cap. 'That goes to the pillar crypts and the shrine. We are going south.'

I shake my head sharply and force my feet to turn around. It's hard to move. I've started sweating. Micky's already well ahead, turning left down a different passageway.

'Hurry, before they all come out of church!' Micky's voice echoes along the walls. His footfall sounds muffled, distant. I stumble after him, and we are out in the open again, at the very end of the central court. The sun is blinding. Someone grabs my arm.

'Lily! Stay near me or you might get lost.' It's hard to focus on Micky. He squints at me. 'Maybe we shouldn't have come this way.' He pulls me along until we're in a porch at the top of a stairway. A man with a crown of lilies strides on the wall. Swirls of flowers and tendrils, a drum beating, a chorus of voices, the clang of metal.

'When we're down these stairs, we can get out through the South Portico,' someone shouts.

Everything is fragmented, the present cut through by shafts of the past. In front, I see lines of women swaying in procession. I want to join them, but a man is blocking my way, holding a tall, shafted double axe. His dark hair flows over his broad shoulders. His skin shines with oil. He raises the axe high. Below, there's a bowl ready to collect the blood.

Where is the sacrifice? It must be near. My heart is beating like a marching drum. The Bull King is close. Is here.

A moment of blackness – a deep, roaring cascade.

*I am rage! This is my throne of power! Who has dared to desecrate it – to steal – to disembody me?*

*Who takes my place and leaves me in endless shadow? I will lay them low – I will keep my power. Give me the blade!*

There's a sharp pain on my cheek, across my shoulder. I think my arm is being wrenched apart. My mind is stretched to breaking point.

Push, push, push at the door. Make it shut. Force him out. Force it closed.

I blink and the light of day seeps back, blurring. Sweat drips down my back. I'm being pulled along a crumbling slope out of the Palace. Micky isn't looking at me. He's dragging me behind him at a run.

'Stop,' I croak. 'You're hurting me!'

He glances back, and I see panic in his eyes. He doesn't stop but slows a little, and I'm able to stumble after him into the shade of a pine tree outside the ruins.

I slump onto the stony ground, trembling. Micky stands above me, breathing hard. He takes off his cap and wipes his forehead. His face is pale, except for one red patch on his right cheek.

'A man's voice was coming out of your mouth! That spirit is taking you over. You need to stay away from the Palace. I barely got you out of there!'

My body is numb, as if all my senses have been switched off, but my head is throbbing. The reality of the man with the axe, his expression, his anger. I know he's waiting for me in the darkness. I keep my eyes open and look up at the distant branches against the brilliant blue sky.

'I'm sorry,' I whisper. I take a deep breath – let it out. 'I felt it was my Palace, my ground, and that I would have it again, and no one would take it from me.'

'That is completely crazy,' Micky says, finally sitting down next to me, 'but I'm getting used to it.' He twists his mouth into what's meant to be a smile. 'The first time was bad, but now I know what is happening. And I know I have to protect you. So listen, Lily. This spirit does not care about you. He only cares about his power. He wants people to worship and make offerings for *him*. He is using you.

The  Bull King wants you where he can control you. Didn't Frank say that you had to keep the door shut?'

I nod. I don't dare speak, or I'll start to cry.

'But you are letting the Bull King tell you what to do. Keep away from the Palace, the tomb, his areas of power. He has more and more control over you. At first it was just your voice, but now it's your body too.' He wags a finger at me. 'And I don't want to be punched by an old Minoan King using your fist again. It hurt!' He touches his cheek tentatively.

'I'm sorry! I had no idea I did that!'

'Don't cry,' Micky says. 'It wasn't that hard. I've had worse from my little brother. Just stay away from here, or they will send you to the priest or to your lunatic asylum in England. Right?'

I nod and wipe my wet cheeks.

'Come. I'll take you back to the Villa.' He holds out a hand to help me up.

# Chapter 24
## 6th March, 1930
## Villa Ariadne

I can't believe I didn't realise what was happening to me. I allowed the Bull King to control me. I knew he was hard to resist, but I underestimated him in his places of power. He was the one filling me with anger when the priest grabbed me. He made me plan the visit to the tomb with Micky.

The Bull King wants me to fulfil his wishes, find his tomb, restore it, carry out the ritual. But will that make him rest or will it make him rise? I feel like a wrung-out rag, and I haven't dared go further than the Villa garden for two days.

Micky got in trouble with his father for lying about being in Heraklion, so he's not allowed to visit me. He's clearing all the debris from inside their house so they can begin to rebuild the walls.

That possession must have been awful to witness. He was polite about it, but I'm sure it was messy. I hate not knowing what I did, but I'd hate knowing even more. Imagine having your body and mind taken over like that.

Hilda and John Pendleton have dinner with Uncle Leonard every evening, and she tries to encourage me to join them, but I'm happy eating in the kitchen with Kosti and avoiding Uncle Leonard as much as possible.

Hilda is worried about me, and I can't blame her. I look awful. Sunken eyes, pale complexion, and I must have bitten my lip at some point because it's bruised and swollen. She wants Uncle Leonard to get the doctor from Heraklion, but I've managed to make him understand privately that a doctor of medicine will be of no help and only cost money he doesn't have. He listens to arguments like that.

I wish I could tell Hilda what was really going on, but it's too risky. Adults don't believe things like this are possible unless they have direct experience of it. And I'd rather not put her, or me, through that.

It's a shame because it means that I can't walk through the site, and I was just beginning to find my way around and understand its complicated structure. Some of the understanding is actually not mine – it's the Bull King's. But I'd like every opportunity to learn. This strange gift has got to be good for something.

I'm also keeping out of the way because the Villa is at sixes and sevens, preparing for the arrival of King Arthur – sorry, Sir Arthur Everett, or 'Little Arthur' as John Pendleton still insists on calling him. He's due on the boat from Athens today. Then he'll be driven to the Villa, where we must all be ready to receive him. Although the Palace of Knossos, the Villa Ariadne and all the land around it no longer belong to him, he still behaves as if they do. That's what John Pendleton says, and Uncle Leonard coughs and looks uncomfortable.

I'm not sure if I want to meet Sir Arthur. Apparently, he likes children, but prefers boys. He's helped the Boy Scouts in England and even adopted a local boy who was ill. And he throws Christmas parties for children in his village every year where he pretends to be the Minotaur. They say his wife died when they were both quite young, and he's never recovered. They had no children of their own, so he shares his life with other children. I hope he's kind.

I've had to sweep out and polish my room with Maria. There were lots of spider webs. The curse paper fell out of *Our Wonderful World: Peeps at the British Empire* as I was cleaning. It makes me shiver. I wonder how to ask Mr Pendleton to create the hieroglyphs that undo it. Or if Uncle Leonard will beat me to it.


I've met Sir Arthur and I didn't make him angry, so that's a decent start. I think the only people who *aren't* intimidated by him are Micky's father and John Pendleton. Everyone else is on hot bricks. Kosti says Manolaki is Sir Arthur's only Cretan friend. Manolaki does everything with a calm manner, and I can understand why Sir Arthur would like him. As for John Pendleton, he's just full of the highest confidence in himself. He sees Sir Arthur as a vaguely amusing background to his own adventures in Knossos.

I wonder what you would make of Sir Arthur. I don't know anything about you, except that you seem to have had an independent, perhaps even a rebellious, streak. Maybe you would have taken Sir Arthur in your stride, whereas I pick up on the nervousness of others, like Uncle Leonard, who is as jumpy as a box of frogs.

When we are introduced, Sir Arthur shakes my hand very formally and asks what I like best about Knossos. I get rather tongue-tied and go blank. Finally, I dredge up the image of the giant pithos that saved me when Papa Persakis was hunting for me. I really don't blame the snake for biting me. I'm sure I'd be cross if someone came through the roof and landed in my bed without announcement. Obviously, I don't tell Sir Arthur about that part.

'Did you know that the site had more than four hundred pithoi?' he says. 'Imagine how many thousands of gallons of oil and wine they could hold. What a tremendous civilisation!' And then he moves on to talk to Micky, who's been allowed off house-arrest to greet Sir Arthur.

After the formal welcome and tea in the dining room (English cakes and small sandwiches, not Greek pastries), Sir Arthur goes straight out to visit the Palace site with Uncle Leonard, Manolaki, John Pendleton and Hilda. Micky stands watching them go, perhaps wishing he'd been included. Then he turns around and looks at me. Everything is quiet. Without saying a word, we go into the garden.

'I have a surprise for you,' he says as we arrive at the pine trees.

'I'm not sure I want any more surprises.'

'This is a good one.' He reaches into his pocket.

As soon as I see her, tears spring to my eyes.

'Is it really Margarita?' But I know it's her. She sits on Micky's shoulder just as she used to and washes her spiky fur and whiskers with her paws. I don't dare touch her in case she turns out to be an illusion.

He gives her a little seed in his fingertips, and she runs down his arm and jumps back into his pocket.

We both giggle. She's just the same.

'How did you find her? Where's she been?'

'I don't know, but I've been working by the house for two days, and this morning I was humming the old tune I sing to her at night –'

'You sing her a lullaby?' I remember he sang to her when she was chased by the snake, but I can't imagine any English schoolboy admitting to singing their pet mouse to sleep at night. I cover my mouth to hide my smile.

'A what?' Micky looks cautious.

'Never mind. Carry on. You were singing while you were working –'

'Yes, I was piling up the rubble from the house, and then she was there, sitting on one of the stones. I thought I was dreaming!'

Micky looks down at his pocket, reassuring himself she's still there.

'I'm so glad!'

'I wanted to show you right away, but Father wouldn't let me come. He said I had to do my punishment for lying.' Micky straightens up, looking serious.

'Is that finished now?'

'No. One more day after today. Then I can return to the site.' He glances at me out of the corner of his eye. 'How are you feeling?'

'Silly.'

'It was not silly! That spirit is frightening. It was good you didn't go by yourself.'

I tuck my hands under my knees and sigh.

'His power has grown, and that's my fault. I thought I had control over him, but it was the other way round. He's been getting into my thoughts and making me do things. I notice it now, but I need to find a way to break his power over me. To shut the door once and for all.'

Micky picks up a stick and snaps it into small pieces.

'Where do you think his power comes from?'

'I felt him when you showed me the site, the first day we met. Remember how I nearly fainted? His power is here, where he ruled, and by his tomb. He's been waiting for a mind that's open – that he can use.'

Micky looks down at the remains of the stick.

"So *you* have to leave?' He shakes his head. 'But you can't go away on your own. There must be something that can break his power.'

I shut my eyes. This will test our friendship to the limit.

'Do you remember the day before the earthquake when I held the sealstone by the tomb? The beautiful stone with sea animals engraved on it? That voice was immediately strong, even stronger than the Bull King.'

I can still hear the liquid words of the woman who spoke to me from the stone.

*Come to me! Swim to me! Down to me!*

Micky is scratching his head.

'A dolphin and an octopus, I think.'

Margarita peeks out of his pocket, upends herself and dives back down. He drops a seed in for her. We're both silent for a while. It isn't a pleasant memory for either of us. I take a long breath.

'I think I need to go to the sea. It changes everything. That sealstone was an offering to the Lady of the Sea. She will drive out the Bull King. She's older, deeper, more powerful. She existed before all the Bull Kings and their axes.'

Micky looks sceptical.

'You are guessing from something you saw when you held the sealstone?'

'Something I heard. Something I felt,' I correct him.

'Lily, can you swim?'

I shake my head. No one has ever thought to teach me. I've always been told to *Stay away from the river!*

'So what will you do, and how will it help?' Micky must get some of his calm and patience from his father, but I can see he's struggling.

'I don't know,' I admit. 'It might not help, but I need to try. Maybe we can find a little boat?'

Micky raises his eyes to the heavens.

'I am not stealing a boat for you, Miss English. I'm already in trouble.'

'I know. I'm sorry. It was only a thought.' I'm hearing strains of a chant at the back of my mind. It beckons me.

'What if the Bull King is making you want to go to the sea?' Micky is frowning and chewing on a grass stem at the same time.

'No, he wants me to go to his tomb. The sea is where his opposite is. That's all I can sense. He is the Bull. Then there is another, opposing power in the sea, the Lady. I have to find her.'

'Isn't that going to make the problem worse? You will have two spirits in you!'

'Maybe. But I don't think so.' I feel increasingly certain, in fact, and I want Micky to stop coming up with potential problems. 'Where is Kaltsóni?' I say to divert him. Also I've been missing that dog.

'He's tied up at the Taverna. He keeps finding hedgehogs in the Palace. They are coming out of their nests after the winter. I don't want him to scare them.'

'You have hedgehogs in Crete? I thought they only lived in England!'

'I will show you one day. There are lots of them.'

Across the garden we hear Sir Arthur's insistent voice coming from the Villa. The Palace tour is over.

'I must go, or Father will be angry.' Micky scrambles to his feet and runs off without a backward glance.

# Chapter 25
## 8<sup>th</sup> March, 1930
## Villa Ariadne

Uncle Leonard comes into my room right after breakfast. I wonder if he'll apologise, and decide that, if he does, I should try to be more forgiving. It's not pleasant holding a grudge. But, with Sir Arthur here, my uncle just wants to remind me about my duty to behave myself, not to get in trouble on the site and certainly not to talk about the situation that led to my coming to Crete. If asked, I'm to say that I've come for my health, the climate suits me and I find the archaeology fascinating.

I give him the silent treatment and a hard stare. He looks deeply uncomfortable and leaves my room quickly. Uncle Leonard is actually in my power now, in more ways than just that old curse. If I start talking, he could lose his job. Not that I want to talk about my private family business with Sir Arthur, but it is a useful tool to have at my disposal should I need some assistance from Uncle Leonard in getting myself to India.

I hope you appreciate all the trouble I'm going to so that we can be together again, Mother. I hope you actually want to be reunited.

I'm about to go to the Taverna to find Kaltsóni when I glimpse a familiar figure through the window, heading towards the front door. I dash through the hall and hide behind the partially closed dining room door, my heart hammering. Papa Persakis is coming – perhaps to tell Sir Arthur lies about me.

I hear Maria open the front door to him. They speak in Greek, and the only part I understand is 'Kyrie Everett.' I need to know what the priest says to him.

Sir Arthur's commanding voice fills the hall as his footsteps ascend the stairs from the lower floor.

'Who is it? What do they want? Ah, Papa Persakis. Good morning, come in. Maria, thank you. You may go.' Her footsteps retreat towards the kitchen.

Sir Arthur tries a few pleasantries about the earthquake, but the priest interrupts.

'I have something to show you, please.'

'Ah – some more old coins? I only give money to the children for those, Papa, you know that.'

'No – this is not coins.' The priest clears his throat. 'We speak in private?'

'We don't have secrets here. It's a public archaeological excavation. But you may show me whatever it is in my office. I've finished my site log for yesterday, and I can spare a little time.'

The slap of the priest's sandals follows Sir Arthur's polished leathers into the library. Sir Arthur keeps his door open so he can see everything that happens in his Villa. If I can get nearer, I might be able to hear their conversation. I don't want to get on the wrong side of Sir Arthur, but knowing what the priest says is worth the risk.

I'm quite good at walking silently, having had a lot of practice. So I'm able to slip along the wall to a position in the passage next to the lavatory, just out of sight of Sir Arthur's office. If anyone comes, I'll pretend to need the loo.

'Where did you find it?' Sir Arthur is saying.

'Not me. A boy, near the road by the vineyard after the earthquake. Maybe the earth threw it out of its hiding-place.'

'Which boy? I must know exactly where it was found. It's extremely important.'

'He will show you. I take you to him. But how much will you give me for this ring?'

'I beg your pardon?' Sir Arthur barks.

'It is, how you call it, priceless. Important to you. See it has figures on it. A special scene with many figures. How much you give me for it?'

'My dear Papa Persakis, I cannot buy it from you! That would be illegal. Don't you know the law here in Crete?'

'But no one will know, Kyrie. The boy won't say. He is silent. I make sure. It was found on the land you bought, Kyrie. You buy it for twenty million drachmas and take it for your museum in England.'

I've never heard an old gentleman swear before, but I'm sure that's what Sir Arthur is doing, in some language or other.

'Papa Persakis – you shouldn't tempt me like Satan! And if you think I'm going to buy anything for twenty million drachmas, you are sadly misinformed about my means.'

Sir Arthur is drumming his fingers on his desk angrily.

'It is worth that or more, Kyrie.' The priest sounds sulky.

'Well, let me see it properly then, if you're so sure of its astonishing value.'

I wonder if I'll feel the power of the Bull King from the ring, even from a distance.

But there's nothing. No heightening of desire to visit the site, no righteous anger at the desecration of his tomb, no control exerted over my mind.

The library is silent except for the scratching of a pencil and the shuffling of sandalled feet. I wait, barely breathing for what seems like hours.

'Thank you, Papa. Take it away and show it to the Ephor at the museum. It's a very interesting ring, and he must see it as soon as possible.'

'He is not there, Kyrie. He's gone to Dreros. So I leave it tonight with you. You make more of your notes and your drawings. See how special it is. I trust you, Kyrie. I come back tomorrow. We talk then about the cost.'

'Very well, but I will not be buying until the Ephor has had first option,' Sir Arthur says, 'and certainly not for anything close to twenty million!' But there's a different tone to his voice. His desire for the ring is obvious.

I slip into the lavatory as the priest walks out of the office. He pauses in the hall, says something in Greek, perhaps a blessing on the house, or a curse, opens the door and is gone.

I'm breathing fast. Everything feels wrong. I have to see the ring to understand what's happening.

*Strike while the iron is hot*, as Nanny used to say. So I sidle out of the lavatory and knock on the open library door.

Sir Arthur is bent over the ring, which is lying on the desk blotter, catching the sun.

'Hello, Sir Arthur. I'm sorry to bother you.'

He looks up frowning, sees me and blinks.

'Ah, yes. Lily, isn't it? We haven't had a proper talk yet, have we? But I'm rather busy at the present moment.'

'Is that a *ring*? It's so big!' I make my voice sound younger than it usually is. As I've mentioned, it's useful, on occasion, to look small and fragile.

'Yes, my dear. A most interesting ring. Quite remarkable. Unique. I believe it might rewrite some of Minoan religious history.' He's barely able to contain his rising excitement.

'It looks beautiful,' I say, approaching the desk.

'It is. It is.' Sir Arthur picks it up carefully between two fingers. 'I have a magnifying glass in one of these drawers. He opens the right-hand drawer and rummages. 'Here we are.'

Sir Arthur is silent as he gazes through the glass.

When he looks up at me again, his eyes are bright and his moustache twitches.

'Extraordinary! Just as I thought.'

I still have no feeling from the ring, although I'm only a foot or two away.

'May I look at it, please?'

'Of course, you must see!' Sir Arthur exclaims. 'This is an historic moment. You should remember it your whole life. Are you interested in mythology?'

'Yes, sir. I've read some books about it.'

'Good, good. Come closer. Hold out your hand. Now take the magnifying glass in the other one. Don't drop it!'

The gold ring is warm. It lies quiet on my palm, like the inanimate thing it is, beautiful but meaningless.

I look at it through the magnifying glass to pretend interest. The scene is confusing, with several figures and what look like large stones and trees. But at the bottom there is a woman in a low boat with a prow that could be a bird or a horse. And I've seen her before.

'I don't think I understand what is shown,' I say, handing back the ring and the magnifying glass carefully.

'No – of course not. It will take weeks of study to work out what it means, who it represents, but surely the goddess is here in this image, as I thought!' He places it very precisely down on the blotter again. 'Yes, I was right about her. She is the key.' He draws his chair closer to the desk and raises the magnifying glass.

'Which goddess?'

He looks up at me again, reluctantly. I'm interrupting the study of a new wonder.

'The great goddess of the animals, the mother goddess, the goddess of the sea and the Underworld, they are all one, all connected, and here she is expressed, I believe in her three aspects – water, earth and air. You see her in the snake goddess figurines, using the serpents in rituals, and in many ways throughout Minoan art. She commands the animals. She embraces Crete as the Sea Goddess. Now, I must begin a serious study, Lily. Please ask Kosti to bring me a cup of tea.'

'Yes, Sir Arthur. Thank you for showing me.'

'Not at all, not at all. Good to see a child interested in these things. Many simply run around chasing balls. My ward, James, used to spend all his time hitting or shooting things. A fine lad, but not a scholar. Goodbye.'

I'm dismissed. I go to the kitchen with the message for Kosti then head to the Taverna.

A very useful spying mission. I've discovered several important things.

The ring on Sir Arthur's desk is not a real Minoan ring, but a forgery. Papa Persakis is trying to pass it off as genuine. But no one in their right mind would believe that the priest could make that forgery. Never. So another person is involved – and working out who that might be isn't difficult.

What *is* going to be difficult will be convincing anyone, particularly Sir Arthur, of the truth. He's already obsessed with the ring. The other difficulty will be finding the genuine ring. Because there certainly is one, and it belongs to the Bull King.

The other important piece of information is the identity of the spirit who spoke to me from the sealstone: the Minoan goddess who rules the wild beasts, the Underworld and the sea.

Luckily that's where I'm going. I don't know how Micky has organised a day off to go to the coast, but he's left a folded note for me at the Taverna with a message that it will happen tomorrow, and I must be ready at first light.

# Chapter 26
## 9<sup>th</sup> March, 1930

I don't think I shut my eyes at all last night, afraid I'd oversleep and miss our chance to reach the sea. I'm wearing almost all my clothes. It's very cold. Micky wears his cap, coat and the haversack over his shoulders. But there's no Kaltsóni at his side. He only speaks in a whisper until we're well away from the buildings.

'I hope you're ready for a long walk?'

'Yes. How far?'

'Maybe five miles or more. Over rough ground it might take two or three hours. We can have one rest.'

He's more serious than usual. No smiles. We go silently past the buildings and on to the rough road northwards.

'Do you have Margarita with you?'

'No. I do not want her to get hurt. She's in her cage at the Taverna.'

'How did you arrange this with your father?'

'He thinks we are getting the bus to Irákleion to see my family.'

'But you will get in trouble again!'

'We'll go and see them after we've been to the sea. So maybe I won't.'

I wish I could tell Micky why it's so important for me to do this, but, although I'm sure it is necessary, I have no idea what I'll have to do.

'Thanks for helping me.'

He makes a dismissive sound.

'I hope it works.'

It's obvious he doesn't want to talk, so I keep my mouth shut and follow him through the dim light, trying not to turn my ankle on the uneven ground as we leave the road and head across the scrubby fields.

Soon we're in territory I've never seen before. Up hills that must have been steep enough before the earthquake and now are covered in rubble. I have to scramble on my hands and knees in places. By the time we've climbed the third hill, it's full morning sun, and the sea looks close – azure blue, tipped with white, glinting with energy. Alive.

'We can stop here. I think it's past seven now. You have walked quite well.'

Micky's trying to sound much older than me. There's definitely something wrong.

He hands me some bread and a boiled egg and sits down looking out to sea, eating silently.

'What's wrong, Micky? You aren't usually this quiet.'

'I'm worried, of course.'

'What about?'

'You – you idiot! What if you die or go completely mad and everyone thinks I'm responsible?' He takes off his cap and screws it up in his fist. 'You want to go out in a boat. But what are you going to do there? Do you have any idea of how dangerous the sea is?'

I look at the crust of bread I'm struggling to eat.

'I'm not going to die. I'm not going to go mad. That's why I'm going to the sea, to stop that happening. I'll be fine, I promise.'

'You have no idea! People die all the time, even when they say, *I'll be fine*.' He imitates me in a childish voice. 'And I can't tell anyone, because everything you do has to be secret. Then I am the one who gets in trouble!'

'Has something happened? I haven't told you about the ring –'

Micky throws a small stone down the hillside.

'Papa Persakis wants me to come for private lessons. He thinks you are bad for me. He's been talking to Father.'

'But – but your father won't believe him, will he? He won't stop us from seeing each other?'

'Father is worried because I lied to him the day I didn't go to church. So he might. He certainly will if he finds out what we are doing now. He will let Papa Persakis give me those lessons to make me be obedient. In Crete we obey our parents, and we show respect. Unlike you English.'

A couple of goats wander past as I stifle a cross reply.

'Uncle Leonard is not my father. And anyway, your father won't find out,' I say, hoping it'll be true. 'Did you know that Papa Persakis visited Sir Arthur yesterday?'

I tell him about the priest trying to sell the ring illegally.

'Twenty million drachmas? The man is crazy!'

'Even more crazy than me,' I agree.

'So it's definitely a fake?'

I nod. 'But there is no way of proving that to Sir Arthur or anyone at the museum. They won't believe me.'

'Unless we find out who made it. We need evidence. Or to force them to confess.'

But neither of us can think how.

Micky smooths out his cap and pulls it on his head. We start walking again.

As I watch him striding in front of me, head down, shoulders hunched with worry, I make a decision. I'm not going to put Micky through any more ordeals. I should be managing by myself, as I've been doing all my life since you left. It was wonderful to have a friend for a while, but people with my 'gifts' are too difficult to be friends with. From now on, I'll stop involving Micky. It puts him in too much trouble and danger.

This will be our last expedition together.

My legs are very tired when we eventually reach the rocks that hem the beach, but my mind is alive with energy. When I was on the big ship, I didn't notice the huge power and vitality inside every drop of water. But here, on this shore, I feel it pulling at me.

'Lily!' Micky beckons me from the top of a flat boulder. I join him.

'My friend, Elias, said we can borrow his boat. Over there.' He points down to where a few small, brightly-painted rowing boats are pulled up on the beach.

'What is this place, Micky? Was it important in the past?'

Micky looks around and shrugs.

'It's Karteros, but in the old days it was called Amnisos, after the river.' He points to a snaking stream of water splitting the beach. 'Zeus came down from the cave where he was born, and this is the place where his umbilical cord came off,' he says, matter-of-factly.

'Zeus, the King of the Gods?'

'Yes, he was born on Mount Ida.' He waves a hand at the jagged, looming mountains behind us.

'And these stones?' They seem to have shape and purpose, like the corridors of Knossos.

'This was a temple to Zeus.'

No wonder I feel so agitated.

'Theseus and Odysseus landed here, if you believe they existed. And that island,' Micky says, pointing to a long lizard-like shadow off the bay, 'is Día, where the Minoans kept their ships in three harbours. Some people say this is the place where Minos threw his gold ring into the sea to make Theseus prove that his father was Poseidon.'

If only I could describe to you what's happening in my head! I feel the river flowing into the sea, joining the land with the water, the water with the land. I can feel the age-old conflict between the waves and the shore. On land, there's an entire sea-faring community: trading, fishing, rope-making, boat-building, diving for shellfish. Beyond it, the great sea, full of life, churning in its creation. Two forces: one seeking to exploit, one to consume. Endless cycles of absorbing, defending and devouring. The river running between the two, like a rope tying them together.

My eyes jolt open. Micky has grabbed my arm to stop me falling backwards. I slip down the stone and sit on the sand, pushing my hands into its cold grains. I don't look up at Micky, but I feel him standing over me with his arms folded.

'Are you sure this is a good idea? Because it seems very stupid to me.'

I keep my eyes on the sand. The tiny broken pieces of past lives in shell and rock.

'I think it's the only way. I need to leave the land and let the sea take over.'

'That does not sound safe. What do you think is going to happen? I can't rescue you here. I don't swim either.'

I close my fists and clench the sand inside. The mountains and hills stand watching me.

'All you need to do is keep me in the boat, Micky.'

He barks a laugh. 'It's not that simple! When you were possessed by that Bull King, you were stronger than your body should be. I could barely hold you. And it's going to be harder on a boat. We might both drown.'

The words that come out of my mouth aren't from my conscious mind.

'I either go into the water from here on foot, or I go by boat. That's why I'm here.' I push myself to my feet, trying not to show the trembling that has taken over my whole body. 'Let's go.'

Micky stands looking at me, then turns to the beach and the blue-grey distance of seemingly endless water.

'Why are you here? Why is this happening?' he whispers, to himself, I think, so I don't answer. He shoves his hands deep in his coat pockets and strides off towards the boats.

I follow him, a few paces behind, trying to stamp some strength into my still trembling legs. It's not easy walking on the sand. We stop to take off our shoes and socks. Micky rolls up his trousers.

'This one.' He approaches a small rowing boat, white and blue, very worn, the paint coming off in big flakes. On its side a name in Greek: *Delfíni*.

We leave our shoes and coats in a pile on a rock.

Micky's already pushing the boat down the wet sand until its bow is tipping in the surf. I wait. Whatever happens next could be disastrous if I don't maintain some control, some power over my own mind. I need to prepare.

'Just give me a minute,' I call to Micky.

I walk back to the scrub and grasses at the edge of the beach and find what I need: flowers in shades of yellow, white and blue. I don't know their names, except for the daisies – Margaritas. As I pick them I think about their life, and all the things that depend on them – bees and butterflies and all the other creatures that use them for cover and food. Then I turn back to the sea.

Micky pulls the boat close and helps me in as it pitches in the surf. He throws me the rope and clambers aboard. Everything rocks alarmingly.

'Put your weight in the middle, on that front bench!' Micky shouts.

He's sitting at the back, pulling the oars into position.

'Have you taken this boat out before?'

'Yes, but not alone. There isn't much wind, so I will manage,' he grunts, straining the blades through the water.

We jerk forward into the bay, Micky facing the shore and me facing the sea.

# Chapter 27
## Karteros

The clouds disperse as we reach the centre of the bay. Waves rock the boat insistently.

It's the right time.

'Micky, you just have to keep hold of me, please.' I give him my left arm. 'I'm sorry if it goes wrong. I'm sorry for everything. But please, just keep hold of me no matter what I say. And stay out of the water.'

He nods mutely and grips my wrist.

I stand up and face north, to the great Mediterranean Sea. My eyes are shut, so I feel as if I'm floating, but I can also feel Micky's fingers holding tight. In my other hand is the bouquet of flowers.

'Lady of the Sea, accept my offering and help me, please.'

I throw the flowers as hard as I can. Then, I open the door of my mind and wait. Part of me can hear the sea breathing – the other part Micky muttering.

I float between the two worlds.

The water slaps against the side of the boat, the wind blows, and the warmth of the sun vanishes.

A presence arrives.

*You call me with flowers when others have offered lives, riches, golden rings. You bring the remnants of a spirit with you. A strong man. One I have known before.*

The voice in my head is deep – but certainly feminine. Liquid, both warm and cool, sliding into the creases of my mind.

'I have given myself too much to the earth, to the blood of the Bull and his power. I wish to speak to you now, not serve his needs.'

*I have spoken to many over the ages, many powerful men and clever maids. Why should I speak to you?*

I don't have an answer. The voice is so big, so full. I feel tiny, battered, like a mere petal on the breeze, no more substantial than the foam.

But even the foam and the petal come from somewhere, are formed and have some purpose and meaning.

'My father gave me this gift, then died. My mother left me behind and travelled over the sea. I've been used by a jealous spirit of the land. I ask for your help, Lady of the Sea, so I can be free to find my mortal mother, so we can be together.'

A long silent pause.

*You little understand this ancient gift, given by your father. You are young and ignorant. Yet you have commanded the crocodiles. They are mine, but you have already usurped that power!*

'I didn't mean to!'

*Young one, you do not know what you ask or who you offend. You called on Poseidon when you should have acknowledged me! You should have brought me the great ring as an offering. The ring I myself brought up from the depths.*

206

The golden offering – the payment for passage to the Afterlife. I should have known.

*But I will teach you. Teach you how to make proper offerings, how to serve me, how to harness the power of the Sea and the Beasts. How to walk in the Underworld. I will teach you, but you must come down to me. Come.*

Something is tightening around the centre of my chest, as if it's encircled with a living rope, pulling me out of the boat into the water.

I cannot obey the voice, or the strangling force, because my arm is almost being pulled out of its socket. Somewhere in that other reality, in a boat rocking on the waves, Micky is clinging on to me for dear life.

'Let her go!' he shouts.

I open my eyes, but they don't see only the physical world any more. Around the beautiful Cretan bay, the gulls wheeling overhead, the peeling paint, other things are visible. I'm kneeling, bent over the side of the boat. Micky is clinging to the bench, mouth open, shouting. But I only hear the demand of the Lady of the Sea – *Come!* The pull on my chest is almost unbearable.

The tentacle of a giant octopus is wrapped around me, suckers holding me tight, dragging me closer and closer to the churning water. Another tentacle reaches over the side of the boat, feeling for my leg.

Just off Día, a flotilla of reed boats has gathered. Their prows stand high in the water. Men pulling long oars are coming for me. Men who serve the Bull King. They slice through the water so quickly pushed on by the waves.

I will be taken by one or the other of these forces. One or the other.

Then I remember Uncle Leonard.

If I'm hurt or killed, Uncle Leonard will be attacked by a crocodile and consumed.

The ships are coming closer. The men hold coils of rope. They are preparing to catch me.

If I have to go, it'll be better to go into the beauty of the sea, into its rocking embrace. And there I can ask the Lady of the Sea to hold back the crocodiles.

I turn to Micky. His eyes are wide, his chest is heaving with effort. I think I manage to smile.

'Don't follow me.'

In one sharp move I twist my hand up across his grip and let the octopus pull me in.

A funnel of water consumes me. The octopus releases its suckers and shoots downward into darkness. I'm sinking, but I'm not afraid. I can see the bubbles of my breath rising and popping above me in the blue, stained-glass horizon. It's calm under the rocking waves. I hear the voice in my head, like a chant.

> *I circle the earth, hold its sway*
> *Give birth to all*
> *Devour, devour*
> *Come to me, Come to me*
> *swim to the deep*
> *return to the water*
> *turn into the water*

More and more voices join in. The sea song is washing me – washing away the expectations that hung around me like ropes and chains. Status, respectability, behaviour. None of it matters. None of the things my grandfather, or

Uncle Leonard, or even Sir Arthur value are of any real importance.

I want to sing too. I open my mouth.

It fills with sea water, and that is when I no longer hear the chant. It's replaced by another voice. Familiar – and frantic.

*Lily! Kick, for God's sake, kick! Move your arms! Push yourself up! Kick now, or I'll give you a good kicking myself, you stupid girl! Didn't I tell you to stay away from the water? Don't you know anything?*

I move my legs, but they feel extremely heavy, and the light above is fading.

*Keep going!*

My heart hammers. I begin thrashing my arms. I gulp more water. It's getting dark.

*No, don't panic, you idiot! Push with your legs! Get up towards the light. NOW!*

Frank says some rude words I will never forget, but it has the desired effect. I snap out of my drowning panic, and, with all my strength, I push myself up through the cold, heavy water into the air, spitting and coughing.

*Now put your arms out wide and kick your feet. Kick! Keep your head above the water!*

My hair is all over my face, so I can't see. But I can hear thumping in the distance. I can't stop coughing. My heavy clothes pull at my cold arms and legs.

*Lily! Keep your mouth shut. Breathe through your nose and kick, you stupid girl!*

I can't keep afloat. The waves are slapping me down. My legs and arms are lead. Salt water floods my mouth.

*Stop being pathetic! Hold on! Help is coming.*

I try to see between the waves, looking for Micky in the boat. But it's not the help I'm expecting.

Dorsal fins break the water around me. There's a blow of air, then another and another.

Dolphins surround me. There are so many it feels as if the sea is full of living stones with gleaming eyes. Two of them hold my sleeves in their beaks. The yellow bands along their sides look like rays of sunshine. The water fizzes with their clicking language.

The pod pushes me with beaks, flippers, bodies. Some dive under my feet, pushing me upwards. Eventually I'm able to get my arm over one and hold on to the fin. Her tail sways gently. She takes a breath, showering me in a fishy spray. Her eye regards me curiously. We glide towards the shore until I can feel the sand under my bare feet. I try to balance and manage to stand. There's an eddy of water around my legs, and my dolphin is gone.

They're all leaving, surging out to sea, the sharp call of their underwater whistles and clicks dispersing back into the swirling water. I see them leaping in the distance. Their loss feels like the extinguishing of a fire.

I pull my cold, heavy legs through the surf and onto the beach, turning to look for the boat in the bay.

It's not far off, maybe sixty yards. Rocking gently.

Empty.

The sun is shining on the water. The waves lap against the side of the boat. No head, no arms anywhere.

I wade back into the bay. 'Come back! Come back,' I cry, slapping the water. 'Get Micky! Save him!'

I'm shouting so much, I start coughing and spluttering again. Then I'm a bit sick.

Three women in red and black skirts come up behind me and try to pull me back to land, but I push them away. I try to submerge, because if the dolphins came once, they can come again and save Micky.

One woman holds me around the waist. Pulling me back to the beach.

'*Koíta*,' she says, pointing at the rowing boat. '*Koíta!*'

The Greek word finally makes sense. I look.

Micky is pulling himself up on the far side of the boat. He heaves himself inside, streaming with water. He coughs.

He's been holding on to the other side, looking for me in the water.

My vision blackens around the edge as I sink to the sand.

Next thing I know I'm lying on my side, and Micky is sitting next to me, his coat around my shoulders. The women are gone. I don't know if they were real or part of the spirit world.

'At last you are awake!' He takes something out of his bag. 'Here, drink this. It will warm you up quick.'

'What is it?'

'*Tsikoudia.*'

I'm none the wiser.

He takes a sip and shakes his head like a dog who's been in water. 'Go on, try it.'

It burns my throat but afterwards tastes of raisins, and it does warm me right through.

'More?'

'No, thank you.'

I watch him take another gulp. His cheeks turn red, from cold or the drink I don't know. He puts the stopper in the bottle, takes off his shirt and starts to wring out the water on the sand.

I watch him. The way his muscles move over his arms, the heart beating under those ribs. I nearly lost him.

'I'm sorry, Micky. I'm really sorry!'

He gives me strange look and shakes his shirt back into shape. 'Sorry for pulling my arm off, and diving into the water and being rescued by dolphins?'

I nod, tracing a spiral in the sand to avoid meeting his gaze. 'I thought you'd drowned trying to save me. I shouldn't have asked you to come.'

'And miss the best moment of my life? Do you know how long I've wanted to see dolphins? I always watch them from the rocks when I'm by the sea, but I can't swim so I've never seen them close. It was beautiful!'

My mouth is wide open, so I shut it.

'They were really real? You could see them?'

'They were real – so many! Beautiful!' He's grinning from ear to ear. 'Can you call them again?'

I stop smiling, remembering Frank coming just when I needed him.

I shake my head. 'They only came because I was about to drown. I feel like a football after a cup match.'

Micky laughs.

'The spirit who was talking through you had some strange ideas. But I'm glad you decided not to go down to serve the 'Lady of the Sea'.'

I shake my head.

'No, and I'm not going to be the mouthpiece for the Bull King either. I'm just Lily. And I'm hungry. Did you bring any more food?'

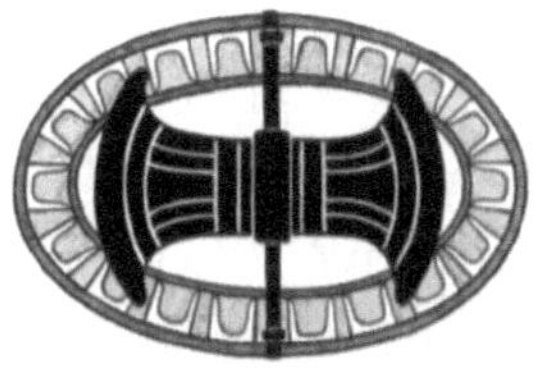

# Chapter 28
## Heraklion

We stay on the beach in the weak sunshine until we dry out a little, and a few hardy tourists begin to walk up and down. Then we trudge back towards Heraklion to visit Micky's mother and try to retrieve his honest reputation.

The city is living in a double reality, too. Many buildings partially collapsed, others untouched. What law decided whose home survived or not is unclear. Micky is silent as we walk along the cracked streets.

When we eventually arrive at Micky's aunt's house, there's no one at home and the door is locked. We wait outside for a while, hoping someone will come back. Eventually a neighbour arrives and explains that the family have gone to a distant village where a relative has taken ill. They'll certainly not be back today.

The *tsikoudia* has definitely worn off. I feel every bruise on my body. I just want to lie down and sleep. Micky starts off down the street towards the town centre. I limp after him.

'What do we do now?'

He thinks for a few paces.

'Visit the museum. Then we can tell Father that we did something useful. You must pretend that you're interested when he asks you about the displays.'

'Won't we have to pay? I don't have any money.' I'd rather just sit on the pavement and shut my eyes.

'No. I know the guard. He will let us in. I hope.' Micky looks at me sideways. 'Although we look awful.'

I don't reply. I'm sure he's right.

Luckily it's not far to the museum. I force myself up the steps. Micky starts a friendly conversation with the guard while I lower myself onto a nearby bench. The guard looks at me curiously. I shut my eyes, remembering my visit to the Ashmolean Museum when the old man at the desk gave me a toffee.

I feel so much older now. What riddle did he ask me? *What have I got in my hand?* A simple trick for a child. My childhood is behind me. I nearly drowned trying to regain control of my own will. The spirits are still there, but I'm not in their power any more.

Tiredness is making me feel reckless. When I open my eyes, the guard is still watching me. I stare back at him until he looks away.

Micky beckons.

'Some of the rooms are closed because of the earthquake, but we can look on the ground floor.' He leads me into a room lined with cases full of large painted vases.

I wonder why Micky enjoys seeing objects behind glass when he's had the chance to hold artefacts fresh from the soil. The thought of all the remnants of so many lives brings on a fresh wave of exhaustion.

'I'm going to find the lavatory. I'll be back in a minute.'

Micky points to a dark corridor beyond the first gallery. In the gloom, I eventually work out which is the right door and spend some time in front of a small mirror trying to comb my hair with my fingers. The person looking back at me is as pale as a ghost, but at least the eyes are determined. I splash dried salt off my face with fresh water.

I'm half-way back along the corridor, heading for the gallery, when I'm grabbed from behind. Before I can shout, a hand is clamped over my mouth and my arm is twisted so I can't move. I squirm and try to stamp on the man's foot, but he's tall and strong.

I'm being dragged back down the passage, my legs thrashing. I try to bite the hand, but it's pressed too hard against my teeth, hurting my lips. He pushes me through a door.

'Let her go, and then stand by the door please, Papa Persakis. I was not expecting you to abduct her in that manner. Lily Ash, I apologise for his rough treatment. Please sit down.'

Papa Persakis says something angrily in Greek and releases me so suddenly, I nearly fall over.

Monsieur Girardon stands behind a desk in a bright artist's studio, full of drawing tables and fragments of fresco and plaster casts. He regards me coolly.

I wipe my mouth and glare at the priest, who crosses himself and leans against the door, arms folded, unblinking. My lips feel swollen. I can taste the tang of blood. I remain standing and turn to Monsieur Girardon, who's now sitting at the desk, hands interlinked, a half-smile on his face.

'So, Mademoiselle Lily, you've come to visit us to inspect what we are doing?'

I shake my head, not yet trusting my voice. I lick my lips. A large window providing lots of natural light fills one wall, but there are bars across it. No escape that way. On the desk are fragments of mosaic and half a Minoan ceramic cup, but no useful weapons.

'You *haven't* come to spy on us? I must say, I find that hard to believe.' Girardon cocks his head. 'I wonder why you're here, then? Not enough antiquities for you at Knossos? Want to inspect more gold?'

'I'm not interested in gold.'

Girardon looks at me, his lips pulling back into a false grin, and then he begins to chuckle.

'Not interested in gold. You must be the only person in the world who isn't! Why, even the priests on Crete are interested in gold. Aren't they, Papa Persakis?'

'I have seven children and a wife to feed,' the priest says in his high, anxious voice. 'I can't feed them all on donations from that poor village. And the English come and steal our buried riches!'

'Enough,' Girardon hisses.

There's a moment of silence. A fly bumps noisily against the window glass.

'So you're not interested in gold. Not to be bribed, unlike most. You are a strange puzzle, Lily Ash. And an inconvenience.' He looks at me over his glasses. 'You are always where you shouldn't be. Always putting your hands on things you should leave alone.'

His own hands are steepled, his look calculating.

'I think I understand one thing about you, however. You are a lonely little girl. You would not want to lose your only friend.'

Girardon lets the sentence hang in the air while my stomach turns. He looks me straight in the eye.

'Of course, we know you have been lying about my work to Monsieur Ash and Sir Arthur.'

'I didn't –' I begin, but he cuts me off.

'Any more interference, or any hint of suspicion about my artefacts, and Micky's father will lose his job on the site. He will be sent back to the small village where he came from, along with all his family.'

'You can't do that – he's the foreman!'

Girardon raises his eyebrows.

'What if questions were asked about his honesty? What if some of the artefacts went missing and were found in his possession? These things happen all the time, and it's so often the Cretan workers who are at fault. So often. For how can you trust these poor people who will do anything for meat and wine?'

'The whole site relies on Manolaki! He's worked there all his life!'

'True. But who do you think Sir Arthur will believe – the Artistic Director of the National Archaeological Museum or an uneducated farmer who started out washing pot sherds?'

He draws a line under a set of figures on a piece of paper in front of him.

'I give Sir Arthur what he wants.' Girardon smiles thinly. 'He is a man under my control, and it would be good for you to understand that before anyone,' he pauses, 'comes to harm.'

He points the tip of his pen at me.

'I don't know how you get your information, Lily Ash. Only the Devil does. But from now on you must control yourself. I'm all too aware of your uncle's straitened circumstances. His job can be lost in an instant.' Girardon clicks his thin fingers. 'And then where will you go?'

I'm too shocked to reply. The room is still and silent until Papa Persakis shifts against the door.

Girardon leans forward.

'I think you and I understand one another now.'

I glare at him in reply.

'Lily! Lily, come out!' It's Micky knocking and calling at the lavatory door down the corridor.

'Ah, of course, it's your *chevalier* come to rescue you,' Girardon smirks. 'Remember – even a hint of what you know, and I will make sure dear Manolaki Angelakis and all his family disappear from Knossos for good.' He returns his gaze to the desk. 'You may go.'

The priest is barely able to move out of the way in time as I run for the door. I don't want to spend another second in that room with those horrible, corrupt men. And if they think I'm under their control, they're in for a nasty surprise.

Micky is just outside the door.

'Lily! What were you doing in there? That's not the lavatory, silly!' Micky tries to peer through the closing gap of the doorway.

'I took a wrong turn. Come on, let's get out of here.' I grab his arm.

'What? Where are we –'

'I'll tell you everything, but we have to go, now!'

He knows me well enough to stop arguing and head for the museum exit.

We find a bench in a little park overlooking the high Venetian walls, and I tell him everything. He listens, swearing occasionally, and, when I get to the plan about discrediting his father, he looks angrier than I've ever seen him.

'That thieving bastard. He thinks he has everyone dancing to his tune!'

'He knows that adults don't believe children, and that rich people don't trust the poor.'

'It's the poor who should never trust the rich! Money eats their souls,' Micky replies.

'What are we going to do? Your father must keep his job. And my uncle –'

He would feel so humiliated, having to pack up his trunk and leave in disgrace.

Micky shrugs the haversack onto his shoulders. 'Let's get back to Knossos. I'm hungry, and no one can think on an empty stomach.'

We talk all the way back. By the time we arrive, cold and very hungry, we have a plan.

# Chapter 29
## 10<sup>th</sup> March, 1930
## Villa Ariadne

'I'm glad you've decided to talk to me again, Lily. I've been worried. You really do need a mother's touch. When you arrived back with Micky yesterday, you looked like a street urchin.' Uncle Leonard takes a sip from his teacup. 'So, once I've been paid by Sir Arthur, I'm going to hire a governess – someone to educate you and teach you how a lady should behave.'

I stare back at Uncle Leonard.

'A governess is not a mother. Mothers do more than brush hair, wash clothes and teach decorum. And anyway, I can do most of that myself, as you can see.'

I shake my clean hair back from my face, determined not to get into another runaway argument with him. There's important business, and this talk of neatness and manners is just a distraction.

'Well it wouldn't do any harm,' Uncle Leonard says gruffly. He wants to be seen doing something for me.

'That's not necessarily true,' I reply. I can't help it. 'But I have important information for you,' I continue before he can start arguing the qualities of governesses.

'Oh? Yes?' He takes a bite of his marmalade-covered toast.

'I have found a tomb. It belongs to one of the most powerful rulers of Knossos. I will show you where it is so that you can discover it and excavate it.'

'A tomb?' Uncle Leonard's hand is stuck half way to his mouth, the remaining toast shaking gently.

'Yes. You understand my abilities by now, I hope. I've found a site below the Palace, on the sloping hill by the vineyards. The spirit of the Bull King spoke to me there. It's his resting place so it must be a rich and interesting burial and –'

'Stop! Tell me about it without the reference to spirits.'

I glare at him.

'Don't you understand yet? They aren't evil. They aren't good. They're traces of thought energy. The more they were honoured and worshipped, the longer and stronger their spirits remain. Because of my father's abilities, I can hear them. They have their own motives. I can't tell you about the tomb without talking about the spirit because I wouldn't know it was there if he hadn't spoken to me. So – I'll tell you the way I need to, Uncle.'

His mouth is hanging open. He realises eventually and shuts it. Then he folds his hands, perhaps to stop them from shaking.

'You seem different, Lily.'

'I am. You won't want to hear about why, but you should listen to me about this tomb. It could make you absolutely essential to Sir Arthur and ensure you keep your job.'

'My job isn't at risk, is it?'

'It might be. I heard Girardon complaining about you.'

'What? Where? To whom?' Uncle Leonard is half-out of his chair with anger.

'I'll tell you everything after I've shown you the tomb. You know my abilities. Just trust in them for once, without being afraid or wanting to stifle them. The visions aren't deceptive. The spirits aren't necessarily harmful. It's only if you deny them that they start using their energy to damage things.'

Uncle Leonard sits down again.

'So you want to show me this tomb – now?'

'Yes, that would be best. The sooner the better.'

He stares at me.

'What's happened to you, Lily?' He puts his hand out as if to touch mine, then lowers it. I don't think I've ever seen him look so confused.

'We can talk after you've seen the tomb. Meet me outside the front door in a few minutes.' I walk calmly out of the dining room.

Micky and I had decided not to draw unwanted attention by looking like a raiding party. We are taking separate routes to the site of the tomb. And I decide it's best not to tell Uncle Leonard about the other people who'll be there. Best keep him on his toes. He's more likely to do what we want if there are witnesses.

Uncle Leonard follows me silently around the east side of the site until we start picking our way over the hill above the vineyard.

'You know your mother was always climbing trees,' Uncle Leonard says as we scramble over the earthquake-tumbled ground. 'Always impossible to find at dinner time.'

He sounds almost fond. This snippet of information about you sounds like a peace offering, so I accept it as such. It's nice to hear something good about you – even if he didn't necessarily mean it that way. 'I notice you're always up in the trees or sliding down scree,' he says conversationally.

'The outdoors tends to have fewer spirits or old objects with vibrations, so I find it more peaceful.' That silences him. We concentrate on the uneven ground for a while.

'My mother didn't have this ability, I suppose?'

'No,' he says shortly. 'It definitely came from your father. The people of the Highlands are known for having second sight.'

I would like to continue questioning him, but we're getting close to the tomb, and, as well as the call of the Bull King, I can hear human voices. I hope it's Micky and his father – and no one else.

I signal for Uncle Leonard to stop moving and be quiet, and he does, standing awkwardly on the side of the hill. Clambering forward slowly, I reach a jumble of large rocks interspersed with scrub. Good cover.

The voices belong to Micky and his father, coming down the path from the road. Kaltsóni follows at Micky's heel. I'm about to emerge when I see another figure, about fifty yards behind, scurrying from tree to tree. The outline of him is unmistakable.

Papa Persakis.

Behind me I can hear Uncle Leonard slipping on the unstable rubble and muttering to himself. I turn and gesture him to get down, to be quiet. He looks affronted but stoops down on the crumbling hillside. Soon he will look as dusty as I did yesterday.

I peer out again. Micky and his father are about twenty yards down the hill, surveying the vineyard. Manolaki, under his ever-present straw hat, peers at the stones strewn across the jumbled field. I can't see the priest any more. No doubt he's hiding by one of the olive trees lining the road. Or perhaps he's made it to the hut and is spying on us from behind one of its ruined walls. Kaltsóni will get his scent soon.

My mind is empty of plans. Resisting the Bull King's demand requires my strength and attention, but I also need to warn Micky.

I pick up a small stone and throw it down the slope towards him. Micky doesn't notice, but someone else does. A shadow moves out from behind the cottage wall. It's a boy. He stands up, shades his eyes and looks towards my hiding-place. I pull back.

Even from that distance, I'm sure it's Nikos, the finder of the ring. Is Papa Persakis coming to speak to him? Have we interrupted their secret meeting? I take a deep breath and concentrate. Try to focus on my memory of you. I can't help Micky unless I block out the Bull King. I shut my eyes. Place my hands on the ground. With a great effort, like lifting a huge rock onto the top of a wall, I firmly close the door of my mind.

There's relief as the pressure vanishes, followed by a wave of exhaustion. The sun beats down on the back of my neck. I'm covered in a cold sweat. I wipe my forehead on my sleeve, panting a little.

Barking and loud voices erupt from the road. I peer round the rock again. Behind me Uncle Leonard is edging out. At least *he's* being quiet.

'Who is it?' he mouths.

'Micky, Manolaki and the boy, Nikos, who lives here. Can you translate what they are saying?'

'The boy told them to get off his father's vineyard, and Manolaki is saying that the land now belongs to the British School at Athens, and, as workers for them, they have the right to survey it.'

'The priest is there too, somewhere,' I say wearily.

'Who?'

'Papa Persakis. I don't know what he wants, but I think we should go back,' I whisper. But Uncle Leonard is not listening to me. There's a commotion by the hut. Someone is screaming.

The priest blasts out of his hiding-place like a whirling dervish, his arms waving in the air, emphasising his height. His black hat has fallen off and his hair stands up wild and straggly. Even from a distance I can see his fixed eyes. But it's his voice that freezes my blood.

*'Honour shall return to me! Bring the offerings. Prepare the sacrifices! I will sail to the ends of the earth! All power and riches shall return to me! I will rule again!'*

The deep, proud voice of the Bull King is coming out of the priest's mouth. And he's running, in his black robe, at full speed up the slope of the field straight towards us, one of his hands clutched above his head in a fist.

The Bull King, having been refused entry by me, has found another host open to the other realm. The priest is now his servant.

He lunges past us, a gleam of gold on his raised hand, and scrambles madly towards the tomb. Kaltsóni is barking from the road. Someone has tied him to a tree with a long rope. Micky is running up the hillside, his father clambering behind him. Uncle Leonard and I intercept them.

Micky judders to a halt. The usually calm Manolaki looks alarmed. He takes off his hat, nods to Uncle Leonard.

I meet Micky's eyes.

'The Bull King has him,' I say, not for Micky's sake. He understands very well what is going on, having heard that voice through my lips before. Manolaki crosses himself, and Uncle Leonard is stock still, staring after the priest who is now digging frantically with his hands amongst the stony debris covering the site of the tomb. I hope my uncle isn't going to have another episode of war mania.

'He's trying to return the ring to his tomb which is buried under those rocks. It was part of his grave goods,' I explain for the others. 'The Bull King won't move into the next spirit realm because all his offerings were robbed and scattered.'

'What was that? A huge Minoan gold ring?' My uncle's archaeological instincts seem stronger than his shock. 'We can't let him rebury that! It could be lost!'

Manolaki crosses himself again.

'Lily and Micky, you go and stand further away down there. Kyrie Ash and I will try to help Papa Persakis. He is not in his right mind.'

But we don't move.

'Kyrie Angelakis, I'm afraid I'm probably the only one who can help Papa Persakis,' I say. 'And I need Kaltsóni to help me.'

Before Manolaki or my uncle can begin their objections, someone runs into the side of me, and I'm thrown down on the stones, winded.

Nikos has made his way up the slope unnoticed. Having knocked me flat on my back, he is now crouching over me. Since I last saw him, someone has given him a black eye. He's shouting, incomprehensibly as far as I'm concerned, but I clearly understand his intentions, because his small hand is holding an ancient dagger against my neck.

# Chapter 30

We're all frozen, except for Papa Persakis who continues to scrape away at the hillside with his bare hands, grunting and exploding with the Bull King's words. It is the Bull King's dagger at my throat. I can feel its power. Nikos, or his father, must have found it in their field. Thought it would be useful. Sharpened it.

Manolaki recovers first and begins speaking to the boy as if he were a frightened dog, while inching very slowly closer, gesturing with his hands to lower the knife. But Nikos is not going to be deterred from slitting my throat that easily.

His reply is breathless with anger. I understand only *kakó* – evil. He thinks I'm responsible for the possession of the priest.

Manolaki is down on his knees out of the boy's reach, his voice more authoritative. And all I understand is *mikró korítsi* – little girl. He is reaching out slowly again, but there is a demand in his words. *Dós' mou!* Give me.

The dagger's blade, held by two little hands, presses harder against my throat. My heart is pounding. Everything is very clear and sharp: the blue sky and one white wisp of cloud over the hill, the wide wings of a bird gliding down the slope, the golden brown of the boy's eye, pooling with tears of frustration and fear.

Whatever sacrifices were performed for the burial rituals at the Palace, they were not child sacrifices. I'm sure of that. The Bull King can't be directing the boy as well as the priest at the same time, even with his sacrificial dagger. Papa Persakis, sharing his terrible ideas about me, has frightened Nikos and made him hate me.

The boy's face close to mine makes it hard to think. I don't want to die, but the effect of my death on others frightens me even more. Nikos' life would be ruined. Uncle Leonard would be attacked by crocodiles and eaten.

And Micky. He should not have to watch me die after all the times he's helped me and everything we've been through.

I close my eyes and open my mind's door.

I call for Frank, who saved me the day before. Frank, who came across miles and miles of sea from England.

But it's not Frank who answers.

I hear the Lady's creatures before I open my eyes. They slide out of holes, homing in on the people on the hillside, the warm bloods. Their thoughts slip like silk across the land. Their obedience to her is complete.

The pressure on my throat has lessened. I open my eyes a slit. Four snakes – two orange striped, two brown and grey – rear up around us. I know that it's a ring of protection, not harm, but I think I'm the only one who sees it that way.

The boy presses the dagger against my neck with renewed force. I stare into his wide eyes.

'They will leave when you let me go,' I promise him, but the words have no effect. Why haven't I learnt more

Greek? The snakes' tongues flick in and out, and their bodies rustle against the loose earth and dead leaves.

Micky is about ten feet from me, close to the long, swaying leopard snake, his anguished face grimed with dust.

'Control them, Lily! Show Nikos you are good!' He starts appealing to the boy in Greek – too fast for me to understand.

I close my eyes and try to reach into their reptilian minds. Their tongues bring smells: human sweat, insects, a mouse very close by. I try to bind them to my will, but they obey another. The Lady is even stronger than the Bull King. She demands my service in return for the curse. I must pay for my insolence. There must be a sacrifice.

Something crashes down next to me. Someone is screaming. I'm half-way between worlds. The pressure on my throat is gone, but my arms are heavy, bound by something.

I take a deep breath. Another. Open my eyes.

Nikos is lying on his front, arms behind his back, and Uncle Leonard has hold of his wrists. Blood stains the sleeve of my uncle's shirt.

But I can't get up to help him. Two orange striped snakes are spiralling around my arms, their tongues licking the air near my face. The other snakes have disappeared. Micky is on his feet, scanning the hillside, a new fear written across his face. There's silence, except for the voice in my head.

*You are my priestess now. These are your assistants in worship. You have provided a sacrifice.*

I sit up, holding my arms out straight.

It's as if I'm floating, as if the snakes are lifting me. I'm on my feet and power is surging through my body.

But I've just understood which creature has been chosen as an offering to the goddess.

'No, I'm not!'

I want nothing to do with any spirit who demands the sacrifice of a life. I push and push and fight and fight. Sweat runs down my face, my arms tremble. Suddenly Kaltsóni is at my side, warm and real. Leaning against me and growling at the same time. He anchors me. Guards me.

The floating feeling is gone, the snakes uncoil, slither away, leaving two long narrow scratches on my arms. I collapse, crouching with my hands over my head. The searing presence leaves my mind, but not, I know, for ever.

The dog is licking my face. Someone is holding my hand.

'She's still in a trance. We need water to splash on her,' Uncle Leonard says, 'and I need rope to tie up this boy.'

'Shhh please, Kyrie,' Manolaki whispers. 'Shhh.'

Another voice approaches – the priest's, unnaturally lowered into the words of the Bull King.

'*My knife. My knife,*' he chants as his steps get nearer, crunching on the stony ground. '*A dagger for the sacrifice.*'

Kaltsóni barks, sharp and piercing. I wrench my eyelids open. It's Micky holding my hand. All my limbs feel like lead.

The dagger lies on the ground where Nikos was forced to drop it. Restraining him requires all Uncle Leonard's limbs. Manolaki has disappeared.

The priest is coming quickly, stomping down the treacherous slope. He's nearly on top of us.

'Get the dagger,' I say. 'Quick!'

Micky scrambles to pick it up. He holds it tentatively.

'Throw it!' I shout. 'As far as you can!'

Nikos renews his struggles, straining towards Micky. Uncle Leonard holds on grimly, his sleeve now completely crimson.

Micky's arm draws back and the dagger flies, glinting, through the air until it clangs down between some rocks about ten yards away.

I force myself to my feet, take a step forward. The priest is right in front of us, his face transformed from the thin, ratty, impoverished, corrupt Papa Persakis to a powerful, driven creature, somewhere between flesh and spirit, intent on one purpose: the gathering together of his body and his property. His face constricts and grimaces.

Manolaki springs out from behind a rock. He barges Papa Persakis sideways, sits on top of him, forcing his arms down. But the priest is taller, and the spirit gives him unnatural strength.

'Help me!' Manolaki calls, and Micky runs forward holding the remains of the rope that had restrained Kaltsóni.

Soon father and son have the priest pressed down on the ground with his arms tied behind his back.

But the Bull King remains, shouting his ancient pride and greed. There's only one way to be rid of him. I call Kaltsóni to my side, kneel beside Papa Persakis and put my hand on his head.

'Rest, spirit. All your offerings will be brought. A new sacrifice will be made for your journey. Rest now. All that is lost will be found.'

*'How can you promise this? My body and my treasures are scattered. Men dare touch them, dare steal my honour, and I burn with rage!'*

'Rest, spirit. I promise to do this for you. We will find your treasure.'

*'You are not strong enough. You do not know the rituals. You are too young.'*

'You will teach me, Great Bull King. As the Lady of the Beasts and the Sea has taught me her chants and shared her power.'

*'How can you serve two masters? I cannot trust you!'*

'I serve no one. I do this of my own free will. I do what's best for all.'

*'If you do not bring back my treasure and my bones, I will take you instead. I will consume you. Your dog guardian cannot save you. You cannot hide from me.'*

'I guarantee it with my own blood. Here – my blood is now spilt in your domain.' I wipe the blood from my scratched arm on the stone. 'May it be the seal on our agreement. I will return with your offerings. Now leave this man, Great Bull King. Leave him.'

I press my hands on either side of the priest's head – feel it tremble. Kaltsóni whines, shifts to press his body between mine and the priest. We all shake with the spirit's passing.

I'm as weak as a baby. I lie down on the hillside panting like the dog beside me. When I open my eyes, the priest is sitting with his hands still tied behind his back. Manolaki grips the rope, looking thoroughly unnerved.

'He'll be calm now. The spirit is gone.' From Manolaki's expression, I don't think my reassurance helps much.

Further down the hill, Uncle Leonard is sitting in exactly the same position as before, with Nikos on the ground under his knee.

'Let him up. He can't do any harm now.'

The boy has stopped crying, but he won't look at me, even as I help him to his feet.

'He's had a very strange, disturbing dream. That's what we must tell him.'

'I'll talk to him,' Micky says.

Uncle Leonard gets up stiffly and looks down at his arm. It's hard to tell if the bleeding has stopped or not, the sleeve is so saturated. His hands have begun to tremble, so I sit down on a rock with him and undo the sleeve button.

The cut along his forearm is long but not deep. The blood is beginning to clot. The scratches on my arms look minor by comparison.

'I shall live. 'Tis but a scratch,' he murmurs. All the same, he lowers his head between his knees for a moment. We sit like that for a while with Kaltsóni at our feet.

He looks up eventually and shakes his head. 'Let's get off this cursed hillside. You look like you've been run over by an omnibus.'

More of his strange sense of humour.

He takes Nikos by the arm and picks his way down the hillside followed by Manolaki and the priest. They go like lambs towards the hut.

Micky doesn't follow. He has turned towards the tomb.

'Come on. We have to find her.'

I look at him – my friend, wild-eyed and desperate.

'Find who?'

'Margarita, of course! I saw her run up there away from your snakes.' He wipes his nose with the back of his hand and starts climbing.

'They smelled her! I heard their thoughts!'

He turns to look at me, frowning.

'Next time, try to stop them rather than listen to them! Margarita went down a hole and so did those snakes. Come on!'

My legs don't feel able to move an inch, but I grab Kaltsóni's collar and force them, one step at a time up and up, until my chest is as tight as an iron band. Micky has stopped. He bends over a large, smooth stone sticking out diagonally from the hillside.

'Look.' Micky points under the protruding rock where the priest had made a shallow tunnel by scooping out stones and dirt. 'I think she went in there. She took off like an octopus.'

I giggle in spite of everything.

Micky looks at me seriously.

'She did! She was terrified!'

The hole looks too narrow for Micky's shoulders.

'I'll go in,' I say. 'It's my fault she got scared.' I do feel guilty, even though I never asked for the snakes to come. But I really don't want to go down the tunnel into the Bull King's tomb. What if he ignores our agreement and overwhelms my mind?

'No.' Micky pulls me back. 'Stay out of that tomb. What is the point of training an animal if you don't put it to use?'

He inches his head into the mouth of the tunnel and begins to sing the long, haunting notes of the lullaby.

*Nani, nani my child.*
*Come Hypnos make her sleep*
*and sweetly lull her.*
*Come Hypnos from the vineyards*

take my child from my hands.
Take her to the sheepcote
to sleep like a little lamb,
to sleep like a little lamb,
and to wake up like a little goat.

He stops for a moment and we listen, lying on the ground. Even Kaltsóni is completely still.

'I think I hear something, but it could be earth sliding down the tunnel.'

Micky nods and starts singing again. The hole is so black that we don't see her until she's right in front of us. Margarita, dusty, quivering, but alive.

We make a big fuss over her.

'I thought the Lady took you as a sacrifice,' I whisper, stroking her spiky fur with the tip of my finger.

'What?'

'Nothing. She's the luckiest mouse on the whole island.'

Micky smiles crookedly.

'She had a quiet life until you arrived. Here – hold her a minute,' he pops her on my shoulder. 'I think I saw something in that tunnel. You stay here.'

I try to object, but he's already sliding his head and chest down on the loose soil. He pushes himself in until all that's above ground are the soles of his worn-out shoes.

'Don't go any further, Micky!' I cry, suddenly fearful that he'll fall into the tomb – or worse, be taken over like the priest. Kaltsóni whines and starts to dig the soil around his shoes.

'Don't worry. I have it. Pull me out.'

There's no strength left in my arms, especially as I'm trying to keep Margarita on my shoulder. Eventually Micky shimmies himself back up and out, covered head to toe in soil.

His right hand is a fist, and he has a huge grin on his face.

'Look at this.'

He opens his palm. Amongst the gravel and soil is a gleaming gold ring, its carving vibrating with life.

# Chapter 31

'Put it back, Micky! That's the Bull King's ring, and he'll be angry if you remove it!'

Micky looks at the glowing ring and rubs it between his thumb and finger.

'I thought you said it was fake.'

'There is a fake one, but this one's real. They made a copy to sell to Sir Arthur and had the real one to sell here. But the Bull King made me vow to return all his grave goods.'

Micky glances quickly at my face to check that I'm not joking.

'Really, Micky, he wants his ring. He wants his dagger and all the other offerings and sacrifices, so he can move beyond this world. Which will be a good thing for everyone!'

I take Margarita off my shoulder and hold her out to Micky.

'Take her, give me the ring, and I'll throw it back down there.'

'The carving is of the Lady of the Sea, so doesn't the ring belong to her?' he asks, still gazing at it.

'It's the Bull King's offering to the Lady to accept him into the Underworld, the Afterlife, but it was separated from his body by robbers. The earthquake brought it to the surface again. She's been looking for it, or a substitute offering or sacrifice, ever since.'

'Is *that* what was happening when you jumped into the sea?'

'Yes – in a way.'

The hand I'm holding out is trembling. Micky ignores it and puts the ring on his middle finger.

'Wish I had a camera.'

I nod, trying not to show the panic I feel. 'You'll remember it.'

He looks at the engraving carefully again.

'It is beautifully carved.'

Then he sighs and takes it off his finger, examining the gold beads on the band.

'You are right. It will only cause trouble.' He takes Margarita in his other hand and puts her in his pocket. 'I'll throw it back in now.'

'Goodness me, what are you doing under there? Is that a gold ring?' A voice behind us bellows.

We've been so enthralled by the ring we didn't hear John and Hilda Pendleton scrambling down the hill, and now they are standing just below the stone of the tomb, staring at us. Kaltsóni wags his tail enthusiastically at them. No use as a guard dog.

We both freeze. Micky's hand closes around the ring. Mr Pendleton leaps up towards us like a mountain goat.

'Let me have a look, please. Yes, right now. And where *exactly* did you find it?'

John Pendleton takes the ring from Micky's hand.

What to say and what not to? I'm too exhausted to decide.

Micky takes over.

'We didn't find it. It was Nikos Papadakis. We were looking for Margarita. She was lost when Papa Persakis attacked.'

It's a long explanation. Hilda looks horrified, but John Pendleton has thoughts for nothing but the ring. The same desire as Sir Arthur's lights up his face.

'And you say that Manolaki and Mr Ash are down in that hut with the mad priest and the finder of this ring?'

'You must go and help them, John,' Hilda holds out her hand to me, 'while I get these children back to the Villa. Lily, you look absolutely wrung out!'

'I'm fine,' I lie, getting up off my knees. 'It's Uncle Leonard who needs help. He's got a cut on his arm. We'll look after the ring if you could go down and help him.'

'Heavens! It's a good thing we came along when we did, John. John! You can't go down that tunnel! It might collapse!'

'It's a tomb! I'm sure of it!' He's on his knees peering down into the blackness. 'If only I had a torch! It must have been opened by the earthquake. By the size of these stones, it's an important one.'

He gets reluctantly to his feet and brushes off his shorts with the hand that isn't gripping the ring.

I hold out my hand.

'I'll keep it safe, Mr Pendleton. I think they will need both of you in the hut. They wouldn't let us help. Didn't want us to get hurt.'

I let the sentence hang, my hand still stretched out.

'Yes, we will look after it and stay out of the way,' Micky adds, looking uncomfortable.

'The priest was obsessed with the ring. Seeing it might make him worse,' I insist.

John Pendleton hesitates. He stares at the ring, holding it close to his one working eye. There's a long pause. Then he looks at us and smiles broadly.

'I have a safe pocket for this. That'll keep it out of sight. Best for it to be catalogued straight away and kept secure.' He slips it into the breast pocket of his jacket and pats it happily. 'If you can't make your own way back to the Villa, wait for us here. Come on, Hilda.' He's already striding towards the hut, gold ring secured, to the rescue.

Hilda hurries after him, glancing back at me.

'Micky, look after Lily until I return,' she calls.

We both watch them all the way to the hut and see the door close after them.

'Damn it!' I kick a stone down the hillside.

Micky gets up, holds his hand out to me.

'If we can't give the Bull King back his ring, at least we can find his dagger.'

Micky has a good idea of how far he can throw, so it doesn't take long to find, lodged between two stones. There's a new scratch down its hilt.

'I think you should hold it,' I say. Who knows what will happen if I pick it up. I might feel the bloodlust of the priests or the terror of the sacrificed bulls and sheep. Either way, it would be too much.

He holds it tentatively between two fingers. The bronze glows dully against the white stones. We silently make our way back up to the tomb tunnel, and, without a word, Micky lies down and throws it in.

Then we begin walking to the Villa.

After I've slept for a couple of hours, been woken up by Kosti and eaten some sandwiches, I'm told that all the adults are in Sir Arthur's office, so I creep into the room. Uncle Leonard, arm bandaged, in a fresh suit, looking the picture of respectability, is in full flow, explaining the whole affair. The priest had a fit of madness, and the boy, Nikos, was influenced by him to attack foreigners. Uncle Leonard doesn't mention anything about me, the snakes or the Bull King. Manolaki stands silently by the wall, Micky at his side. Sir Arthur is holding the ring and turning it this way and that. I can't help wondering if he is actually listening, his whole attention seems to be on the engraving.

'I am sure –' John Pendleton begins, but Hilda digs him in the ribs. 'Ah, I mean to say, Mr Ash, Manolaki and I believe that the Papadakis field is the site of a very important tomb of the middle to late Minoan period, and we should excavate it soon, before it's robbed further.'

Uncle Leonard clears his throat. 'There may be many more tombs and structures in that field. We should survey it properly. The ring is of unknown provenance. The priest had it when he accosted us in the field, but it seems that in his unstable mind he decided to rebury it in the tomb. Then, thanks to Lily and Micky, it was retrieved and the tomb discovered.'

'Wonderful. Well done to Micky and Lily,' Sir Arthur says, giving us one of his moustache-jumping smiles. 'But there's something very curious going on here.'

He picks up his magnifying glass.

'Papa Persakis showed me this ring before – and wanted a huge sum for it. As if I didn't know it's illegal to buy any artefact unless it's been offered to the Ephor and the museum first,' he says pointedly. 'But it wasn't this ring. The engraving was slightly different.' He peers at the ring and at the sketch in his notebook. The room is silent. 'One must be a forgery. But which is which, and where is the other?'

Micky and I glance at each other. Uncle Leonard clears his throat again.

'It may be that the priest can answer that question, now that he has returned to his right mind.'

'I wouldn't trust what he says if he's been trying to sell antiquities illegally,' John Pendleton says. 'We should search his home for the other ring and look at them side by side.'

'This is the real ring,' I call out. I can't stop myself. I'm tired of hiding. I step towards Sir Arthur's desk.

Sir Arthur looks at me impatiently.

'You have some information about it that you haven't told your uncle?'

'I'm able to see the past,' I say. My voice is breaking, but I carry on. 'I can tell you what is ancient and what isn't.'

John Pendleton barks with laughter.

'What a splendid fantasy!'

Uncle Leonard puts his hand on my shoulder.

'I think Lily has been over-stimulated by events –'

'No, Uncle! You know what I can do! Test me if you want. Blindfold me and see what I can tell you.'

I cross my arms to stop them trembling.

Everyone is staring at me.

'This ring must not leave the country,' I insist. 'It is the real ring of the Bull King and it must stay here with his remains.'

'Lily is telling the truth,' Micky says softly at the back of the room.

I'm looking at Sir Arthur in what is probably a very challenging way. But he's smiling, and there's a gleam in his eye.

'Well, who can resist such a possibility? I know my dear old colleague, Mackenzie, would have believed you, and, for his sake, let us entertain the possibility that you are gifted in this way.'

He gets lightly to his feet. It's hard to believe he's eighty years old.

'You may all go, and, after supper we will set up the experiment.'

The audience remains the same: Sir Arthur, the Pendletons, Uncle Leonard (twitchy as a bag of rabbits), Micky and his father. It's Manolaki who brings out the objects for me to hold.

Suffice it to say I'm able to identify which are the old pieces of pottery, the excavated animal bones, the ancient seals and daggers versus the reproductions and modern pieces. All with a large black blindfold completely covering my eyes.

When the blindfold is taken off, many eyes are fixed on me. Manolaki looks pale, and John and Hilda are whispering to one another.

'Don't tell anyone outside this room,' I say. 'Please. I don't want to become like an animal in a zoo, and I don't want to be tested all the time. You must trust me.'

Sir Arthur steps forward and takes my hand, smiling.

'My dear, what you have is a great gift. We will not throw pearls to swine. This Ring of Minos, the Bull King, will remain here in Crete.'

There's a murmur of assent. Uncle Leonard coughs and steps forward.

'Lily should rest now. She's been through such an ordeal and done so well.'

I feel tears springing to my eyes. I don't think he's ever praised me before.

Hilda whispers in John Pendleton's ear again.

He purses his lips, considering. Then nods.

'Leonard and Lily – we'd like to invite you to excavate with us next season at Tel el Amarna. We believe the skills both of you possess will be invaluable,' John Pendleton says. Hilda is beaming.

Uncle Leonard turns bright red. I hug Hilda because Egypt is on the way to India. There's just the small matter of a curse to sort out.

'We may need your help with some hieroglyphs before then,' I say, with a glance at Uncle Leonard.

'And I,' Sir Arthur interjects, 'will be asking for your assistance with some of the objects I've acquired from a certain source. When we return to Oxford, I'll be in touch. In the meantime, thank you, Lily.'

He sits down in his chair and folds his hands together in a satisfied way.

'Micky has helped me so much,' I say. But I can't look at him because I'll probably cry. To be believed, to be accepted, to be valued. It means everything.

I want to see that acceptance in your eyes when I eventually find you, Mother.

## Chapter 32
### 12th March, 1930

Micky, Kaltsóni and I are sitting in our usual place under the pine trees, overlooking the site. The afternoon sun is strong, and I'm feeling woozy from sleeping for eighteen hours. Kaltsóni is also sleepy – he did a lot of work yesterday. Micky, on the other hand, has plenty to say. I'm struggling to concentrate on his words.

'Lily! How will we return the ring to the tomb?'

I lie back and rest my head on one hand.

'We can't do anything. They're taking it to be studied at the museum in Heraklion. The Ephor will decide if it's real or not, without asking us. Then –' I shrug.

'But you said you made a vow to the Bull King to return all his offerings!'

I pick up a dry stem and begin splitting it down the middle, trying not to think about the Bull King's threats.

'I had to. It was the only way to release his grip on the priest's mind. I hope he'll accept all his grave goods remaining in Crete as fulfilling that vow. The rest is beyond my power. The archaeologists will be there now, deciding how to excavate. The remains will go to the museum.'

Micky looks at his hands. 'But something could be in my power. My father has influence. He and the Ephor respect one another. I will talk to him.'

I feel an immediate lifting of worry. Manolaki will understand the importance of being respectful. He heard the Bull King's voice.

'Thank you, Micky.' My eyes swim, and I turn away, finding it hard to speak. 'I've never had such a good friend.'

Micky doesn't say anything for a while.

'I've never had so much excitement. Like watching moving pictures, maybe.'

'I don't know. I've never been to a picture house,' I admit.

'Me neither. Maybe we can go to the one in Irákleion soon?'

I don't dare answer as I can't trust my voice. But I know I'm smiling ridiculously widely.

'I want to ask you something –' Micky stops. Glances at the sleeping dog. Starts again. 'I saw how Kaltsóni helped you – kept you from being taken over. How did you know he could do that?'

'When I first went to the field where the tomb is, I brought him along, just for a walk. But he seemed to know what was happening when the Bull King spoke to me. He lay alongside me, and it was as if he anchored me to the here and now. To myself.'

We're both giving him a pat, and, even in his sleep, Kaltsóni rolls over so we can scratch his lovely soft belly.

'This kind of dog is on pottery decoration from thousands of years ago. The same curly tail, the same ears.

It's an ancient breed.' Micky stretches out the dog's tail, and it springs back to a curl, wagging rhythmically.

'Maybe that's why Kaltsóni understood what I needed.'

Micky nods – looks away towards the Palace.

'He chewed through the rope yesterday so he could reach you. He should be your dog. He should go everywhere with you and keep you safe.'

'No, Micky! He's yours. He loves you!'

'I have Margarita.' He pats his pocket gently. 'Besides, Maria's cat doesn't like Kaltsóni, and when her cat is unhappy, Maria makes bitter food. So it's better for him to live in the Villa with you.'

'That's not true! Maria always makes delicious –'

'Lily, for once, don't argue! Kaltsóni is yours. He is meant to look after you, that's clear. And if he is with you, I won't worry.'

There's a moment of silence except for my sniffs as I try not to cry.

'*Se efcharistó pára poly, Micky.*'

'Excellent! I understood. Your Greek is finally getting better! You're welcome, Lily.'

I try to slap him, but he dodges, laughing. Kaltsóni bounces up, hoping for a game. We throw sticks for him to fetch until it's time for Micky to help his father.

Kaltsóni and I walk slowly back to the Villa. My mind is already in a Heraklion picture house, sitting next to Micky.

'Lily –'

Uncle Leonard is standing just inside the doorway, as if he's been waiting for me.

'Leave the dog tied outside and come to my room, please. I have something for you.' He looks on edge. He's been scratching his wrist at the end of the arm bandage.

Kaltsóni accepts the inevitable and lies by the door. I follow Uncle Leonard down the steps and into his bedroom.

'Please – sit.' He's pointing to the only chair by the small desk. I pull it out and turn it round. He's pacing the room.

'I understand that you're still angry with me for what happened when your mother was sent away, and –' He stops walking for a moment and points at me with a long finger, 'you are right to be angry. Your life was made worse by Father's decision, by his judgemental spirit.'

He seems to have come to the end of his thought and stomps across the room again.

'But,' he continues, 'you don't know everything. And maybe knowing more will help you understand why he was so harsh, even if it's too late to change what happened.'

He takes a long deep breath.

'While I was away studying at Oxford University, a terrible accident occurred. Your mother was sixteen. Our parents went out for the day. Our younger brother died when she was meant to be looking after him. And Father never forgave her for Francis's death.'

'Francis? I don't know anything about Francis!'

'No. They made sure of that.' Uncle Leonard shakes his head in an imitation of his father's angry mannerism. 'Father and Mother kept his photographs and personal effects in a private trunk. It was too painful for them to see his image around the house. He was their last child and their favourite.'

'But how could it be my mother's fault?' I shout. 'He wasn't a baby, was he? How did he die?'

Uncle Leonard puts a finger to his lips and sits down on the narrow bed, pressing his hands between his knees.

'He was by the river at the bottom of the garden with the dog. He thought it would be fun to throw a stick in and watch him swim. The river was in flood. Buster was swept away, and Francis went in to try to save him. His leg was caught in a submerged tree branch and he drowned.'

Uncle Leonard closes his eyes.

'Rosetta was inside at the time. She simply took her eyes off him for a few moments, and he made his foolish and courageous decision. Buster managed to pull himself out further downstream. Our parents never forgave the dog or your mother. Rosetta went off the rails after that. The blame, the grief, the guilt sent her a bit mad.' He looked down at his hands. 'She left home, and she met your father.'

I feel sick with understanding. It nearly engulfs my mouth, but I manage to swallow.

'What did Francis's friends call him?'

Uncle Leonard's eyes meet mine. I think he knows.

'Frank. They called him Frank. He knew lots of boys in the village. He was always getting up to mischief.'

At that moment I imagine I feel the familiar tug of Frank's insistent mind which hasn't visited me since he saved me from drowning in the Aegean Sea.

'He still is, Uncle. He still is.'

I try to explain, without too much detail, the contact I've had with Frank, and I think Uncle Leonard finds it a comfort. He is silent for a while, his eyes shut, but I see the tears seeping out.

I get up from the chair and head for the door, hoping I can reach out to Frank one last time in the quiet of my bedroom. But Uncle Leonard has not finished. He takes my arm and makes me sit down again.

'You must understand, I promised to destroy them, but I never could. I've kept them all these years, even when I thought you were a delinquent and belonged in an asylum at best.' He looks at me with a crooked smile. 'How could I guess the truth? It was too much for my prosaic mind.'

'What did you keep, Uncle?'

He looks over at his trunk at the end of the bed.

'I'll show you.'

He brings a small key out of his breast pocket.

The trunk is stacked with books and a few summer clothes he's not yet unpacked, but he just pulls them all out and dumps them on the floor. Then reaches right down to the bottom.

'Here.'

A plain rectangular tin box, painted black. Perhaps it once contained ammunition.

'Open it.'

It's full of letters, all in the same hand. The one on top has a stamp with a rupee symbol on it. I take it out of the envelope with shaking hands. It's dated 1st December, 1929.

I look up at Uncle Leonard but he has his hands over his face.

So I start reading.

I'm still reading now, in my own bedroom, working my way forward from the very beginning when you got on the ship to India in 1922.

Uncle Leonard was not up to conversation when I opened the box, but perhaps I'll go and find him after dinner. I think I'll be able to speak to him properly, without resentment, for the first time.

I don't know if Frank will talk to me again. I'm almost afraid to try. But I'm glad he's finally been acknowledged and his story told. Imagine dying and having your memory wiped out, your name never mentioned. No wonder he stayed behind! Good thing too, as he saved me from drowning twice. My uncle and a friend, although never an easy one.

I hope he'll be able to move into the next realm now, even though I'll miss him.

But here are all the letters you have written spread out on the floor around me. My own mother's words – just for me. Like an embrace.

I've been walking the labyrinth alone in the dark all these years.

I'm near the centre now.

I'll find you there, and we'll walk out together.

# Notes

I have always enjoyed writing historical fiction based on a scaffold of facts, and this book is no exception. As *An Ancient Haunting* is set within living memory, it's important to distinguish between the two. Many fascinating people worked in and around Knossos in 1930. My story operates as an alternative reality.

But I do want to pay tribute to those who inspired this book, whose lives are definitely worth exploring:

**Sir Arthur Evans** – director of the Ashmolean Museum, Oxford, purchaser of the site of Knossos, millionaire, single-minded interpreter of Minoan culture and religion through his book *The Palace of Minos at Knossos*. It was this book, found in my high school library, that started me on a lifelong fascination with the Minoans.

**Émile Gilliéron fils** – Swiss artist who worked with Evans for three decades, restoring artefacts, filling in the gaps in frescoes and producing replicas. He became Artistic Director of all Greek museums. During his lifetime, his honesty was questioned by scholars, who believed him to be forging artefacts for sale, but Arthur Evans trusted him. He was the one who took the Ring of Minos to the Athens Museum in summer 1930 for assessment of its authenticity. It was declared to be a fake. His Italian wife, Ernestina, was an artist in her own right.

**Emmanuel Akoumianakis and his son Michalis** – Emmanuel (aka Manolaki) became the foreman of Knossos and was called 'my old wolf' by Sir Arthur Evans, who trusted and relied on him. He was skilled at spotting sites worth excavating by examining the above-ground features.

During the WW2 invasion of Crete, he died defending the hill to the east of Knossos and was buried within sight of the ruins where he'd worked all his adult life. Michalis (known as Micky) was a site messenger, later becoming a lawyer and working with the Resistance against the Nazis. In 1944, he and his sister Phyllia assisted Special Operations Executive (SOE) agents Patrick Leigh Fermor and Billy Moss in abducting the German general who had taken up residence at the Villa Ariadne. There are many retellings of this daring action. Micky is invariably remarked on for his thoughtfulness and quick thinking.

**John and Hilda Pendlebury** – met at the British School at Athens and soon married. John was a man of huge courage, vitality and mischief. He worked in both Egypt and Crete (as curator of Knossos), where he walked across the whole island mapping archaeological sites. This knowledge led him to become an important resource to the SOE during WW2. He was tragically shot and killed in 1941 during the invasion of Crete. Hilda, formerly a schoolteacher, accompanied John on his excavations and was known to be an intelligent archaeologist and very 'game'.

**Father Nikolaos Pollakes** – Greek Orthodox priest of Knossos district. Tried to sell the Ring of Minos to Sir Arthur in 1930 for 20 million drachmas, having bought it from the father of the finder, Michalis Papadakis. Sir Arthur considered Father Pollakes to be 'of unbalanced mind'. In 1931, he was prosecuted by Spiridon Marinatos, the Ephor, for engaging in 'illegal activities concerning antiquities'. The case was proved and Father Pollakes was removed from his parish.

It wasn't until 2005 that the Ring of Minos resurfaced, having been hidden by the priest's wife in the 1930s. Their house was inherited by Georgios Kazantis, who renovated it and found the ring in a jar, hidden in an old fireplace. He took it to the museum which declared it genuine. You can see it on display in the Heraklion Archaeological Museum. Two copies of it are held by the Ashmolean Museum.

The southern Aegean is subject to a great deal of tectonic activity. An earthquake measuring 6.8 occurred on the 14th February, 1930. Over fifty deaths were reported.

*Nani, nani my child* – is a traditional Greek lullaby. It was recorded as part of a European Union Project – 'Languages of the Cradle'. You can hear it sung on this website: www.reverbnation.com

It has been a privilege to research the people associated with the excavation of Knossos. Although my story focuses on the British archaeologists involved, it is important to recognise the work of Minos Kalokairinos, who discovered the site in the late 19th century, and was followed by countless other archaeologists and scholars from Greece and around the world whose efforts have illuminated the fascinating character of the Bronze Age in Crete.

My interpretation of the culture and, in particular, the religious practices of the Minoans does not reflect any particular school of thought but is based on both research and imagination.

A short list of books exploring some of the events, characters, discoveries and issues follows:

*Labyrinth: Knossos, Myth & Reality*, Andrew Shapland (ed.) Ashmolean Museum, 2023

*Sir Arthur Evans and Minoan Crete: Creating the Vision of Knossos*, Nanno Marinatos, Bloomsbury, 2015

*Mysteries of the Snake Goddess: Art, Desire, and the Forging of History*, Kenneth Lapatin, Da Capo Press, 2003

*Minotaur: Sir Arthur Evans and the Archaeology of the Minoan Myth*, J. Alexander MacGillivray, Jonathan Cape, 2000

*The Villa Ariadne*, Dilys Powell, 1973

*Ill Met by Moonlight*, W. Stanley Moss, George G. Harrap & Co Ltd, 1950

*A Handbook to The Palace of Minos at Knossos with its Dependencies*, J.D.S. Pendlebury, Cambridge University Press, 1933

# Acknowledgements

I am greatly indebted to Dr Kostis Christakis, Curator of Knossos, for taking me on a tour of the Villa Ariadne and sharing his deep knowledge of the site. Also to Dr Andrew Shapland, the Sir Arthur Evans Curator of Bronze Age and Classical Greece at the Ashmolean Museum, for generously sharing his expertise and for assistance in accessing and understanding the Evans Archive. I'm grateful to Anna Streetly for her superb illustrations, to Mike Ashton for his great graphic design, and to Ann Mason for her excellent editorial skills. Electra Rhodes and Alison Lester provided wise advice on early drafts which proved incredibly important.

The number of people who have assisted in the creation of this book, either through editorial help or by propping me up when I needed encouragement, is huge. This list is inevitably incomplete: Writing West Midlands & Room 204 friends, Susannah Stapleton, Caroline Lawrence, Ted Eames, Sarah Ibberson, Karen Robinson, Honor & Lou Bleackley, Lucy, Vivienne & Pearl Armstrong-Blair, Clara & Liz Van Hoose, Alex Hodgson, Amy Boucher, Hector Panos, Marc DeMarchena, Christine Low, Liz Lefroy, Christopher Sweeney, Imogen Maxfield, Sarah Lamsdale, Helen Garrett, Hilary Stock – *Efcharistó!*

Particular thanks to Mum – for sharing a love of Greek art and culture, Freya – for providing delicious cake when I needed it, John – for being my Shrewsbury Library buddy, and Jim – for being an inspirational river rescuer and NTS. As ever, deep thanks to Michael for his enthusiastic support and loving encouragement.

Without museums and libraries, this book would not exist. I am grateful to all those who look after the innumerable, wonderful stories of human history – particularly the staff of the Heraklion Archaeological Museum, The Ashmolean Museum, Gladstone's Library and Shrewsbury Library.

# Praise for books by Kate Innes

### *Greencoats – historical fantasy set in WW2*

'*Greencoats* beautifully combines the genres of historical fiction and fantasy. The magic feels real and the reality magical. Tense, compassionate and lyrical, I devoured this in a weekend. Highly recommended for middle grade readers.' **Caroline Lawrence – author of *The Roman Mysteries***

'A magical element is introduced through spirits within the trees and skilfully woven with the realistic human stories to create a wonderful world.' **Rubery Book Award Shortlist Review – 2022**

### *The Errant Hours – Arrowsmith Trilogy Book One*

'Kate Innes's glorious first novel is a lyrical joy. Up there with the best of Patricia Bracewell and Elizabeth Chadwick, it offers utter immersion in an intricate, plausible world. A must read.' **Manda Scott – author of the *Boudica* series**

'*The Errant Hours* is a beautifully crafted epic tale of adventure, love  and courage, worthy of the greatest Medieval minstrels.' **Karen Maitland – author of *Company of Liars***

### *All the Winding World – Book Two*

'Will enchant readers new to the period and delight those who know it well.'  **Historical Novel Society**

### *Wild Labyrinth – Book Three*

'This is work of the highest creative historical imagination. A wonderful book.' **Alix Nathan – author of *The Warlow Experiment***